The Heir's Treasure

by

JoMarie DeGioia

PUBLISHED BY:

Bailey Park Publishing

The Heir's Treasure

Book One of the
Bridgewater Brides Series

by

JoMarie DeGioia

England 1815

Chapter 1

Philip Wilton, Baron Wilton, sat at a table at the Inn at Salisbury and patted his flat stomach, a sigh of satisfaction escaping his lips. Having just consumed a hearty meal of venison and potatoes, he pushed the plate from him and brought his mug of ale to his lips. Taking a swallow, he gazed about the dining room. It was practically furnished, with simple wooden tables and chairs. The room was nearly empty, two men the only other diners present. A fire burned in the hearth, since the spring evening was a bit chilly.

That afternoon Philip had taken his leave from Bridgewater Park, his cousin's grand estate situated in Somersetshire. The Earl of Bridgewater—an older gentleman whose wife had borne him two daughters before learning that she could bear no more children—apparently took pleasure in counting Philip as his heir, the man who would one day possessed both his title and his vast fortune. It was a shame that Philip's own father had taken such little interest in Philip when he was alive.

Philip's mother had passed away when he was a small child, and his father had employed a veritable army of nurses and tutors to see to his care. No doubt the man had found the task of caring for his own son unpleasant. Philip had been all but ignored by his father, and when the man passed away ten years ago Philip had barely noticed his absence.

His own estate was seen to by solicitors; he knew little of his holdings and cared even less. This upcoming trip to London to meet with the solicitors was all the time that he would allow such matters to consume.

A fit young man approaching the age of twenty-five, with thick blond hair and brilliant green eyes, Philip was well-aware that he had little trouble attracting the interest of any woman upon whom he turned his dimpled grin. He kept himself far from ladies of Society, however. The so-called "marriage market" held little appeal for him, and as he was a baron of moderate fortune he drew little attention from marriage-minded females at present.

He much preferred carousing with his friends at the gaming houses and pubs, drinking and gambling and wenching to his heart's content. Closing his eyes for a moment, he once more thanked God for his cousin's robust health, knowing that when he finally came into the earl's fortune and title, he would be all but hunted down and forced to the altar.

That brought his former mistress to mind, a silly girl with the largest breasts he had ever seen. The girl managed to find herself a tradesman to marry three weeks earlier and, after an exhausting and immensely satisfying farewell, Philip had released her from any attachment. While he had enjoyed having a young woman available for his pleasure, he couldn't deny his relief at no longer having to suffer the seemingly endless chatter that nearly always preceded their trysts. On this particular evening, he looked forward to dallying with any doxie who caught his fancy.

Two serving girls, Philip couldn't recall their names, eyed him appreciatively from where they stood near the kitchen door. They were very alike in looks, both with dark hair and eyes and ample bosoms. Philip nodded in their direction, holding up his empty tankard. Smiling widely, the girls hurried to his table.

"I will serve Lord Wilton," one of the girls said quickly, filling his mug.

"Nay," the other pouted, setting her pitcher of ale on the table. "I wish to serve Lord Wilton."

Philip looked from one to the other, a delicious idea flitting through his mind.

"Perhaps," he intoned with a wicked grin, "we can come to some arrangement that would benefit all parties?"

The girls wore identical smiles. One came to rest in his lap, wiggling and giggling as the other came behind him to run her hands over his shoulders and through his hair. Philip felt a tingle of anticipation course through him as he imagined the pleasures that awaited him were he to take the two wenches abovestairs. A musical, feminine voice broke through his lascivious musings.

"Sir," the unseen girl cajoled, "if you would but listen to reason, you will see this matter can be easily resolved."

"Nay," the innkeeper answered, entering the dining room. "You pay now or you go."

Philip watched absently as a slender figure followed on the innkeeper's heels. He leaned to one side to get a better view of the slight girl standing toe to toe with the burly man. His breath caught at the untamed beauty before him. The girl's golden hair, its braid little more than a memory, floated about her shoulders as she argued her case with the innkeeper. Her dress, a bit rumpled, hugged her curves. As he watched with growing interest, the girl placed her clasped hands in front of her and stared up at the innkeeper with the most captivating amber eyes.

"Please, sir," she begged. "My maid is already abovestairs in her room. She does not travel well."

"I care not fer yer maid's problems," the man said. "Ya' secured yer rooms and ate yer meal before ya' told me of yer situation. Settle yer bill now or get out!"

A flash of anger appeared in her amber eyes. "But you refuse to listen to reason," the golden maid countered. "I am on my way to visit my relations. I'm quite certain that they will reimburse you for my expenses."

Mr. Wick, the innkeeper, rubbed his chin thoughtfully. He looked the young woman up and down, and Philip could well guess his thoughts. Surely he believed she was but a trollop of little consequence, and any "relations" were surely of the masculine persuasion who would hardly reimburse him for any kindness shown the chit. Philip figured Wick was probably correct.

"I don't care how ya' get the money," Wick said with finality. "But you'll pay me before ya' are abed."

"I'll pay fer the wench," one of the dining room patrons said suddenly, drawing Philip's attention.

Philip shrugged off one serving girl's grasp and gently pushed the other from his lap. Giving her bottom a playful slap, he sent her and the other away from him. He leaned forward and ran his gaze over the bedraggled young woman once more. Never before had he seen such a lovely girl. The thought of one of the brutes touching her soured his belly. He stared in dismay as the other diner joined the discussion.

"Nay," the man cut in, coming to his feet. "I'll pay what the chit owes."

The girl looked from one man to the other, her rosy lips pursed slightly in obvious distaste. Philip couldn't blame her. The men were dirty and unkempt and not the best men to gift with her splendid little body. She held her hands out in front of her, her lashes fluttering as she offered them a small smile. The façade almost fooled Philip. Almost.

"Gentlemen," she began, her tone deferential. "I appreciate your kind offer."

"Pay me first," Wick cut in, his eyes narrowed on the two diners. "Pay me before ya' take the wench abovestairs. I'll not have her skippin' out in the middle o' the night with yer gold in her pockets."

The man's meaning penetrated the girl's mind in that instant. She gasped aloud, her eyes round. Philip found her show of dismay enchanting, if a bit overdone.

"Sir, you do not think that I…?" she stammered. "That I would ever secure my own comfort in such a manner?"

"We got a deal," the first man said, grabbing her by the wrist.

The sight of the man's grimy hand on her creamy flesh made Philip cringe. He came to his feet. "I'll settle her bill."

All heads turned in surprise. The girl's full lips parted as she gazed at him. Those incredible amber eyes slowly raked his form, from his fine brown jacket, over his tan breeches, to his booted feet. Her interest nearly burned through his clothing as her gaze traveled to his face once more.

"Wilton wants the wench," he heard the first man grumbled.

"We saw her first," the second added. He turned to face Philip. "We'll share her, mate."

Philip shook his head at that. His eyes locked on the girl's as he crossed to where she stood. Not taking his gaze from hers, he pulled several pound notes out of his pocket and handed them to the innkeeper.

"I daresay this should cover it, Wick," he said, finally looking at the man.

"Well, I suppose," the man began. Philip's gaze dared argument. "Yes, of course, Baron Wilton," he rushed out.

Philip nodded at Wick and turned his attention on the compelling bit of baggage. She stared up at him, a blush covering her smooth cheeks. That false smile returned.

"I thank you for your assistance, sir," she said with a curtsey. "If you would but give me your name and address, I will see that my relations repay your kindness when I reach my destination."

Philip gazed down into her flushed and beautiful face. His eyes settled on her rosy lips as she ran the tip of her tongue over them in her nervousness. Desire flared through him as he imagined tasting those lips.

"There will be no need for that, I assure you," he said, his voice husky.

She gasped once more, and then she glared up at him, sparks fairly flying from her eyes.

"I am not some doxy you can tumble," she snapped. "If you think you can take advantage of my situation, you are sorely mistaken!"

With that, she spun on her heel and rushed from the room. Philip could only stare after her as laughter came from the other two patrons.

"Yer welcome to her, Wilton," one of the men chuckled.

Shaking his head, Philip left the dining room, contemplating the wisdom of trailing after the golden beauty with the flashing eyes.

***

Lady Margaret Penworth—Maggie, as long as she could remember—ran into the sleeping chamber and slammed the door, letting out a cry of frustration. That afternoon, when she'd realized that she lacked sufficient funds for their journey to Somersetshire, she was reminded of just how little she knew of the ways of the world. Her life, which up until now had been filled with jovial gents and coddling matrons, was altered forever. And now to be thought a trollop? A light-skirt to be sold to the highest bidder? She crossed to the bed and sat, suddenly exhausted.

She and her lady's maid, Joan, had traveled from Sussex this day, and the journey had come on the heels of the darkest tragedy she could have imagined. Her mother had passed away less than a week prior, leaving practically nothing but sadness and a tiny cottage for her daughter. Maggie had never known her father, a baron of little fortune who had died sometime before her birth. But for the stipend her mother assured her would continue to pay for the cottage's upkeep, Maggie had little to recommend herself for anything other than being a paid companion to one of the widows populating their little corner of Sussex.

The steward of the estate on which the cottage was situated, a Mr. Lavery, had wasted little time in making his base desires known to Maggie, confirming her innate distaste of the man she'd sensed upon reaching her thirteenth year six years earlier. The knife that she now carried on her person for protection had offered enough of a threat to keep the vile man from her. But his insistence that her mother had hidden a treasure in the cottage had assured her that his mind was as twisted as his looks.

At her mother's parting request, Maggie traveled to impose upon the Earl of Bridgewater and his family. Maggie truly had no one left in this world save for the man who was once married to her mother's sister. Her uncle had always been most kind to her, and upon learning of her mother's death he had insisted that she come stay with them at Bridgewater Park.

She knew little of his situation, save that he lived with his second wife and two little daughters. Maggie longed to feel a part of a family, distant though these Bridgewaters were. She couldn't ignore the tiny spark of hope that the relation would give her a bit of security now that she was thrust out of the tight circle of her mother's protection.

Maggie thought back to the troubling incident in the inn belowstairs, and realized that the very handsome gentleman who had paid her bill expected a certain payment for his generosity. Being a lady of virtue, she could only imagine the demands he wished to make upon her fair person, but she presumed that he and the disgusting steward were of a like mind. She shivered again, burying her face in her hands.

The door opened suddenly and her handsome benefactor strode into the room. Maggie lifted her head and stared at him in shock.

"How dare you enter a lady's room?" she cried, coming to her feet. "Please leave at once!"

The intruder smiled crookedly and shook his golden head.

"I think not," he said, closing the door. "There is the little matter of repayment to discuss."

Maggie watched as he crossed to her. Even as innocent as she was she recognized the intent in his gaze, having seen the same look in Mr. Lavery's eyes time and again.

"You cannot think to take advantage of my position?"

The gentleman nodded, silencing her. He gazed down at her, and then grasped her gently by her arms.

"I promise you, miss," he began, his voice smooth. "You will experience as much pleasure as I."

He bent his head to hers as she stared up at him, mute. She suddenly pulled out of his grasp.

"I will not be used in this manner!" she shouted, stepping back from him. "If you will give me your name and address I will see to it that you are compensated."

The man chuckled.

"There's no one else here, miss," he said with a smile. "You don't have to perpetuate that ridiculous story."

Maggie blinked at him.

"Ridiculous?" she repeated, dumbfounded. "Why, of all the arrogant, self-serving reprobates."

"Easy," the rake cut in, his green eyes sparkling. "You may injure my delicate feelings."

She arched a brow at him. She took a deep breath in an attempt to rein in her anger toward the rascal.

"Please leave my room, sir," she said in what she thought was a reasonable tone of voice. "Leave me your name and address."

"Ah, very well!" he exclaimed, throwing up his hands in defeat. "I am a gentleman, miss, and do not force my intentions on any woman."

Her shoulders slumped with relief and he let out a grunt of apparent irritation. As she watched him warily, he walked to the chair beside the bed and sat.

"What do you think you're doing?" she asked, aghast.

He stretched his long legs out in front of him, crossing his arms over his chest.

"You cannot expect me to return to the dining room just yet," he intoned, a very pretty smile on his face. "I have a reputation to uphold."

She gave a snort to that ridiculous statement. She reached up to brush her tangled curls away from her face. "As you wish." She shrugged her shoulders. "I have had a long day, sir, and a longer evening. You may sit there in comfort while I ready for bed."

Holding her chin high, she took herself behind the privacy screen and began to remove her dress. She heard him shift and grumble as she hurried through her evening's ablutions.

"I suppose you have a protector," he drawled after a few moments.

"A what?" she asked absently.

"The man of whom you spoke," he went on. "Your, um, 'relation.' I suppose he's keeping you? He's a lucky gent, if that's truly the case."

Maggie froze in that moment, slamming her brush down on the washstand in the next. She stepped from behind the screen to see him leaning back in the chair. She turned her head to follow his line of sight and realized he must have had a clear view of her.

"Were you watching me as I removed my dress and petticoat?" She sucked in a breath and faced him again. "As I brushed my hair?"

"Any healthy young man would have taken advantage of such a show, miss." He flashed a dimpled grin at her that made her want to slap his face. "I won't tell your protector if you won't."

Chapter 2

"How dare you make such an insinuation!" the gorgeous girl hissed, her hands braced on her slender hips.

Desire shot through Philip like a bolt of lightning. Her figure was clearly visible to him through her chemise, and quite exquisite. She was slender yet curved in all the right places. Her breasts were full but not overlarge, and he suspected that they would fit his hands quite nicely. Coming swiftly to his feet, he crossed to her. He gazed down at her, at her rosy parted lips, and was nearly lost.

"You are incredible," he said, his voice low.

She stared up at him, and seemed to be as lost in the heat between them as he. He lowered his head, brushing his mouth over hers. The touch of his lips must have shocked her back to her senses. She pulled back and slapped him. He blinked in surprise. Suddenly, he threw his head back and laughed.

"Ah, a spirited wench!" Philip exclaimed. "This could prove most interesting."

He grasped her arms again and brought his lips to hers once more, tasting her sweetness. The girl's senses were apparently overwhelmed as Philip used his considerable expertise on her.

She leaned into him, a soft sigh escaping her. Philip moaned, surprised at the pleasure he felt from merely kissing her. He started to deepen the kiss, his tongue brushing over her lips. She recoiled immediately, backing away from him.

"Get out of my room, sir," she said shakily.

Philip suspected that something other than anger made her voice quiver. He took a breath to regain his senses. The kiss had affected him like none before.

"I paid your bill, miss. You owe me."

She took several more steps away from him, though her stance was far from timid. No. Her body was rigid and her hands in fists.

"I shall see you repaid. I travel to Somersetshire on the morrow."

"Somersetshire?"

Wariness filled those amber eyes. "Yes. My relations will see to your repayment, sir. You have my word."

"Your word?" He relished the awareness evident on her face as he stepped closer. Her pupils dilated. "Ah, I want more than your word."

That picture of the shy maiden appeared and she fluttered her lashes. Despite the warning trilling in the back of his mind, he couldn't help but be spellbound.

"I see your position, sir. I am not used to such surroundings or situations, I fear. Pray, give me but a moment to collect myself?"

What was this? She capitulated? His pulse pounded and his body hardened.

"You'll pass the evening with me?"

A nod sent her dark golden curls swaying. She turned and glanced over her shoulder, the picture of willing, pliant seductress.

"Pray, leave me to ready myself?"

Philip nodded dumbly and backed toward the door.

"I shall give you as long as you need, miss." He opened the door and stepped into the hall. "Pray call out to me and I'll be here in a trice."

She smiled at him, full and bright, and he blinked. He eased the door shut and stared at it, imagining that delectable body naked of even the thin chemise. A scraping met his ears, and the wood panel squealed as the knob rattled. He knew then. She had caught him.

"Miss?" he asked, rattling the knob. It stuck tight. Bloody Hell, she had caught him! "Miss, open this door!"

"I will not," she stated through the door. "And do not think to force entry, sir. I have a knife and will not hesitate to free you from your manhood should you try it."

Philip dropped his hand from the knob as if it burned him, stopping just short of cupping his cock in response. He stared at her door for several long minutes, uncertain of his actions. He wouldn't break down the flimsy barrier. That was certain.

He thought then of the two willing serving girls belowstairs. Their ample charms held little attraction for him now, as his tastes suddenly leaned toward slight girls with golden curls and flashing eyes. And cunning minds, he sourly added. Grunting in frustration, he took himself off to bed.

"Contrary wench," Philip grumbled to himself as he tried to get to sleep.

Thoughts of the little beauty kept intruding: her wild hair, her rosy lips. He groaned as he recalled the way those lips had softened beneath his, setting him on fire. And the way she'd looked as she'd offered him that shy smile, he mentally added, all tousled and soft and delectable.

When she'd transformed into the maiden, he'd very nearly leaped at her. He'd wanted to pull the chemise from her and run his hands over her creamy skin, to peel off his breeches and bury himself in her softness. That thought soon had him hard and throbbing with desire. Letting out a sigh of frustration, he buried his fist in his pillow and spent quite a long time waiting for sleep to claim him.

He awoke to feminine laughter, the sound sweet in the spring morning. He pulled himself to a sitting position in the bed and stretched with a loud yawn. His dreams had been filled with a certain fair-haired chit and had left him feeling befuddled. The sweet laughter came again, and he realized it originated from the drive in front of the inn. Rubbing his eyes, he swung his legs over the side of the bed and crossed to the open window.

He was surprised to see the golden wench there on the drive, standing beside a modest carriage. He dragged his eyes from her face for a moment and absently noticed that she was dressed as the proper young lady. As he watched, she favored her companion with the prettiest smile he'd ever seen. He knew instinctively that if she ever bestowed such a smile on him, he would happily do anything she asked of him. Her voice reached him.

"Come now, Joan," the girl cajoled. "You survived the first leg of our journey. Surely you can persevere?"

Her companion's shoulders slumped in acceptance as she preceded her mistress into the carriage. The beauty nodded with approval and donned her straw bonnet. Lifting her chin to tie the wide blue ribbon beneath, she froze as she noticed Philip staring down at her from his window. Their eyes held for a long moment, and the girl was the first to break contact. With a nod to him, she tied a large bow beneath her chin and turned once more to the carriage.

"There, there, Joan," Philip heard her say. "We are nearly at the end. Surely you realize that we have but a few hours to ride to Somersetshire?"

Somersetshire? Yes, she'd said as much last evening. A smile curved his lips. He watched as she climbed aboard the carriage, following the vehicle with his gaze as it made its way out onto the road. Now that he knew the girl's destination, it would be quite simple for him to track her down. And track her down he would.

He planned to return to Bridgewater Park when his business with the solicitors was concluded, since he had no desire to stay in London and attend the parties frequented by the *ton*. He hoped to be back in Somersetshire within a month's time, if not sooner. He was quite certain that he would find the girl and persuade her to rid herself of her protector.

And when she was free, he would finish what began in her room at the inn.

***

Maggie had awoken at dawn, eager to continue on her journey to her uncle's. The previous evening's troubling events still plagued her mind, as did the gentleman who both dispatched her difficulties and added to her befuddlement. Joan, after assuring Maggie that she was much improved, had assisted her with her dress and hair. Maggie's pretty day dress was white and covered with a sprinkle of blue flowers, and far suited to her sensibilities and station than the rumpled, ill-fitting gown she had worn the previous day. Joan had quickly fashioned a single braid in her golden locks, twining it into a coil at the back of her head. Several curls floated about her face and brushed her cheeks.

As Maggie stared out the window of the carriage, memories of Mr. Lavery's words and actions of the previous day came back to her. The steward had not only insisted that her mother had hidden a treasure of some sort in their modest cottage. He had alluded to a fancy man, a rich gentleman who had kept her mother there for his pleasure. Cecilia Penworth had been a lady of virtue, Maggie knew in her heart. She would never have taken gold or jewels in such an unsavory exchange. Never.

"It won't be long now, Joan," Maggie said with a nod.

The lady's maid paled slightly and Maggie feared that she would yet again fall ill. She reached out and placed a steadying hand on Joan's arm.

The other woman smiled wanly. "Yes, my lady."

Maggie offered a pat of reassurance. She thought back to the tiny room at the inn, trying very hard not to imagine her handsome rescuer there. In her mind's eye she saw him as he'd made his proposition and earlier, when he'd saved her from certain ruin.

Maggie brought her fingers to her lips. Never before had a man kissed her, and she was surprised to find it pleasant. The touch of his hands on her bare arms, the press of his fit body to hers.... And Lord, he was handsome! Lavery's horrid words, her journey from Sussex, her trouble with the innkeeper. The handsome gentleman's attention—and her very confusing reaction to it—had been the very last indignity she could bear.

Maggie sat up as the carriage rolled over the long drive in front of Bridgewater Park. The grounds were beautiful. The rolling hills looked alive with the colors of spring flowers and rich, green grass. The house itself was impressive, built of sand-colored stone and possessing many pointy-roofed gables. There were more windows in the front facade than she could count.

A well-dressed gentleman and an equally turned-out woman stood at the bottom of the wide steps of the home. As the carriage rolled to a stop, Maggie's eyes settled on the man, pleased to see that he wore a wide smile. Her uncle looked older than she remembered, but still quite robust. His smile widened as she stepped down from the carriage with Joan trailing behind her.

"Maggie," the Earl of Bridgewater greeted her. "How wonderful it is to see you."

"Hello, Uncle," Maggie returned. "I wish to thank you for your hospitality."

"Nonsense," the man said with a wave of his hand. "You will always be welcome here." He paused to run his gaze over her face. "My God," he intoned. "You are the very image of your mother."

Maggie smiled at that. She turned to greet the woman standing beside him. She was some years younger than the earl, and quite a handsome woman. Taking Maggie's hands in hers, she leaned closer to place a kiss on the girl's cheek.

"Hello, Margaret," she said with a small smile. "We were sad to learn of your mother's passing."

Maggie read the tenderness in the woman's eyes and was touched by it.

"Thank you," Maggie returned softly. "That is most kind of you to say."

They walked up the steps and entered the magnificent house. Lady Bridgewater greeted Joan and instructed the housekeeper to show her where she would be settled. Maggie gave Joan's hand a squeeze as her companion went toward the servants' quarters.

Maggie removed her bonnet and followed the couple into the parlor. After ringing for tea, her uncle's wife settled herself on a lovely settee of ivory.

"Margaret, dear." She motioned for Maggie to take a seat beside her. "The girls will be down to meet you a bit later. They are quite excited about your coming, especially Betsy."

Maggie learned that Betsy was nine years old, four years older than her sister Mary. She was sorely in need of a companion, the older woman told her. Really a governess of sorts.

"The girls have a nurse and a nanny both," the earl put in. "And Betsy has a tutor. But Lady Bridgewater and I believe that you could instruct her on matters her tutor cannot."

"Instruct her on matters, Uncle?" Maggie asked, sipping delicately at her tea.

"Yes," his wife said. "You could teach her needlepoint. Embroidery."

Maggie nodded enthusiastically. "Oh, yes! My mother saw to my mastering all of the ladylike pursuits. And the vicar near our cottage had seen to my education in more practical matters."

Lady Bridgewater gave a firm nod. "Wonderful," she allowed. "You ride, I suppose?"

Maggie told her that she did indeed ride, and quite adequately.

"Capital!" the earl said. "I'm afraid Betsy balks at learning to ride sidesaddle."

Maggie laughed lightly. "I remember when my mother taught me," she said. "I thought it was quite silly to ride sidesaddle when I was perfectly able to ride astride."

The earl nodded with a smile of his own. "You were a handful when you were young, Maggie."

Maggie saw the affection in his eyes and was pleasantly surprised. She wondered anew why he had stayed away from the cottage for the last few years, but thought it forward to ask such a question of the man who so generously opened his home to her now. The thought of such generosity brought her handsome if irksome benefactor to mind.

She set her cup aside and folded her hands in her lap. "Uncle, I'm afraid that I had a bit of trouble on the journey from Sussex."

"What is this?" the earl asked worriedly. "What sort of trouble?"

The man's wife regarded her closely. Maggie blushed under their scrutiny. She cleared her throat and continued.

"I, um," she faltered. "I'm afraid that I did not have sufficient funds to settle my bill at the Inn at Salisbury. A young gentleman paid the innkeeper in my stead, and I was wondering if you could reimburse him for his trouble?"

"Certainly, Maggie," he said with a small smile. "I was quite worried when you mentioned some sort of trouble."

Lady Bridgewater nodded her head in agreement. "Do you know the name of this gentleman, Margaret?"

Maggie shook her head. "I'm afraid that he didn't give me his name nor where we could find him." She turned to face the earl once more. "He is a man of title," she went on. "A baron, I believe."

Her uncle patted her clasped hands. "I'll track the man down, my dear."

That gave her pause. Would the rake tell her uncle of her dishevelment, of her sharing the space of her room for even that brief time? And what of her threat to him?

"Such assistance shall not go without reward," the earl went on. "Why, he aided your mother's greatest treasure."

Maggie's brows shot up in surprise to hear the man use Cecilia Penworth's name for her. She was immediately reminded of his visits to the cottage when she was small. He had taken her riding, she recalled, and had spent many afternoons taking tea with her and her mother. Her eyes filled with tears as her mother's fair image floated before her. Lord Bridgewater saw her tears and correctly surmised their cause.

"There, there," he soothed. "I realize you miss your mother. We'll be your family now." He looked at his wife. "Is that not so, dove?"

Lady Bridgewater wore a small smile as she nodded. "Yes, dear," she said. "Margaret is a member of our family now."

Maggie returned the woman's smile. She was at last able to set aside the prospect of someday soon being in the vexing baron's company. For the time being.

When Maggie was shown to her chamber, she felt her delight clear to her toes. The room—far larger than the one at the cottage—was decorated in yellow and white and the stripes in the wallpaper matched the plump pillows on the large bed. A vanity sat against one wall, its drawers ready to receive her accessories, hair ribbons and such. Maggie let her fingers trail over the fine furnishings, silently giving thanks for the earl's generosity. She couldn't be more pleased with her room or her situation.

Before they were to go into the dining room for dinner, Maggie was introduced to Betsy and Mary. Betsy, a girl with light brown curls and blue eyes, chatted excitedly to her. Maggie smiled and nodded as the girl enumerated the many activities they would do together.

"We can go riding, and on picnics," Betsy gushed.

"Easy, child," the earl cut in, favoring the girl with an indulgent smile. "You'll exhaust poor Maggie before you even begin."

Betsy apologized with a giggle. Maggie looked down at Mary. The child had curls nearly the color of Maggie's own, and the round face of a cherub. Crouching down to the tot's level, Maggie touched her cheek.

"Hello, Mary," she said. "And do you wish to join us on our outings, too?"

The little girl nodded shyly and stuck her finger in her mouth. Maggie shared a smile with the earl and his wife. Bidding the children goodnight, Maggie watched as Lady Bridgewater sent the children off to bed with their nurse. Betsy stopped and turned in the doorway, her eyes on Maggie.

"Tomorrow we'll go riding, Maggie?" she asked pleadingly.

"Certainly, Betsy," Maggie answered. "That would be lovely."

Flashing a dazzling smile, the child skipped out of the room to follow her little sister to the nursery.

Chapter 3

Philip sat in one of his favorite pubs in London, staring morosely into his mug of ale. The pretty golden maid was on his mind, along with the stack of paperwork awaiting his attention at his townhouse. One of Philip's acquaintances, a handsome rogue possessing a reputation with the ladies that rivaled his own, sat beside him at the table. The man, Viscount Rawlings, eyed Philip closely, clicking his tongue.

"My God, man," he chided. "You're not given to brooding. What the devil ails you?"

Philip looked at the dark-haired man as if he just noticed his presence. "Hmm? Ah, nothing. I was merely thinking about… Never mind."

"Interesting," Lord Rawlings said. "Thinking of a girl, perhaps?"

Philip shot him a look of irritation.

"Ah!" Rawlings cried, a glint in his eye. "Anyone I know?"

"Let it go," Philip said without anger.

Rawlings shrugged his shoulders. "No matter, mate," he said with a crooked smile. "I daresay one of the wenches in this fine establishment will surely send her image flying from your mind."

Philip's well-trained eye quickly scanned the room, seeing the usual assortment of amply-endowed and accommodating serving wenches. "Not bloody likely," he muttered.

Rawlings arched a brow at that. "Well, now. You must tell me her name. I must hear all about this chit who has so captivated you."

Philip took a long sip of his ale and set the tankard down once more. He leaned back and sighed. "There isn't much to tell, I'm afraid," he said. "I came across the girl on my way to town, at the Inn at Salisbury. She was low on funds and I paid for her lodgings."

"The girl was most grateful, was she not?" Rawlings offered, a devilish grin on his face.

"Yes," Philip said. "But she refused my advances."

"She refused you?" The other man was apparently astounded. "You paid for her!"

Philip raked his fingers through his hair and shook his head. "She's a puzzle." Pride kept him from divulging her barring him from her chamber, however. "And never a more comely wench have I seen. She has golden hair and the most amazing eyes." He stopped then, smiling widely. "And the most pleasing figure, as well. I know only that she has gone to Somersetshire. To her protector."

Rawlings nodded sagely and motioned for the serving girl to refill their tankards. She smiled at the gentlemen, showing a wide gap between her two front teeth. She giggled when Rawlings gave her bottom a slap to send her on her way. He looked back at Philip.

"The answer is quite simple, friend," he told Philip. "Find the chit. Bed her. Once you've sampled her charms she will no longer hold your interest."

Philip pictured the girl as she stood in that chamber, delightfully disheveled and utterly enchanting. He was once more seized with the confounding desires to bed her and learn her secrets.

He shook his head and drank more of his ale. "I fear the girl's hold on me will only get stronger."

"Well, well," Rawlings chuckled. "Perhaps I shall accompany you into Somersetshire and have a go at the girl myself."

"No," Philip said sharply. "She's mine."

Rawlings wore a look of surprise at Philip's outburst. "We've never been at odds over a doxy. What of her protector?"

Philip shrugged, forcing an easy smile on his face.

"I have the utmost faith in my abilities to win her from the man."

Rawlings laughed heartily at that.

Philip watched his friend rise and accompany the gap-toothed serving girl abovestairs. After declining a similar offer from another of the girls present—a first in his memory—Philip took himself back to his townhouse to work on his ledgers.

***

The days turned to weeks, and Maggie grew accustomed to life at Bridgewater Park as well as the Bridgewaters themselves. Much of the day the children spent their time in their nursery or the schoolroom, leaving Maggie time for her own pursuits of riding and needlepoint and the like.

Her aunt—for that was how she thought of Lady Bridgewater now—saw to a new wardrobe for her, with many day dresses and tea gowns. Several fancier gowns were also made for her, as they planned to attend the wonderful country dances held in the neighboring towns. Apparently loathe to return to London for the Season, Lady Bridgewater had assured Maggie that they were certain to find her a suitable young gentleman there in the country.

"You are nearly nineteen years old, my dear," the woman said again as Maggie endured another fitting in her chamber. "You have no need for a Season and all that it entails. I promise you the squires residing in Somersetshire will fall over themselves to court you."

Maggie flushed at that praise, thinking herself quite ordinary despite the woman's assurances. But the dresses were indeed beautiful, and she felt a tingle of excitement at the prospect of wearing one of them to a dance. Sussex had never offered much opportunity for anything but the rustic celebration around harvest time. And certainly no gentlemen there ever fell over themselves for a dance with her.

She stood on a stool and gazed at herself in the cheval mirror, at the gown of ivory wrapping her figure. Lady Bridgewater ran her eyes over her, finally giving a firm nod.

"Stunning," she announced, to which the seamstress voiced her agreement.

Betsy entered the room just as the seamstress took her leave. "Ooh, Maggie!" she cried. "You look like a princess!"

Maggie laughed. "Thank you, Betsy."

"All of the gentlemen will wish to dance with you," the child stated. "Will you teach me some of the dances, Maggie?"

Maggie told her she would be happy to, at which the girl beamed.

Lady Bridgewater turned to take her leave. "Betsy, do not dally much longer. Margaret needs her privacy."

"I'll stay but a few moments, Mother," the girl promised.

Maggie rang for Joan and the lady's maid assisted her out of the gorgeous gown. Betsy sat on the stool Maggie had vacated, her feet swinging back and forth.

"Philip's coming for another visit," she said.

"And who is Philip?" Maggie asked absently, changing into one of her new tea gowns with the maid's assistance.

"Father's heir," the girl said. "He's our cousin, too. Second, I think. Or third. He'll be the earl someday."

Maggie nodded, sitting at her vanity to run her brush through the curls at her cheeks. "That's nice."

Maggie gave Joan a nod and the maid took herself out of the room. Betsy stood and crossed to the vanity to rifle through the ribbons in one of the vanity drawers.

"He's a baron already," she went on. "Baron Wilton."

Maggie froze, her brush held in mid-air. She slowly lowered it. Wilton? Why, that was the name of her handsome benefactor, wasn't it?

"Betsy," she said, turning to face the girl. "What does Philip, um, Baron Wilton, look like?"

"Oh, he's most handsome," Betsy said. "He has blond hair and the greenest eyes."

Maggie squeezed her eyes shut as the room appeared to spin.

"Is something wrong, Maggie?" Betsy asked worriedly. "You look ill."

Maggie opened her eyes and managed a smile for the girl's benefit. "I'm fine, Betsy. Just a slight headache, is all. It's nothing that a cup of tea and some of Cook's lovely biscuits won't fix."

"Oh, thank goodness," Betsy sighed dramatically.

The little girl left Maggie then to have milk and biscuits abovestairs in the nursery.

Baron Wilton was coming here. And he was the earl's heir? Lord, what a mess. While she was pleased that the man would be reimbursed for his settling her bill, she was exceedingly vexed by the circumstances of their prior meeting.

Would he tell the earl that the men at the inn, himself included, took her for a doxy? And what of their kiss? She groaned. She had intimated that she would grant him her favors, for the Lord's sake! And that was before threatening his... She groaned again.

Praying she had a few days to accustom herself to his arrival, she closed the vanity drawer and rose. She brushed her hands over her skirt and went downstairs to the parlor for tea.

A few days later Maggie fetched Betsy from the schoolroom after luncheon. They were to go riding and Maggie hoped to cajole the child into the sidesaddle. She walked down to the stables, with the little girl happily skipping along beside her. Betsy soon lost her smile as Maggie told her what they were about.

"I don't wish to ride in that silly manner," Betsy pouted, stamping her foot in the straw.

"Come, sweetheart," Maggie pleaded. "Do give this a try? For my sake?"

Much to Maggie's great relief, the girl gave a small nod. Instructing the groom to saddle the child's mount before she could change her mind, Maggie mounted her filly and rode out into the beautiful spring afternoon.

It had rained the previous evening, and the ground was soft and muddy. Taking evident care, Betsy slowly rode her horse out behind Maggie's. Maggie looked at her over her shoulder, sending her a smile of encouragement.

"There, dear," Maggie called. "You look marvelous."

Betsy snorted in disbelief. "This is most uncomfortable, Maggie," she whined. "Why can't I ride astride?"

Maggie rolled her eyes and took a calming breath. "You are an earl's daughter," she told her for what felt like the hundredth time. "You are a lady. You will ride as a lady would."

Betsy pouted. "Well, it's silly."

Their exchange continued as they made slow progress. Maggie steadily lost her grip on her patience with every plodding step. Perhaps she could think of a different tact to use with Betsy. She pressed her lips together, holding back a biting response to the child's incessant complaints.

***

Philip sat and brooded in his carriage as it traveled away from London toward Somersetshire, troubled by his continued fascination with the little golden chit, as he had come to think of the girl from the inn. After making several inquiries in town, he learned that no one of his acquaintance kept a mistress in Somersetshire, at least not one fitting her distinct description. Perhaps her protector resided elsewhere, he reasoned.

Nearly a month had passed since their meeting at the inn, and in all that time he hadn't taken a woman to bed. For the first time in his life, no other woman would do. This fact amazed him for, while he had a healthy respect for women, he had always felt that one was as good as another. He suddenly recalled the two serving girls at the Inn at Salisbury. Surely two such experienced maids could rouse desire in him.

After taking luncheon at the inn, he once more declined the offer of female companionship. Cursing to himself, he climbed into the carriage, bound for Bridgewater Park.

His carriage rolled up the long drive in front of
Bridgewater Park. He alighted and, seeing no one about, chose to
go directly to the stables. His confinement in the carriage, as well
as his continued fixation on the golden chit, had him yearning for
a long hard ride. The groom greeted him and saddled his favorite
horse. Giving the man a nod of thanks, Philip rode out.

After several passes along the steepest trails, he slowed his
mount to an easy stride, his mood at last brightening. He
breathed in the fresh air and smiled up at the beautiful blue sky.
The sound of laughter soon drew his attention. Feminine
laughter, his mind amended. He reined in his horse and glanced
about, quickly spotting the two riders well away from him. He
recognized Betsy easily enough, but his eyes narrowed as he
sought to ascertain her companion's identity.

She was a slender girl, he saw, and much older than Betsy.
Had the earl engaged a governess? He vaguely remembered the
talk of a distant relation coming to the park in the near future.
Was this woman her?

A flash of white petticoat caught his attention as the young
woman lifted her skirts. His well-trained eye quickly spied the
shapely legs beneath before the skirt dropped back into place. In

growing interest, he turned his mount and leisurely made his way to where the two riders sat on their horses.

***

"Do you see how easily my legs rest in the saddle, dear?" Maggie asked Betsy, readjusting her skirts with a quick flick of her wrist. "And do you see how graceful my seat?"

Maggie held herself regally in the saddle. Betsy nodded grudgingly.

"Yes," she allowed. "But, I can't... There, you see? I can't reach the reins with my legs twisted like this!"

Maggie shook her head as she clicked her tongue. "Don't fret, sweetheart," she said, leaning over. "I'll simply grasp them and—"

"A bee!" Betsy cried suddenly. "Oh, a bee!"

The little girl began to wave her arms frantically to rid herself of the insect, sending her horse and Maggie's into a state of mild panic. Maggie's horse reared up and, as she was leaning far over to the side, she slipped from the saddle.

The horse continued to prance and paw the muddy ground. With a yelp of dismay, Maggie found herself face down in the sticky mud. She quickly sat up, her skirts twisting around her legs as she tried to cover herself. She looked up to see the horses and the child staring down at her.

"Oh, you look so silly!" Betsy giggled. Apparently the bee left both her presence and her mind.

The sound of deep, masculine laughter joined the child's. Maggie turned to see a pair of long legs striding toward her, clad in buff breeches and fine boots which were rapidly becoming covered in the same mud as was her face and hands. She squared her shoulders and slowly brought her eyes to his face, knowing in her heart that it was the infamous Baron Wilton.

Her dreaded suspicions were confirmed.

He gazed down at her sitting in the mud. Thankfully, her face was nearly covered and barely visible to him. Utterly forlorn, she lowered her gaze. This, apparently, caused another shout of laughter to escape him.

"Forgive me, miss." He chuckled as he held out his hand. "Please allow me to assist you."

She shot him a look of contempt as she pushed his offered hand away from her.

"Come, Betsy," she said in a harsh whisper, coming to her feet.

He assisted Betsy and the little girl now stood uncertainly beside her horse. Maggie brushed her hands over her muddied skirt, accomplishing little in way of improving its conditions.

He turned back to Betsy then. "I'll see to the horses, Betsy."

Maggie walked briskly back to the house, with Betsy hurrying after her. No doubt he would fall all over himself and make some sort of effusive apology within her aunt and uncle's hearing.

Oh, she hadn't thought she could have a less auspicious encounter with him than the one at the inn, yet she'd had to deal with him while she was sprawled inelegantly in the mud. Just wonderful.

Chapter 4

Philip returned to the house. Thinking to change out of his traveling clothes and muddied boots before greeting Lord and Lady Bridgewater, he mounted the grand staircase, bound for the suite of rooms kept expressly for his use. As he turned at the top of the stairs, he noticed something out of place. The door to one of the other rooms was ajar, arousing his curiosity. His rooms were well away from the guests' quarters, and this put an interesting question to his mind. Could this room belong to the governess he'd seen riding with Betsy? Or perhaps she was the distant relation the earl had indicated?

He stopped at the door and knocked softly. No answer came from within as the door eased open on silent hinges. He peered into the room and spied the pile of muddied clothes on the floor. Lifting his gaze, he opened his mouth to call out a greeting. The words froze in his throat at the sight before him.

The girl's face was turned away from him, her back arched as she rubbed the towel over her hair. Philip ran his eyes over her figure, pleased and surprised both. Her waist was narrow, her full breasts straining against her thin chemise. She was very well-made for a governess. She removed the towel then, her golden locks cascading down to cover her back. He sharply drew in a breath as recognition dawned on him.

"My God, it's you!"

She whirled toward the doorway, her eyes wide as she clutched the towel to her bosom.

"How dare you enter a lady's room!" she cried.

Philip chuckled as he closed the door, and then he sent her a lazy smile.

"Well, well," he drawled. "I daresay this seems very familiar."

She took a step back from him as he slowly advanced on her. No fear showed on her visage, just that spark that sent his blood pounding. He glanced about the pretty chamber.

"I see no knife. My manhood shall persevere, I wager."

"Please leave my room this instant, sir!"

"Sir?" he teased. "Surely you should address me as 'My Lord,' should you not?"

The girl bristled, her eyes narrowing. "I, sir, am not a servant," she pointed out, her chin held high.

Philip crossed to her, running his eyes over the creamy flesh visible to him above the low neckline of her chemise. His gaze soon settled on her face.

"Aren't you Betsy's governess?"

"No, not precisely," she returned. "You see, I—"

"Are you a guest, then?"

"No," she said in answer.

That gave him pause. Surely she was not the earl's relation? Another thought flitted through Philip's mind. The earl hadn't installed a mistress here at Bridgewater Park? No. He was certain that the man would never do such a thing.

Philip suddenly realized his great fortune. Here at Bridgewater Park he had found the girl who had so captivated him for these past weeks.

He flashed a wicked smile at her. "This poses a very interesting notion to me, miss," he said, reaching out to run his fingers lightly over her arm.

She pulled away from the contact. He shrugged and dropped his hand to his side.

"There still remains the matter of repayment for my assistance at the Inn at Salisbury," he pointed out.

The young woman glared at him. Philip watched the gold flecks in her eyes as her ire grew, mesmerized.

"You shall be rewarded for your trouble, sir," she said. "But not in the manner you're expecting, I wager."

Able to wait no longer, Philip grabbed her to him and pressed his lips to hers. The girl dropped her towel and placed both hands against his chest, pushing him away from her.

"I am not some common trollop here for your amusement!"

Philip let his eyes run over her. Common? Lord, she was magnificent.

"I agree," he said, his voice a caress. "You aren't common in the least."

She blinked up at him, apparently confused. He reached out to brush his fingers over her hair, her cheek.

"Your hair is like golden silk," he said softly. "Your eyes are a most unusual color." He cupped her cheek with his hand. "And your mouth," he whispered, running his thumb over the curve of her lower lip. "Ah, your mouth would make a man forget his name."

He captured her lips again, rubbing gently. She placed her hands on his chest once more. But instead of pushing him away, she curled her fingers around the lapels of his jacket. He moaned softly as she closed her eyes and parted her lips.

"That's it," he murmured, tunneling his fingers through her hair. "Open your mouth for me."

She did, a sigh escaping her when his tongue slipped inside. She reached up behind his neck and ran her fingers through his thick hair, whimpering in pleasure.

His mouth left hers to nuzzle her ear, her neck. He ran his hands over her, molding her tightly to him. He cupped one breast with his hand.

"I knew you would fit me perfectly," he rasped.

Her nipple harden against his palm and he gave a shudder. She suddenly went rigid in his arms, alarm cutting through the passionate haze. He dropped his hand and she stepped back from him.

"I don't welcome your attentions, sir," she whispered, shaking her head.

Philip laughed, a strangled sound to his ears.

"That's not true," he said. "Not if that kiss was any indication."

He reached for her once more. She quickly recovered herself and pushed his hands from her.

"Arrogant brute. Leave my room this instant!"

He growled in frustration. He took a deep breath and glared at her.

"Very well," he said finally, raking his fingers through his hair. "But know this. Bridgewater Park may be a large estate, but there is no place you can hide from me. Nor from your response to me."

He turned on his heel and left her. He cursed fluently as he entered his chambers, slamming the door. What was the chit about? He wanted her and he knew damned well that she wanted him. He was certain she was well-versed in the art of lovemaking. Her kisses were all the evidence he needed to that end.

Perhaps she was hired without the earl's being aware of her character. He would ask them about her, he decided. He would ascertain her place in the household. After swiftly changing his clothes he went downstairs in search of the earl and his wife.

He found them in the parlor, awaiting tea time. The earl stood and clasped his hand in a firm handshake.

"Philip, my boy," the man said. "Good to have you back at Bridgewater Park."

Philip smiled widely. "Good to be back, sir."

Philip greeted Lady Bridgewater with a kiss on her hand and sat down on one of the settees that flanked the fireplace. The three of them spoke of London and of his very uneventful trip back into Somersetshire. After a few minutes of conversation, Philip thought to bring up the subject that was so plaguing him.

"Lord Bridgewater," he began. "Have you engaged a governess for Betsy?"

The other man raised his brows. "What?" he asked. "A governess? Why would you think such a thing? Betsy has the nurse and her tutor."

"Well, sir," Philip said, clearing his throat. "I was out riding and I saw a young woman with the child."

The earl's laughter brought him up short. Philip looked from him to his wife, perplexed.

Lady Bridgewater smiled warmly at him. "The young woman you saw is not Betsy's governess," she provided in answer, "although she does suit that purpose quite well."

Philip shook his head as he puzzled over that.

"My boy," the earl cut in. "The girl you saw… Ah, here she is now."

Philip stood as the earl did, his head turning to the door. His breath caught as he met the newcomer's gaze. He smiled crookedly at her, at which she raised her chin and looked away from him. She smiled at Lady Bridgewater in greeting and crossed to the earl.

"Hello, Aunt," she said, her voice as smooth as her creamy skin. "Uncle."

She returned her gaze to Lord Wilton, apparently quite satisfied by the look of utter amazement he suspected he wore. His mouth fairly hung open in shock.

"Maggie, dear," the earl greeted her warmly. He took her hand and turned her to face Philip. "I wish to introduce someone to you. This is my heir, Baron Philip Wilton. Philip, this is my niece, Lady Margaret Penworth."

Philip bowed to her, at which she curtsied. She favored him with a cheeky grin and turned back to her uncle.

"I'm well acquainted with Lord Wilton, Uncle," she said. "Although I didn't know his name at the time we first met."

"Well, well," the earl returned, his curiosity piqued. "And where have you met before this?"

The girl sat, the men following suit. She brushed her hands over her skirt and smiled once more.

"You see, Uncle," she began. "This is the very gentleman about whom I told you. The man who came to my assistance at the Inn at Salisbury."

"No!" Lady Bridgewater said in surprise. "This is truly a great coincidence, is it not, husband?"

"Truly," the earl agreed. He turned to Philip. "Is this true, son?"

Philip couldn't take his eyes off of the girl. The pink of her dress made her skin appear flushed. Her hair floated about her shoulders in shining curls which escaped the braids at the back of her head. Lord, she was lovely. Philip finally found his voice and turned to the earl.

"Yes, sir," he said. "And I was most happy to come to her aid, I assure you."

"This is quite diverting," the earl said. "You see Philip, Maggie came to us and told us of a mysterious stranger who settled her bill. A young lady of breeding could get into any sort of trouble traveling about these days."

Philip shot a quick look at her. A young lady of breeding? Damn, had he been completely wrong about her? The earl's voice broke through his reverie.

"So you see, Maggie," the older man went on. "There is no need to search out your benefactor."

Lady Bridgewater smiled. "Quite diverting, isn't it, Margaret?"

"Oh yes, Aunt," Maggie answered, reaching for her cup of tea.

Philip took his own cup and slowly brought it to his lips, his mind working. Lady Margaret? The earl's niece?

Lord Bridgewater asked after Philip's business in London, at which he spoke with the man yet he had no notion of what he said. The ladies chatted about the weather and Betsy's improvements at her various endeavors, laughing gaily as Maggie recounted the story of the bee. Philip had trouble concentrating on what the earl said as well. Maggie's sweet laugh and lovely face was a constant draw of his attention.

Her every movement was graceful, her bearing genteel. He felt like the lowest creature on God's earth to have thought so ill of her. And to have forced his attentions on her! But she had given as good as she got, and he wasn't only thinking of her passionate kiss abovestairs not an hour earlier.

Tea time passed quickly. Philip stood over Maggie as she set her cup aside. She arched a graceful brow at him in question.

"Lady Margaret," he began with a smile. "Would you like to take a turn in the garden?"

The girl looked nervously at the earl and his wife, obviously unsure of the wisdom of her being alone with him. He could scarcely blame her reticence, given how big a fool he'd been up to this point.

"Go on, Maggie," the earl urged. "You children enjoy the afternoon."

Lady Bridgewater nodded her agreement. "We'll see you at dinner."

Maggie stood and looked at Philip, uncertainty still etched on her delicate features. He offered her his arm, and she gingerly placed her hand on him. He walked her to the glass doors which led out into the formal gardens behind the great house.

"I am a fool," Philip said when they were finally alone.

Lady Margaret simply nodded, a smile teasing the corner of her mouth. Philip growled playfully at her.

"You don't have to take such enjoyment in this," he complained, a grin on his face. "I've never been so wrong about a girl in my entire life."

She shrugged her slight shoulders and crossed to the rose bushes adorning one long wall of the garden. She reached out and lightly fingered a dark pink blossom, bending her head to smell its fragrance.

"You're not completely to blame, Lord Wilton," she said softly. "The state in which you found me at the inn did little to recommend me."

"Nonsense," he said with a wave of his hand. "I should have taken you at your word. Though you did surprise me more than once that night. And please, call me Philip."

"All right." She turned back to him and smiled sweetly. "Philip."

He studied her for a moment, slowly shaking his head. "I was right about one thing."

"What's that?" she asked, tilting her head to the side.

He couldn't tell her what he had professed to his friend Rawlings, that she could tighten her hold on him without so much as trying. He would never dare give a woman that much power.

"How are you related to the earl?"

"His first wife was my mother's sister," Maggie answered.

Philip nodded as they continued their walk, recalling something to that effect being said some time ago. He suddenly stopped and turned to her.

"Lady Margaret," he began, taking her hand in his. "You must forgive me. For my horrible assumptions as well as my improper overtures. Please tell me you forgive my boorish behavior?"

"You're not the only one with fault, Lord Wilton. What, pray, of my threat?"

"Idle, I presume?" She said nothing to contradict him, however. "I deserved such treatment. So you will forgive me?"

She stared up at him, her lovely eyes round.

"Very well," she said finally. "I'll forgive you on one condition."

He arched a brow at her, a smile teasing his lips. "And what would that be?"

"You must call me 'Maggie,'" she said with a nod.

"Done!" he said, bringing her hand to his lips.

She blushed over his gallantry and gently pulled out of his grasp.

"You know, Maggie," Philip said as they renewed their stroll. "We're related in a fashion. You may even say we are cousins, though distant ones."

Maggie nodded. He stopped and gently grasped her shoulders.

"I'll never again do anything to compromise your virtue," he vowed. "You have my word that I'll present myself as a gentleman at all times."

She stared up at him, then nodded her acceptance. Philip let out a breath. He bent down and placed a chaste kiss on her brow.

"Come," he said, turning toward the house. "I suppose we should ready for dinner."

To his delight, Maggie permitted him to lead her back into the house.

Chapter 5

Long after dinner, Philip offered to escort Maggie to her room. She had felt his gaze on her time and again, and wondered what he was thinking behind those sparkling green eyes. She was well aware of his strong masculine presence too, and of his arms that had held her so closely that afternoon. And his kisses! She blushed hotly. Putting such thoughts out of her mind, she bade goodnight to Lord and Lady Bridgewater and placed her hand on Philip's arm.

They slowly climbed the staircase, he apparently as lost in his own thoughts as she. Philip stopped suddenly, bringing her up short. She looked up at him, her brow slightly furrowed.

"Your room," he said in answer to her unasked question.

She laughed nervously and opened the door. He followed her inside and gazed down at her for a long moment.

"Good night," he said finally.

She nodded, still staring up at him. He brought his lips to her brow as he had in the gardens, placing a gentle kiss there. He then kissed the tip of her nose. He pulled back and stared at her lips. Groaning, he brought his mouth to hers.

"Maggie," he murmured, brushing her lips with his. "Ah, Maggie."

He captured her lips, kissing her deeply, his tongue mating with hers. Maggie returned his kiss full measure, wrapping her arms around his neck and pressing herself against him. He buried his face in the crook of her neck, placing teasing kisses on her soft skin.

"Maggie," he rasped. "You set me on fire."

"Philip," she whispered, letting her head fall back.

"We can be together, Maggie." He trailed his lips over her flesh, to the swell of her breast. "Nothing has to change."

His words broke through to her. She came to her senses and deftly stepped out of his grasp. He blinked at her.

"Nothing *has* changed," she whispered. "You still possess the lowest possible opinion of me."

"No, no," Philip said, reaching for her. "You misunderstand me. I thought that now we—"

"You thought that, although I'm the earl's niece, I'm still a light-skirt meant solely for your pleasure," she said. "Well, I'm not. I am a lady of virtue."

He held his hands out in front of him, pleading. "Maggie, let me explain."

She buried her face in her hands as tears of shame and anger stung her eyes. There was nothing he could say that would explain his behavior.

"Leave me, sir."

"Good night, Maggie," he said softly, taking his leave.

Maggie wiped her eyes, her sobs finally quieting. Sniffling, she stepped out of her beautiful gown and set it aside for Joan's attention. Sitting at her vanity, she readied herself for bed. As she pulled the brush through her thick curls, her mind worked.

How could she let Philip's gallant words of the afternoon convince her of his high regard? He would never think of her as anything but a trollop. And only because of her great misfortune at arriving at the Inn at Salisbury in less than sterling circumstances. How long would it be before she lost the good opinion of the Bridgewaters as well? Setting the brush aside, she donned her nightgown and crawled into her bed, thoughts of Philip filling her dreams.

The next morning, Maggie arose and readied for the day. Joan assisted her into her riding habit, a lovely outfit of dark blue trimmed with black velvet. It was in two pieces, the long skirt topped by an adorable spencer. The jacket came to her waist, accentuating her slender curves. She sat at the vanity as Joan braided her hair, a brooding look on the face staring back at her in the mirror. She would try her best to avoid Philip. With Betsy occupied in the schoolroom, she looked forward to a wonderful morning of riding with nothing other than her horse and her thoughts to accompany her.

"Do you wish your hair up, my lady?" Joan asked, setting the brush aside.

"Hmm?" Maggie answered absently. "No. I believe I will ride quite furiously this morning, Joan. A braid will do nicely."

Joan nodded and plaited her mistress's thick locks. The maid withdrew a wide ribbon of black velvet from the vanity drawer and tied a fetching bow at the end of Maggie's braid. Maggie smiled and thanked the girl, and then sent her on her way.

She stood and shook out her skirts, finally ready to go downstairs to the breakfast room. Breakfast was an informal meal, with diners serving themselves from the sideboard and seating themselves. It was Maggie's favorite meal of the day, for it always brought to mind the comfortable meals she'd shared with her mother in the cottage. Her heart clenched at the memory even as she took solace in the ritual. Sighing, she turned into the sunny breakfast room. Inside sat the earl and his wife, apparently well into their meal.

"Good morning, Aunt," Maggie said as she breezed into the room. "Good morning, Uncle."

"Good morning, child," the earl said with a smile.

"Margaret," he aunt began, "are you going riding so early?"

"Yes," Maggie answered, walking over to the sideboard and picking up a plate. "It's been quite a while since I have ridden alone."

The earl chuckled as he grasped her meaning. "It will be most pleasant to be without Betsy's companionship for once, eh?"

Maggie returned the man's smile as she served herself a small portion of eggs and smoked ham. "I do admit that I'm sorely looking forward to a peaceful ride."

"Perhaps you can stay out of the mud today," Philip drawled from the doorway.

Maggie stiffened at the sound of his voice and turned. She ran her gaze over his splendid form, clad in a brown jacket and breeches. She recovered herself after a moment, finally giving him a curt nod in greeting. He regarded her closely, at last favoring the others with a bright smile.

"Good morning, all," he said, joining Maggie at the sideboard. "Good morning, Maggie."

"Good morning, Lord Wilton," she returned coolly, turning to walk away from him.

He deftly stepped in front of her, blocking her progress. He leaned closer to her. "You agreed to call me Philip," he said, his voice low.

She pursed her lips. "That was when I thought we could be friends. I now know what you truly think of me."

"Maggie, I don't think ill of you," he insisted, raising his voice a bit.

Maggie looked quickly at the couple seated at the table. She leaned closer to Philip. "I only wish I could say the same of you," she said, spinning on her heel.

Philip served himself a hearty portion of the fare, and then took the seat across from her.

"And what are you about this fine morning, Philip?" Lady Bridgewater asked.

"I thought to go for a ride myself," he said easily, his eyes on Maggie.

Maggie kept her eyes downcast and chewed mechanically, eager to finish her meal and escape his close scrutiny. Her uncle's words reached her.

"Perhaps you could accompany Maggie this morning," the man said.

Maggie dropped her fork to clatter on the table's surface. Philip bit back his laughter as he lifted his tea cup.

"That would be quite pleasant, Maggie," he drawled. "Would it not?"

Maggie looked up then to glare in his direction. "Yes," she said through clenched teeth. "Very pleasant, indeed."

"Capital," the earl said with a satisfied smile. He stood as his wife rose. "Enjoy your ride, children."

When Lord and Lady Bridgewater were well gone, Maggie shot Philip a look of extreme vexation. He pulled back, his hand over his chest.

"Maggie." He grinned. "I daresay you nearly slayed me with that dark look."

"If only I could," she said. "How could you agree to a ride with me? You know that I have no desire to be in your company."

Philip shrugged his broad shoulders and set his napkin aside. "It wasn't my idea, love."

"Don't address me so, you scoundrel," Maggie said, coming to her feet.

She turned to exit the room but Philip was faster. He bounded out of his chair and blocked the doorway.

"Maggie, don't treat me like this," he pleaded. "I give you my promise that I'll be on my best behavior," he added, smiling crookedly.

Maggie snorted at that. "If you please, sir," she said, waiting for him to step out of her way.

He did with obvious reluctance and she breezed past him, her chin held high.

"Maggie, please listen to me," he said as they reached the stables. "I didn't intend to compromise your virtue last evening."

"That is of no consequence," Maggie said as she waited for the groom to saddle their horses.

She tapped the toe of her boot impatiently in the straw as Philip renewed his efforts to win her favor.

"I know that you are a lady," he said, holding his hand out to assist her into her saddle. "You have my word that I will never force my attentions on you again."

Maggie brushed his hand away and allowed the groom to assist her. "Your word does little to assure me," she said, grabbing up the reins.

Philip covered her hands with his then. He flashed what she guessed was his best smile at her. "Maggie," he began, his voice a caress. "It will never happen again. On my honor."

Maggie looked at him closely, and then she shook her head.

"You, sir, have no honor," she said with a flick of the reins.

Philip stepped aside as she rode out into the glorious morning. He mounted his horse and followed behind, darn him.

***

They rode hard and fast, and Maggie easily kept up with the furious pace Philip set. He crouched low over his saddle. She looked over at him once and favored him with the smallest of smiles. He beamed a grin back at her.

Finally, they reined in their horses near a field of wildflowers. Maggie looked at Philip, her breath coming fast. He gave a loud whoop as he dismounted.

"You ride splendidly!"

She arched a graceful brow at him. "You seem surprised."

"I daresay you shall never cease to surprise me, dear Maggie."

She let him assist her down from the horse and he held his hands on her narrow waist for longer than was proper.

"You are truly a marvel," he said, his eyes gazing into hers.

Maggie stared up at him. "I fear I will need to guard my heart where you are concerned."

"Your heart, Maggie?" Her softly-spoken words affected him. "Truly?"

She blushed. "You, sir, are far too charming for a simple young lady to bear," she said lightly.

Philip grinned. "You forgive me, then?"

"I daresay that I would be hard-pressed to stay angry at you, Philip."

He laughed at that. She smiled in response and turned to walk through the meadow. He led the horses to a small stream nearby and let them drink. He turned and watched Maggie as she bent to pick flowers, choosing some of yellow and white and pink. Her braid had come loose during their vigorous ride, and the loosened curls now brushed her cheeks. As she lifted a flower to her nose, he noticed that those cheeks were still flushed from exertion. Never before had he seen such beauty.

"Maggie," he called.

She straightened. "Yes, Philip?"

He crossed to where she stood with her tiny bouquet in her hands. He plucked a pink flower from the bouquet and drew it across her cheek.

"I meant what I said, Maggie," he said. "I'll treat you with the respect you deserve."

Maggie nodded slowly, her eyes wide. He bent his head and brought his mouth to hers. Their kiss was sweet and fleeting. He pulled back and ran his gaze over her. He swore softly and stepped back.

"Come," he said, taking her hand. "We must leave here before I lose my conviction." He winked. "Or my manhood. You don't still have that knife, do you?"

She laughed. Their ride back to the stables was at a more relaxed pace, with several warm glances and smiles exchanged as they rode. He had seen the warmth in her eyes after their chaste kiss and knew that she was weakening toward him. She was starting to matter to him, as astounding as that could be. When had a woman's friendship ever meant so much to him?

He'd bedded plenty of them. Tall ones. Short ones. Plump ones. Thin ones. He was generous in bed, seeing to their pleasure and taking his as his due. But with Maggie, now that it had finally penetrated his thick skull that she was a lady of virtue, he found he still wanted to be in her company.

What was it about this particular girl? She was very beautiful, of course. But he'd been with beautiful women as well. She had flashing eyes and pert opinions and kept him on his toes. Was it the challenge? And if so, just what was driving him?

He couldn't have her. That was certain. She was the earl's favored relative and a sweet girl at her core. The sensual pull toward her he'd felt that very first night hadn't dimmed, unfortunately. If anything, the more he learned of her the more he wanted her.

That thought doused his pleasure in their ride and he kept his muddled thoughts to himself as they returned to the stables.

Chapter 6

Their days fell into a pattern of sorts, with Philip and Maggie often taking rides together in the mornings. Maggie was with Betsy for most of the afternoons, riding with her or teaching her needlework and the like. Thankfully, the little girl finally decided that riding sidesaddle was not so terrible. Maggie suspected that this was solely due to the fact that Philip had informed her that the most graceful ladies rode in that manner.

As for Philip, he spent his afternoons with the earl, making use of the man's sharp mind. There was much he needed to learn, and what better teacher could be had than the man whose holdings would one day be his?

One morning, three weeks after his return to Bridgewater Park, Philip joined Maggie in the breakfast room as he often did.

"Good morning, Maggie," he said in greeting, a smile on his face.

"Good morning, Philip," she returned with a smile of her own. "Pray, what has you grinning so?"

He served himself and sat across from her. "I thought that we could go on a picnic today."

Maggie tilted her head to the side. "Well, I suppose Betsy could do without another needlepoint lesson this afternoon," she offered with a small smile. "The poor child's little fingers deserve a rest from the prick of the needle, I daresay."

They soon finished their breakfast and Maggie instructed the cook to prepare some light fare for their nooning meal. Telling Philip she would be down shortly, she went to her chamber to change into her riding habit. Philip met her at the bottom of the stairs with their bundle of food tucked under his arm. He ran his gaze over her. She wore the dark blue riding habit he so admired and her hair was once more fashioned into a single thick braid

"You do look lovely today, Maggie," Philip said as they strolled to the stables.

She accepted his compliment with an incline of her head, blushing lightly. He packed their parcel into one of the saddlebags and assisted her onto her mount. They rode out into the bright morning.

They stopped at the meadow by the stream, as the spot had long since become their favorite. Philip helped Maggie down from her horse, holding her closely to him for a long moment.

Unable to resist the lure of her perfect mouth, he placed his lips on hers.

"So sweet," he whispered as he raised his head.

"Philip," she said softly, shaking her head.

He sighed and released her. "You'll drive me quite mad, woman."

Maggie laughed and withdrew the blanket from behind her saddle. He took it from her and spread it on the ground, stepping back to allow her to sit. She did, looking about and sighing.

"It's so lovely here, Philip," she said. "I wish we could stay here forever."

Philip silently agreed, thinking there could be nothing more wonderful in the world than loving her on that blanket, the fragrant flowers around them. The crystal clear image of her naked and spread beneath him caused him to groan. Taking a breath to cool his ardor, he retrieved their bundle of food and handed her the package.

The cook had prepared a luncheon of cold roast beef and assorted cheeses, along with some crusty bread. A crock of cider finished their meal. Maggie set out the food while Philip poured them each a glass of cider.

"This looks marvelous," she said, slicing the bread.

Thankfully, he no longer felt the threat of that infamous knife he had yet to see let alone this one.

"Yes," Philip agreed. "There's nothing quite like eating out-of-doors."

Philip removed his jacket and joined her on the blanket. They ate their meal in companionable silence. As Maggie packed up their leavings, Philip reclined on the blanket, his hands under his head.

"Ah," he sighed, content.

Maggie smiled at him and set the bundle aside. She started to stand, but his hand on her knee stilled her.

"Let's dally here, Maggie," he said. "It's too beautiful a day to rush back to the house."

"Very well," she said, settling down once more, her legs tucked under her.

Philip rolled over to lean on one elbow. "Tell me about your childhood. I fear I know very little about you."

She shrugged, running her hands over her skirt in a feminine gesture Philip found most pleasing.

"There's very little to tell, I'm afraid," she began. "My mother and I lived alone. My father died before I was born, you see. The people in our part of Sussex were most kind, however."

"What was that like?" Philip asked. "Living with your mother, I mean?"

Maggie's smile was brighter than the sun and he smiled in response. "It was quite wonderful. She loved me so very much. I had a tutor, of course, to teach me the mundane aspects of being an educated lady in our society. But my mother taught me to ride and work the needle and how to carry myself like a lady."

Philip smiled at the wistful look on her beautiful face.

"I daresay she succeeded in her efforts."

"I miss her," she said, her voice soft.

He placed his hand on hers. "I didn't know my mother."

Maggie's brows shot up. He'd anticipated her surprise. In the weeks they had known each other, Philip never spoke a word about his childhood.

"How can that be so?"

Philip hesitated, loath to discuss the dismal past. But one look into Maggie's guileless face gave him the encouragement he needed.

81

"She died when I was very small. Just three years old."

"So, you were raised by your father," she put in.

Philip let out a harsh laugh. "Hardly. My father had more important matters to see to than the raising of his only child."

"Oh, Philip," she said, her brow furrowed.

Philip saw her concern and was heartened by it, but he wouldn't give any more thought to his neglectful father.

"Don't fret, Maggie," he said with a crooked smile. "I had nurses and nannies and tutors to see to my upbringing. I drove them all quite mad, I'm proud to say."

"I can see you as a little boy," she laughed. "All smiles and mischief and teasing laughter."

He shrugged at that.

"Did you have many friends?" she asked him.

"Friends?" he repeated. "Oh, I had boys to chum around with, I suppose. I still do. Did you have friends when you were growing up?"

Maggie shook her head. "Aside from my mother I had no true companions. My uncle came to visit quite often when I was a child, however. Oh, and I had Joan. My lady's maid."

Philip grinned. "The poor girl who doesn't take well to traveling?"

Maggie apparently caught his meaning, no doubt thinking back to their initial meeting at the Inn at Salisbury. She laughed and nodded vigorously.

"What of you, Philip?" she asked. "Don't you have anyone with whom you are close?"

He raised his brows as the truth settled on him. "I don't."

Maggie touched his hand with hers. "I'll be your friend."

He smiled, touched by the simple words. He realized then that he'd never spent as much time with a woman without bedding her as he had with Maggie. She made him feel… He couldn't put a word to what he felt, but it had ceased being primarily sexual weeks ago.

"Thank you, Maggie," he said. "I've never spoken of my childhood to anyone before. No one has ever asked me, really."

"I'm glad that you can speak to me."

Philip stared up at her, a strange feeling causing his breath to quicken.

"I enjoy talking to you," he returned in a soft voice. "You make me feel as if I matter."

Maggie's eyes widened then, shining as she gazed at him tenderly. "You do matter, Philip."

Philip looked at her, stunned. He swiftly came to his knees in front of her.

"Do I, Maggie?" he asked. "Do I matter to you?"

She placed her hand on his cheek. "Yes," she answered, her voice husky. "Very much so."

"Ah, Maggie," he said, rubbing his cheek against her hand.

Philip kissed her palm, the inside of her wrist. Maggie's breath caught at the gentle yet provocative motion. He cupped her face with his hands and leaned closer until their foreheads touched.

"You matter to me, Maggie," he whispered, bringing his lips to hers. "My Maggie."

He kissed her then, slowly penetrating her mouth with his tongue. Maggie whimpered and touched her tongue to his, setting him on fire. He wrapped his arms around her, pressing her tightly to him. He brought his lips to her ear, nibbling the lobe. She leaned her head to the side as he nuzzled her neck.

"Philip," she sighed, running her hands over his back.

Her gentle caresses increased his passion ten-fold.

"I want you, Maggie," he groaned, gently bringing her down to the blanket. "God, how I want you."

He worked the tiny buttons of her spencer, opening the jacket to reveal her thin chemise beneath. Maggie gasped as he caressed her breasts through the gauzy fabric.

"Do you want me, Maggie?" he asked, his lips trailing over her flesh.

"Philip," she began, breathless.

He untied her chemise and bared her breasts. "So lovely," he rasped, kissing her nipple.

He closed his mouth over the pink bud, sucking gently. Maggie arched beneath him. She cradled his head and held him there, her fingers twisting in his hair. Philip settled himself between her legs, rubbing against her. Their clothes soon became an irritant he wouldn't suffer any longer. He lifted her skirts and caressed her through her drawers.

"Oh, my!" Maggie cried, her eyes closed tight. "That feels so…"

Philip lifted his head from her breast to gaze at her face. Her eyes were closed, her lips parted as she took in shallow breaths.

"Maggie," he said again, coming up to kiss her lips. "My Maggie."

He kissed her as he began to unbutton his breeches, his arousal straining at the tight fabric. Maggie opened her eyes then, shock in their amber depths.

"Philip, we mustn't," she whispered, shaking her head.

"You were made for me, Maggie," he soothed, kissing her cheek, her neck. "Let me love you."

Maggie's body responded to his every touch. Yet suddenly she gave a violent shake of her head.

"No, no," she sobbed.

The fear in her voice reached him. He froze. He couldn't do it. He couldn't compromise her virtue.

"It's all right," he said, cupping her face in his hands. "We'll stop."

Maggie blinked back the tears in her eyes and nodded. Philip kissed her once more, tenderly. His hands shaking, he buttoned his breeches and closed her jacket over her breasts. He let out a ragged sigh.

"Ah, Maggie," he said, kissing her hair. "I'm sorry I frightened you."

She gave a quick shake of her head, sniffling. "I wasn't frightened. Not really," she said. "I knew you would never force me."

He gazed down at her, amazed at her faith in him taken with her opinion of him a scant month earlier.

"Let me hold you, Maggie?" he asked, stroking her hair. "Just let me hold you?"

Maggie nodded, snuggling into his side as he rubbed her back. She cuddled closer to him and let out a sigh. The warm sun on her back combined with the steady rise and fall of his chest soon lulled Maggie to sleep.

Philip studied her face, so beautiful in repose. Her cheeks were flushed, her lips parted. Her thick lashes rested on her cheeks, long and lush. Never had he seen such a beautiful girl. And she wasn't merely beautiful on the outside.

She was kind and sweet—and strong and smart—and made him feel like a better person than he imagined he was. He was still rigid with wanting her yet he was able to put aside his passion, something he never thought he could do. He closed his eyes and smiled, content.

Philip let her sleep for a long while, reveling in the way she felt in his arms. When the sun had moved quite a distance in the sky, he gently and reluctantly shook her awake.

"Maggie," he whispered, brushing her hair back from her face. "Wake up, love."

Maggie opened her eyes and blinked up at him in surprise.

"You called me 'love,'" she said in wonder.

Philip smiled ruefully. "I know you told me not to."

"You may," she said, her lips curving in a smile.

Philip flashed a wide smile at her. He sat up and turned, cradling her in his arms. Her jacket fell open, giving him an enticing glimpse of creamy flesh. He forced his eyes back to her face.

"We should return to the house, love," he told her, as reluctant as ever to let her go.

***

Much later, Philip stretched out on his bed. He thought back to what happened, or what very nearly happened, on their picnic and was amazed once more. Never before had he felt such passion, such wanting. Maggie was still a puzzle to him, innocent and passionate at once. But what was he to do about it?

He wanted her. And she wanted him, thinking back to her uninhibited response to his kisses and caresses. He was in no position to ask for her hand. He had no desire to marry, not for years to come. He had nothing of his own and wouldn't wish for the earl's demise to come into his inheritance. She was a lady, and he couldn't expect her to lay with him with no promise of a future. There was no use for it.

She was out of his reach.

Chapter 7

When Philip awoke the next morning, his mind was set. He would put an end to his flirtation with Maggie. As much as he wanted her, as good as she made him feel about himself, he was not going to continue his pursuit. It would only lead to one thing. And while he was certain that making love with Maggie would bring him the most pleasure he'd ever known, he wouldn't take her virginity. It wouldn't be fair to take her to his bed when he had no intention of asking for her hand.

His shoulders slumped, he dressed and went in search of her.

Getting no answer to his knock on her door, he went down to the breakfast room. Lord and Lady Bridgewater were seated at the table, their empty plates pushed aside. He nodded a greeting to them and crossed to the sideboard.

"I tell you, husband," Lady Bridgewater said with a smile. "She will cause a stir, I am certain."

"She's a lovely girl," the earl allowed, sipping his tea. "But do you truly believe she'll find a suitor out here in the country?"

Philip stiffened as he listened to their exchange.

"There are any number of squires in Somersetshire that are ready to take a wife," his aunt said.

Philip slowly turned toward his relatives. He forced a smile on his face. "Are you speaking of Maggie, madam?"

"Yes, dear," the lady answered. "We're attending a dance this evening, and I predict Maggie will have an offer of marriage before the month is out."

Philip struggled to hold his countenance. The thought of Maggie's taking a husband, a man who would be within his rights to take her into his bed and into his life, caused a sharp pain to settle in his heart. He glanced at the earl, who watched him closely.

"What do you think of Maggie's chances, Philip?" the earl asked.

Philip chose his words carefully. "I believe Maggie will be the most beautiful girl at that dance, sir," he said evenly. "Where is she this morning, if I may ask?"

"She took Betsy on an early ride," Lord Bridgewater answered, that speculative look still on his face.

Philip nodded and sat. He ate his food quickly, eager to be free from the earl's close scrutiny. Philip finished and stood, excusing himself. He strode into the parlor, his mind working.

He couldn't let her marry some country squire. She was his! He would ask for her hand himself. No other man would touch her, would share her love and spirit. Conviction filling him, Philip left the room to speak with Maggie's uncle.

When he reached the breakfast room, raised voices could be heard from within. He held himself still as he realized Maggie was the topic of discussion.

"We will not give her to some country fool," the earl said. "She is a lady. She will have a proper suitor, and not the first man who chooses to ask for her."

"She carries herself like a lady, I'll allow," her aunt returned. "But we know nothing of her birth."

The earl spat a curse. Philip pulled back. He'd never heard such language from the man.

"Her father was a baron," the earl said. "Her mother was—"

"Her mother was a trollop," she cut in. "Margaret will be lucky to make any sort of reasonable match with so muddy a history."

"I thought that she would find someone of high rank," the earl said. "Perhaps she and Philip—"

"Philip?" she cried. "My God, he'll be an earl one day. He has no need to saddle himself with a wife of so lowly a station."

"Maggie is not of low birth," the earl growled.

"She is," the woman said. "She lived alone with her mother. We know nothing of her father."

"Do you wish to know of her father?" the earl asked. "Well, I'll tell you. I'm her father."

Philip slumped against the wall, feeling the blood drain from his face. Maggie was the earl's daughter? Whatever chances she had of finding a suitor were now greatly reduced, no matter her beauty and gentility. This made her illegitimate, and any alliance with such a woman would be undesirable. And what of the earl? If word of it were to get out, he would be ruined by the scandal.

Philip would keep the secret, of course. The earl was as close as a father to him. But, what of Maggie? He still wanted her, but to marry her? He listened closely, as the room had fallen silent after her uncle's declaration.

"You're her father?" Lady Bridgewater whispered. "I should have known."

"I loved her mother," the earl said. "It was a long time ago, and I ended the affair before you and I married."

"You took your wife's sister?" she asked, aghast.

"Yes," the earl stated in a soft voice. "My wife was ill for so many years." Philip heard him sigh. "I won't have you breathing a word of this to Maggie."

"Oh, believe me, husband," she snapped, "I have no intention of letting your little bastard know the truth of her birth."

It nearly broke Philip's heart to hear Maggie referred to in such a manner. He turned and slowly walked toward the grand staircase.

A slight figure caught his eye as he reached the foyer. His eyes widened as Maggie hurried toward him, a smile on her face. Her hair was slightly mussed and her cheeks flush from her ride.

"Philip!" she gushed, grasping his hand with hers. "Good morning to you."

He squeezed her hand. "Hello, Maggie," he said, his throat tight.

She pulled back, confusion on her face. "Is something wrong?"

Philip ran his eyes over her, unable to equate the Maggie he now knew with the illegitimate get Lady Bridgewater had just derided.

"Maggie....," he faltered. "Ah, it's nothing."

Maggie looked at him closely. He flashed a grin at her.

"I hear talk of a dance to be held this evening?" he said, thinking to turn the topic.

"Oh, yes," Maggie returned. "My aunt says that I shall have the men eating from my hand, if you believe such a ridiculous notion."

"I believe you underestimate your worth," he said. "I only hope that you'll save a dance or two for me?"

Maggie laughed gaily. "You, dear Philip, may have three, for that is the most I'm to allow any man," she pointed out with a nod.

He smiled, his mood lightening. Surely he would think of something to set this to rights. She deserved far more than a hasty marriage to a country squire, despite Lady Bridgewater's assertions to the contrary. The trouble was, he had no idea what the solution could possibly be.

***

Lord and Lady Bridgewater stood with Philip in the foyer, dressed for their evening.

"It should be a pleasant evening, eh, Philip?" the earl asked.

Philip nodded absently. He'd thought of Maggie's situation all afternoon, and still no answer was clear to him. Though he paid no attention to the gossip among the *ton*, he knew the power it could wield. He would inherit the earldom at some time in the future, and must maintain the good Bridgewater name. For his children, if not for himself. *Children.*

Girls with Maggie's golden hair or boys with her strength of spirit. He let out a sigh which his relations most certainly took as exasperation for being forced to attend such a country dance.

He wore his black breeches topped with a dark gray jacket. A waistcoat of deep blue finished his dress. He tugged a bit at his white cravat, eager for Maggie's arrival. Just when he thought he would go mad from the waiting, movement at the top of the stairs caught his eye.

"Doesn't Margaret look lovely?" Lady Bridgewater said. "She looks quite the lady, wouldn't you say so, husband?"

Philip heard the sarcasm in the woman's tone and bristled. Maggie was a lady. And Lord, she was stunning! He let his eyes run over her, noting that the creamy gown nearly matched her skin tone. Her curls were styled in a graceful pile atop her head and several glossy tendrils trailed down to frame her face. She wore a smile for the three of them, her eyes sparkling as they settled on Philip.

"Maggie," he said reverently as she reached the bottom step. "You look beautiful."

"Thank you, Philip," she said softly.

He held his elbow out to her and led her out the front door. "I'm very pleased to be your escort this evening."

"Don't think to monopolize Margaret's company, Philip," Lady Bridgewater said firmly. "I daresay she'll have many young men vying for her attention."

"Yes, she will," the earl allowed. "Maggie, you'll take their breath away."

Philip silently agreed. He assisted Maggie up into the carriage, settling himself beside the earl on the seat facing her. The carriage pulled away, bound for the assembly hall and the evening awaiting them.

The dance was held in the nearby town of Taunton, a short ride from Bridgewater Park. Philip gazed at Maggie as they rode, listening with little interest to Lady Bridgewater's instructions to the girl.

"Now remember, Margaret," Lady Bridgewater said, "it won't do to pay too much attention to any one man. You don't want to be thought overly accommodating."

"Yes, Aunt," Maggie said with a nod.

Philip felt the earl stiffen beside him. Stealing a glance at him, Philip noted the man's pain at his wife's insinuations about Maggie's character. Thankfully, Maggie seemed oblivious to the current of tension in the close quarters. Philip sighed and gazed out the window, relieved to have the assembly hall in sight at last.

The party was well underway when the four of them arrived. The hall was quite festive, with candles lighting the space and flowers he couldn't name adding color. Several long refreshment tables were set up at one end, as were chairs around the perimeter. Philip took Maggie's elbow once more as they entered the hall.

The noise seemed to stop as they entered, for the local squires and their families were not accustomed to having Lord and Lady Bridgewater present. Soon, however, all eyes fell on Maggie. She trembled as the people all but gawked at her. Philip felt her fingers twitch and bent his head to hers.

"Nervous, Maggie?" he teased in a low voice. "I believe you have them spellbound."

His words had the desired effect. She smiled up at him, shaking her head at such a ridiculous notion. Philip returned her smile with one of his own and walked further into the room.

They were soon surrounded by the others in attendance. The matrons swarmed around Lady Bridgewater and Maggie, insisting on introductions. Several gentlemen—young and not so young—bowed low to the ladies, their eyes running over Maggie appreciatively. Philip heard the earl mutter a curse and leaned over to him.

"Did you say something, sir?" Philip asked.

"Look at them, Philip," the man answered. "The pups are drooling all over her."

Philip felt his own anger rise as he saw one young man lightly touch Maggie's hand. Taking a deep breath, he turned once more to the earl.

"Shall we get the ladies some refreshment?" he asked.

"Yes," Lord Bridgewater answered absently. "Yes, Philip."

Philip crossed to the refreshments, the earl following him.

***

Maggie smiled nervously at the gentlemen surrounding her and her aunt. One of the matrons waved at Lady Bridgewater, bidding her to join her on the other side of the hall. Maggie's aunt leaned over to whisper in her ear.

"Take care of all I have told you, Margaret," she said in a low voice.

"Yes, Aunt," Maggie said.

Maggie watched her aunt gracefully crossed the floor to join the older women. Maggie turned back to find a tall young man standing directly in front of her. Her aunt had introduced the man to her but Maggie couldn't recall the gentleman's name. He was on the thin side, with a shock of red hair.

"Lady Margaret," he said with a bright smile. "Would you do me the honor of a dance?"

"That would be lovely…"

"Squire Douglas," he finished for her.

"Squire Douglas."

Maggie smiled and put her gloved hand in his. He led her toward the dance floor. Just as the music began anew, a tall figure stepped in front of them. Maggie looked up to find Philip smiling crookedly at her. He schooled his expression and turned to the young man holding her hand. She glimpsed her uncle behind him, two glasses of punch held in his hands.

"Pray, forgive me, Douglas," Philip said with a bow. "But you see, Lady Margaret promised me the first dance of the evening."

"If you don't mind?" Philip added, not sounding like he cared a whit if the man did so.

"I…," Douglas stammered. "I suppose not."

"Capital," Philip said, twirling Maggie away from him.

He held Maggie closely for a moment, and then led her through a slow, graceful waltz.

"You dance divinely, Maggie," he said. "But I shouldn't be surprised."

Maggie shook her head at him, hiding her own smile.

"I didn't promise you the first dance, Philip," she pointed out to him. "And well you know it."

Philip shrugged. "You should have."

Maggie rolled her eyes and sighed. He chuckled as he twirled her about. He spied Squire Douglas at the edge of the dance floor, his eyes intent.

"I daresay young Douglas is quite eager to have you in his arms," he said, his tone light.

"He seems a pleasant sort of young man," Maggie said with a shrug of her shoulders.

Philip said nothing to that.

"Maggie," he said after a few moments, "you take my breath away in this incredible gown."

She inclined her head in return.

"Although," he went on, bringing his lips to her ear, "I believe I prefer you in your thinnest underthings, your hair a wild tumble."

"Philip!" She caught the glint in his eye and shook her head. "You, Lord Wilton, are incorrigible."

He laughed. "Guilty as charged."

The dance ended much too soon. Reluctantly, she followed him back to Lady Bridgewater. Before she could catch her breath, Squire Douglas grasped her hand.

"Lady Margaret," he said with a bow. "Our dance awaits."

Maggie permitted the squire to lead her out onto the dance floor. Douglas began to move about the floor with her through a quadrille.

"You move like an angel," the man said with a smile.

Maggie looked over at the earnest young man. His gaze was intent, his blue eyes bright. He was but a few years older than Maggie herself. He was a pleasant-looking fellow. Her eyes fell on Philip where he stood watching her, causing her heart to beat a bit faster. Any man would pale by comparison to Philip, though. Shaking her head as if to clear it, she turned her attention back to her partner.

***

The evening wore on. Maggie danced with several of the men present, both waltzes and more sedate country dances.

Philip stood and watched as men young and old alike vied for her attention. He waved down one of the servers and grabbed a mug of ale from the girl's tray. He drank it down swiftly and took another. The Earl of Bridgewater's voice caught his attention.

"She's quite popular, isn't she, Philip?"

"Yes," Philip said flatly.

Lord Bridgewater eyed him closely, as he had that very morning.

"I saw you dancing with her earlier," he said.

"Three dances, sir." Philip smiled. "And no more."

The earl laughed, for he too had heard his wife's endless recital of the rules and customs Maggie must follow.

"It's a pity one must follow such rigid rules of conduct, eh?"

Philip looked at the man then, catching the twinkle in his eye. Giving a firm nod, Philip set his mug aside and took quick strides to where Maggie stood surrounded by several young men.

"Lady Margaret," he said with a low bow. "May I beg another dance?"

Maggie looked up at him in obvious surprise. He smiled then and, without a word, she placed her hand in his.

"Ah, Maggie," he whispered when they were once more on the dance floor. "You feel wonderful in my arms."

He held her closer than was proper, but Maggie didn't appear to notice. She smiled up at him and he felt as though they were the only two people in the room.

"I do so like dancing with you, Philip," she returned, a bit out of breath.

"It would appear so," he teased. "This is our fourth dance."

She gasped and held herself away from him. "We must stop. You must let me go."

"Never," he said, his voice husky.

Maggie relented and followed him through the rest of the dance. He would never let her go.

Something whispered in the back of his mind. Was he thinking about much more than a simple dance?

Chapter 8

When Philip finally brought Maggie back to where Lady Bridgewater stood, it was with regret. The fact that Squire Douglas stood beside the woman did little to ease his mind. Silly little whelp.

"Lady Margaret," Douglas said with a smile surely meant for Maggie alone, "Your aunt tells me that you ride quite well."

"I ride adequately, I suppose," Maggie returned with her usual modesty. "I do enjoy it."

"Perhaps we could go riding together one day soon," he said. "You could show me all of your favorite places on your uncle's fine estate."

Maggie looked quickly at Philip, and he knew that she was thinking of their beautiful meadow. Philip glared back at her. Maggie seemed to puzzle over the abrupt change in his demeanor, but he said nothing. She turned back to Douglas.

"I would enjoy that, Squire Douglas," she said.

The young squire beamed at her. "Splendid!" he exclaimed. "You have already permitted me three dances. Perhaps you will join me for a turnabout the room?"

Maggie looked at her aunt, who gave a swift nod of her head. She smiled at Douglas and let him take her elbow. Philip stared at her, his anger rising. He watched her as he thought of their last ride, and of their picnic by the meadow. Let the boy think to take her there. It would be the last thing he ever did.

"Look at her, Philip," Lady Bridgewater said, drawing Philip's attention from Maggie's slender form. "I knew that the young men would be taken with her, but even I'm surprised by such interest."

"Maggie is a remarkable girl, madam," Philip said.

Lady Bridgewater nodded. "She would do well to marry someone like Squire Douglas."

Philip grunted in answer as he raised his arm to signal another server. He grabbed up a tankard of ale from the girl's tray and drank down a healthy gulp. Try though he might, he was not successful in blocking the sound of Lady Bridgewater's voice. The woman went on to extol the young squire's virtues.

"His estate—or I should say, his father's estate—is not large, but quite impressive just the same. Maggie would do well, indeed."

"Surely Maggie could marry higher than a country squire," Philip said. "She's—"

"She's no one, Philip," the woman cut in. "She's well-suited to life as a squire's wife, living as she did in the country. All alone with her mother in a primitive cottage."

Philip arched a brow at her. "Primitive, madam?"

"Oh, very well," the woman conceded. "I'm certain that the girl's father left her well provided-for."

The woman's voice dripped sarcasm, which was not lost on Philip. His gaze settled on the earl then, where he stood talking to some elderly gentlemen. As Philip watched him, he noticed the man's eyes continually settled on Maggie as she strolled about the room. The warmth in the man's gaze told Philip that he felt much more than monetary responsibility for the girl. It was obvious that he loved his daughter.

When at last they called for the carriage, Philip was feeling out-of-sorts. The ale did little to ease his mind, as he'd had to suffer Lady Bridgewater's continual discussion of the young men present and how taken they were with Maggie. He let the earl assist Maggie up into the carriage, all but dragging his feet as he slowly climbed in behind them. Maggie sat across from him, as she had on the trip to the assembly hall. She tried to catch his eye once or twice but Philip repeatedly lowered his gaze.

"Margaret," Lady Bridgewater gushed, "your uncle has had requests from many of the young gentlemen in attendance. Several of them would like to call on you. We'll discuss them on the morrow, and you may then decide who shall be granted an audience."

Philip watched out of the corner of his eye as she gave a nod of her head.

"Yes, Aunt," Maggie said.

"You may see any of the gentlemen you choose, dear," the older woman went on. "Why, Squire Douglas was the first to speak to the earl, wasn't he, husband?"

"Yes," the earl said tonelessly, staring out the window.

"I believe, Margaret, that young Squire Douglas is quite taken with you. I wouldn't be surprised if you receive an offer of marriage before a fortnight has passed."

The other occupants of the carriage said nothing to that.

Philip grudgingly helped Maggie down from the carriage when they arrived back home at Bridgewater Park. She turned to face him as they stood in the foyer, gazing up at him. Philip stood stiffly before her, eager to be out of her presence to puzzle over his odd feelings in private.

"It certainly was a long evening, Philip," Maggie said. "I believe I'm quite done in."

Philip raised his eyes at last and ran his gaze over her face. He knew that she expected him to escort her to her room, as he'd done each night for weeks now. He didn't dare. Not tonight.

"Good night, Maggie," he said, his tone brusque.

He saw Maggie flinch slightly at his coldness.

"Good night, Philip," she said. "Good night, Aunt. Uncle."

"Good night, my dear," the earl returned.

She turned and slowly began her ascent. Philip watched her, his mind set. He knew without question that if he brought her to her room, he would kiss her. And once he started kissing her, he feared he would not be able to stop.

Accepting the earl's offer of a glass of brandy, Philip turned from the staircase, bound for the man's study. Not long afterward, Philip set aside his half-finished his drink and bade the earl good night. In the hallway upstairs, bound for his chambers, he paused for a moment in front of Maggie's door. He raised his fist to knock, changing his mind in an instant. He opened his hand and placed it on the door. Trailing his fingers over the smooth wood panel, he let out a sigh as soft as a whisper. No. He would leave her alone, as she deserved to be. Sighing once more, he went to his room.

He removed his jacket and laid it across one of the chairs. Unbuttoning his waistcoat, he began to pace. He thought back to the dance, to how lovely Maggie looked. He also thought of her many admirers, and of one young man in particular.

"Silly country fool," he muttered, his mind on the red-haired squire.

His ire growing, he tore off his cravat and threw it down. As he unbuttoned his shirt, he thought once more of the boy who had chased after Maggie all evening. He knew the young man would call on her. And if he did, Philip decided, he would certainly fall in love with her. How could he not? She was the sweetest, most beautiful girl in the world. Lady Bridgewater would force the match, that was certain. He sat down to remove his boots. And Douglas would marry her. The squire would take her to his bed and make her his.

"The hell he will," Philip growled, throwing his boot to join its mate on the floor.

He left his room, bound for Maggie's chamber.

***

Maggie had donned a nightgown of thin white lawn and sent Joan from her room. She now sat in front of the vanity. She slowly ran her brush through her hair, her mind on Philip and his very odd behavior since leaving the dance.

Maggie set her brush aside and leaned forward to blow out the candle. A knock on her door stilled her. Before she could reach the door, the knocking came again. She walked swiftly to the door and pulled it open, drawing in a breath at the sight before her. Philip filled the doorway, barefoot. He wore his breeches, his shirt unbuttoned to the waist.

She blinked up at him. "Philip, what are you doing here?"

"I won't stand for it, Maggie," he said, stepping into the room. Maggie as closed the door and turned back to him. "I won't stand for it."

"I don't understand."

He grabbed her to him, bringing his face close to hers. He ran his gaze over her face, his eyes settling on her mouth.

"No one else shall have you, Maggie," he rasped. "You're mine."

He crushed his mouth to hers, his tongue teasing a response from her. Maggie placed her hands on his chest, her fingers splayed. Philip brought his lips to her neck, gently nuzzling her soft skin.

"You're mine, Maggie," he said again. "Ah, God. I love you."

They froze, both stunned as the words spilled from his lips. Maggie leaned back to stare up at him. The truth was there in his eyes for her to see.

"Philip," she whispered, her hand on his cheek. "Oh, Philip."

Philip kissed her palm and placed her hand on his chest. "Touch me, Maggie," he said, closing his eyes. "Touch me."

Maggie let her hands run over his chest, delighting in the way the crisp hairs tickled her palms. She pushed his shirt off of his shoulders, and then brought her lips to his chest and lightly kissed his skin.

Philip moaned at her gentle caress, his fingers twining in her curls. He cupped the back of her head and brought her lips to his once more. Her fingers trailed over his flat stomach, hesitating at the waistband of his breeches. He grasped her hand

and placed it on himself. His arousal strained at the thin fabric as Maggie lightly raked her nails over him.

"Ah, Maggie," he groaned. "Can you feel how much I want you?"

She nodded, amazed. He seemed to be in pain, but if that were so, why was he keeping her hand there? He suddenly flinched, pulling her hand away to bring it to his lips. Philip cradled her cheek with his hand, tracing his thumb over her lips.

"Maggie," he said reverently. "My Maggie."

He kissed her again, his tongue gently stroking hers. As he kissed her, he deftly unfastened the tiny buttons running down the front of her nightgown. He lifted his head as he spread the material wide, gently pushing it off her shoulders to fall to the floor. He swore softly, and then swept her up into his arms.

He placed her in the middle of her bed, pausing only long enough to peel off his breeches before stretching out on top of her. Maggie gasped as his hair-roughened chest brushed across her breasts.

"Philip," she sighed, wriggling beneath him.

He bent his head and flicked his tongue over her nipple. Drawing the bud into his mouth, he gave her what she hadn't known she craved. Maggie sighed again, her fingers running through his hair as she kept him at her breast. He slowly trailed his fingers down to the curls that shielded her womanhood, gently urging her legs apart as he slid one finger inside of her. Maggie brought her legs together, frightened.

"Easy, sweetheart," Philip said softly. "Let me love you."

She relaxed a bit as he stoked the fire he was building inside of her. When his thumb began to circle the tiny nub of pleasure hidden within, she nearly screamed.

"Do you want me, Maggie?" he asked, coming up to kiss her once more.

"Yes, Philip," she whimpered. "Yes, I want you."

"Ah, Maggie," he said, settling himself between her thighs. "That's it, love. Let me inside."

Maggie spread her legs as his arousal probe her very center. She arched instinctively, taking in the tip. He eased inside, then paused. She opened her eyes and stared up at him, puzzled.

"You're mine, Maggie," he said, his voice rough. "Say it."

"I'm yours," she breathed.

He nodded and closed his eyes. With one deep thrust, he broke through her maidenhead and buried himself in her softness. She cried out, her pain sharp.

Philip held himself still as he soothed her with kisses.

"The pain will soon cease," he whispered. "Kiss me."

She nodded and opened her lips to him. As he kissed her, he began to move. He felt hot and hard and he filled her to bursting. It was remarkable.

"Does that hurt?" he asked.

Maggie gave a quick shake of her head as a burst of pleasure shot through her. Philip's thrusts became deeper, taking her higher and higher. She clutched at his shoulders as she neared her climax.

"Come to me, Maggie."

Maggie cried out his name as waves of pleasure washed over her. Philip let go of his control then, driving into her as his own climax shook him to his big body. He collapsed on top of her, burying his face in her hair. Inexplicably, she began to sob softly.

He held himself up on his elbows, his eyes on her face. "I'm sorry I hurt you, love."

"No, Philip," Maggie said, placing her hand on his cheek. "You didn't hurt me, not really. It was just so… It was beyond words."

Philip flashed her an arrogant grin. "You made me feel good too, sweetheart."

He rolled off of her and drew her to his side. Maggie rested her head on his chest, her fingers tracing over his heated skin.

"Philip?" she asked after a moment.

"Yes, Maggie?" he returned, running his hand over her back.

"You said that you love me."

"Did I?" he teased. Maggie picked up her head to gaze warily at him. "Then it must be true."

Maggie smiled and cuddled closer. Philip let out a sigh of intense satisfaction as he hugged her tightly to him.

"I'll handle everything, Maggie," he went on. "I'll need to think of how best to approach your uncle on this. Perhaps tomorrow on our hunt."

Maggie nodded. "I'll be taking Betsy riding on the morrow."

Philip chuckled, causing her to lift her head once more. His smile widened at the befuddlement on her face.

"I daresay you won't feel up to riding tomorrow."

"Why not?"

He stroked her cheek with his finger. "You'll be a bit sore, I'm afraid."

"Oh!" Maggie gasped, flushing.

"Ah, Maggie," he said. "I don't understand how you can be a wanton in my arms in one moment and as shy as a school girl in the next."

Her cheeks grew hotter and she had no answer to that.

"I do love you, Maggie," he said, kissing her.

They held each other for a while, Philip finally breaking the spell with his loud sigh.

"I must get back to my room, love," he said, swinging his legs over the side of the bed.

Maggie watched him as he pulled on his breeches, not bothering to button them. He bent down and gave her a sweet kiss.

"Good night, Maggie," he said. "Dream of me," he added with a grin.

Maggie let her eyes run over his magnificent form.

"How could I not?" she asked, causing his grin to widen.

He winked at her and left, closing the door quietly behind himself. Maggie picked her nightgown up off the floor and slipped into it. She returned to the bed, cuddling into the sheets which still bore Philip's heat, his scent. He loved her!

Letting out a soft sigh, she drifted off to sleep.

***

Philip entered his chamber and closed the door, taking a moment to lean against the wood panel. Never had he felt such passion, such complete satisfaction. Straightening, he once more stripped off his clothes and climbed into his bed. He laid there, staring up at the ceiling and thinking of the declaration he made to her earlier. He did love her. Never in his entire lifetime had he ever said those words to another human being. Not to his mother and certainly not to his father. As far as any other women in his life, he bedded them and rarely saw them again. Maggie was different. His heart knew that.

She was his, and he would find a way for them to be together forever.

Chapter 9

The next morning, Maggie awoke and stretched, a smile on her face. She swung her legs over the side of the bed and stood, and then felt a tenderness between her legs. She thought of Philip in that instant, a light flush covering her cheeks. He was right on at least one count. She wouldn't go riding today.

She rang for a bath and hurried into the dressing room, puzzling over which of her pretty day dresses to wear. No doubt she would see Philip after his hunt, and she wished to look her best. Settling on a lovely dress of sunny yellow, she took her bath and rang for Joan to help her ready for her day.

When Maggie went downstairs to the breakfast room she found it empty. For that she was grateful, as she was certain she wore all that happened between her and Philip clear on her face. She served herself and sat at the table.

She finished her meal and was sipping from her tea cup when her aunt's voice caught her attention from the doorway.

"Margaret," Lady Bridgewater said in short greeting, breezing into the room. "We have a visitor this morning." The woman turned just as quickly to exit the room. "Do join us in the parlor, dear."

Maggie stood and brushed her hands over her skirt, suddenly self-conscious. Surely one of her prospective suitors would not be so impertinent as to call without an invitation, would he? She hurried toward the parlor, and was quite surprised as her gaze fell on the lovely young woman standing beside her aunt.

"Margaret, I would like to introduce you to Lady Sarah Addington. Lady Sarah, this is our niece, Lady Margaret Penworth."

Maggie curtseyed to the woman who was not much older than herself. The lady's hair was a dark, glossy black, and her eyes were clearest blue. She was very pretty.

"I'm pleased to meet you, Lady Sarah."

"And I you, Lady Margaret," Lady Sarah returned with a curtsy of her own.

The dark-haired woman ran her gaze over Maggie, though Maggie couldn't fathom the reason her blue eyes flashed. Lady Sarah raised her chin and took a seat beside the fire. Lady Bridgewater and Maggie joined her there.

"What brings you to Bridgewater Park?" Maggie couldn't help but ask.

Lady Sarah waved a graceful hand in the air, dismissing Maggie's question. "You're the earl's niece?" Her eyes narrowed. "I'm surprised that Lord Wilton never mentioned you to me."

Maggie shook her head in confusion. Just how did this lady know Philip? Once again she read the glint of interest in the lady's blue eyes.

"I came to Bridgewater Park but a few weeks ago," Maggie said. "I wasn't acquainted with Lord Wilton before that time."

"Ah," the other woman said knowingly. "It is no wonder then that he said nothing of you when last I saw him in London."

Maggie looked at her aunt, befuddled.

"You see, Margaret," her aunt began, "Lady Sarah is the daughter of a very good friend of ours, the Earl of Addington. She is very nearly betrothed to our Philip."

Maggie's heart fell to her stomach. Philip had asked for this pretty woman's hand? He was betrothed to another? Maggie closed her eyes as shame settled on her. She had given herself to a man who had no intention of offering for her.

"Margaret, dear. Are you quite all right?" Lady Bridgewater asked.

Maggie opened her eyes and managed a smile for the other two women. "I believe I ate my breakfast a bit too rapidly," she said. "I will be fine, I assure you."

Maggie felt Lady Sarah's eyes on her as her aunt rang for tea. A masculine voice in the hall soon drew everyone's attention to the doorway. Philip strode into the room, a smile on his face as his eyes settled on Maggie.

"Maggie, I have given thought to our situation, and…," his voice trailed off as he realized they were not alone.

"Philip, dear," Lady Bridgewater gushed, coming to her feet. "I'm so pleased that you are back early from your hunt. Pray, look who has come for an extended visit."

Philip turned to Lady Sarah, amazement on his face. "Lady Sarah? What brings you to Bridgewater Park?"

"Hello, Lord Wilton," the young woman said, coming to her feet and batting her eyes in a way that made Maggie wish to poke her fingers in them. "You left London with such haste, I did not have the chance to tell you I had been in contact with Lady Bridgewater. It was very naughty of you to leave me with nary a word."

Philip's brow furrowed. "I don't understand. What has your visit to do with me?"

Lady Sarah laughed, and then she and Lady Bridgewater exchanged a knowing look.

"Philip, dear," the older woman began, "Lord Bridgewater and I believe it is time you took your courtship of Lady Sarah to the next level."

"My courtship?" he asked. "What are you talking about?"

"We would be most pleased if the two of you would announce your betrothal before the Season is out."

"Our what?"

Maggie couldn't hold in her sob. He shot her a glance and she looked away from him.

"Lady Sarah," Philip began, "I don't know what has transpired between Lady Bridgewater and yourself, but I assure you we will not announce our betrothal."

"Lady Bridgewater said that you would be a bit reluctant to make so permanent a gesture," Lady Sarah said. "No matter. I will simply stay here until we can all come to some sort of agreement."

Maggie, her hand pressed to her stomach, rose from the settee. "Please excuse me," she sobbed, all but running from the room.

"Maggie, wait." Philip turned to go after her.

Maggie ran to her room and slammed the door, falling back against it as fat tears coursed down her cheeks. Philip was betrothed, or nearly betrothed, to that woman. What a fool she was to believe he loved her. He'd wanted her. That was certain. And she had given herself to him, willingly.

"More fool me," she said softly.

A knock on her door startled her out of her reverie. Wiping the tears from her eyes, and pulled the door open. A servant stood in the doorway, a missive held out in front of him.

"A message for you, my lady," he said with a bow.

Maggie thanked the man and closed the door once more, puzzling over the masculine handwriting on the note. She opened the note and read the contents. It was from Squire Douglas, requesting an audience with her that afternoon. Philip would have no use for her now that he had bedded her.

Nodding firmly, she walked over to the small writing desk near the window and penned a reply in the positive.

***

Philip sat in the parlor, his mood dark. Lady Sarah discussed the parties in London, Lady Bridgewater hanging on every word. The younger woman spoke of the "hideous" dresses some of the "silly" girls deemed proper for wear. Talk soon turned to weddings and the like.

"I believe in long engagements, don't you, Lord Wilton?" Lady Sarah asked.

"What?" He smiled without humor. "I suppose that if one must be engaged, that would be preferable."

Lady Sarah laughed harshly, setting Philip's teeth on edge. He gave her a small smile and looked once more to the doorway. What must Maggie be thinking? She had looked hurt and angry both, and he couldn't blame her for either condition. Breathing a heavy sigh, Philip turned his attention back to the two women in the parlor.

The Earl of Bridgewater entered the parlor, puzzlement on his face. "Lady Sarah? I wasn't aware you were coming for a visit."

Lady Bridgewater gave a short laugh and insisted that they had discussed her visiting weeks ago. Philip watched the three of them closely, not liking the smug smile on Lady Sarah's face. He glanced at the older woman, noting that she wore nearly the same look. Just what was she about?

After Philip deemed a sufficient amount of time had passed, he excused himself and left the parlor in search of Maggie. He found her in her room, feeling guilt slash through him as he saw the tell-tale redness rimming her beautiful eyes. She started to close the door on him but Philip placed his hand on the wood panel.

"Maggie, listen to me," he said. "I had no idea that woman was…"

His voice trailed off as he took in her appearance. He noticed she had changed into a pretty tea dress of peach. Her hair shone, as if she had spent quite a bit of time brushing the silky curls that framed her face.

"Why are you dressed so?" he asked.

"That, sir, is none of your concern," she replied tartly.

A dark thought flitted through Philip's mind. Why, she looked to him like a woman expecting a visit from a suitor!

"Is that whelp coming here today?" he asked.

Maggie took a step back from him, her hands on her hips. "Squire Douglas is calling on me this afternoon, yes."

"The hell you say!" Philip growled. "What are you thinking, permitting him to call on you?"

Maggie glared back at him. "I can see whomever I choose, Lord Wilton."

He grabbed her shoulders and gave her a slight shake. "Maggie."

Maggie shook free of his hold, her chin held high. "I suggest you return to your fiancée," she said.

"She's not my—!"

Maggie closed the door on his reply mere moments before breaking into fresh sobs. Cursing fluently, Philip left her alone.

That afternoon, Philip did his best to avoid Lady Sarah, closing himself in Lord Bridgewater's study. The earl joined him there shortly before tea time.

"What an interesting turn of events, Philip," the man said. "Did you know of Lady Sarah's visit?"

"No." He raked his fingers through his hair and took a deep, calming breath. "I have no idea why she's here or why she's acting the way she is. I've made no promises to her."

The earl eyed him closely. "I've heard talk of your reputation in town. Could she have misinterpreted your attentions, son?"

"Hardly," Philip said in answer. "I barely spoke to her when I was in town."

"Well," the earl said, "I know my wife is for the match."

Philip's green eyes narrowed. "There will be no match between myself and Lady Sarah Addington."

The earl laughed without humor and rose. "I don't envy you your predicament." He turned to the study door. "Oh, there has been another interesting development. Maggie's squire has called."

Philip spat out a curse, earning a look of triumph from the earl that he refused to contemplate. He left the room then, Philip trailing behind him.

Tea time was a trial on Philip's patience, for Lady Sarah sat as close to him as was proper. She eyed him like a bird after a juicy worm. Looking away from the woman's intent gaze, Philip let his eyes caress Maggie's slender form, perched daintily on the settee near Squire Douglas. The red-haired young man told an amusing story, at which Maggie bestowed one of her lovely smiles on him. Philip fumed in silence.

At last Maggie turned from her very pleasant conversation with Douglas to find Philip staring at her. Unable to help himself, he thought back to the incredible night they shared. Her sweet words and passionate caresses were fresh in his mind, and if the tenderness in her gaze was any indication, they were in her mind as well.

Philip was heartened by that tenderness. He did love her and, if the warmth in her gaze was any indication, she felt the same. His lips formed her name, causing Maggie's lovely eyes to widen. She gave an almost imperceptible shake of her head, turning back to the young gentleman seated beside her.

Squire Douglas smiled at Maggie, and then set his cup aside. "Lady Margaret, I would so enjoy taking a turn in your uncle's lovely gardens. Would you join me?"

Philip all but willed her to deny the boy and Maggie hesitated for a moment. But she soon glanced over at Lady Sarah. The woman was practically draped over him, her hands clutching at the sleeve of his jacket. Maggie turned back to Douglas and agreed to take a stroll with him in the gardens. The young man rose and, bowing to the others, gently grasped her elbow. Philip watched as the man led Maggie to the glass doors at the back of the house and into the gardens beyond.

Philip rose from his seat and crossed to where the earl sat, conveniently affording himself full view of the garden through the window.

Nodding absently to the conversation around him, he couldn't keep his eyes from following Maggie as she walked beside the young squire.

***

"I admit I have never enjoyed an afternoon as much," Douglas said to Maggie when they were alone. "I'm most pleased that you agreed to see me."

"I've enjoyed your visit," Maggie said.

They strolled about, finally coming to rest on one of the stone benches placed about the formal garden. Squire Douglas took Maggie's hand in his, letting his thumb caress her palm.

"Lady Margaret," the man began, his eyes on her face. "Forgive me if I am being a bit forward, but may I call on you tomorrow?"

Maggie froze, unsure of her actions. Would she be encouraging his attentions if she told him he could call? She had no true notion of what was proper among this particular level of society. While she found him a pleasant person, and quite easy to talk to, she held no romantic feelings for him. Her heart belonged to Philip. But nothing would come of their union now.

She looked up into Douglas' face and gave him the smallest smile. "I would like that."

The squire's face brightened. He brought her hand to his lips and placed a chaste kiss on the back of it.

"Shall we go riding?" he asked, helping her to her feet.

"That would be most pleasant," Maggie answered.

After he gave his farewells to Lord and Lady Bridgewater and the others, Maggie accompanied him to the entryway at the front of the house. Bowing gallantly, he left her. Maggie closed the door, turning to find Philip standing close behind her.

"Philip!" she gasped in surprise.

Her surprise soon gave way to anger as she noted the disapproval on his face.

"I saw you in the garden," Philip grumbled. "I can't believe you would welcome that fool's attentions."

"I merely agreed to go riding with him tomorrow," she said with a shrug.

Philip grabbed her arm and pulled her close, his eyes boring into hers. Maggie blinked back tears as she struggled to keep her resolve.

"Maggie," he pleaded. "Why won't you listen to me? What happened last night, what I said?"

"I will never again believe a word you say to me, Lord Wilton."

She pulled out of his grasp and hurried to the bottom of the stairs.

"Maggie!"

She ran up the stairs.

That evening after dinner, during which her aunt and Lady Sarah had dominated the conversation, they all adjourned to the parlor. Settling herself on a chair beside the glass doors, Maggie gazed out at the darkened garden. She'd enjoyed her stroll with Squire Douglas. He could prove a likeable sort of friend. Yet, when Philip had held her close in the foyer after his visit, she'd very nearly fallen into his arms. He had her, mind and body, and she knew it would be nearly impossible to break his hold on her.

Maggie turned her attention to the others once again. She couldn't withstand Philip's intense gaze on her any longer. The hour wasn't very late, but she excused herself and rose to go to her bed chamber nonetheless.

"Maggie," Philip said, coming to stand beside her. "Let me escort you."

She shook her head firmly. "You have a guest, Philip. I'll see myself to my room."

She bade the others good night and left Philip staring after her, his mouth agape. In her chamber at last, Maggie sat down at her vanity, too preoccupied to think of changing for bed at the moment. She didn't even ring for Joan to assist her. She slowly unpinned her hair, letting her fingers twine through the curls as she closed her eyes. After a while, she stood and began to unhook the back of her gown.

Philip suddenly burst into her room, quickly closing the door behind him. She turned toward the door, her eyes round.

"Philip, leave my room this instant!"

"I won't," he said, coming to tower over her. "You will listen to me, Maggie."

She shook her head. Philip's eyes raked over her and she saw desire flare in their green depths. Maggie stared up at him as if mesmerized. She opened her lips to him as he brought his mouth to hers. Their tongues touched, setting her on fire. He grabbed her to him as he ran his lips over her cheek, her neck. Maggie leaned her head back as he kissed the hollow of her throat, her eyes closed in blissful surrender.

"Ah, Maggie," he said, his voice hoarse. "I love you."

His words penetrated Maggie's mind in an instant. She stepped out of his grasp, crossing her arms as she turned her back on him.

"You'll say anything to get into my bed," she said, her voice breaking.

"That's not true," Philip insisted, placing his hands on her shoulders.

She shrugged off his touch and turned. "What you feel for me is lust, Philip," she said. "That's all it will ever be."

He shook his head firmly at her accusation, his brow furrowed.

"I love you, Maggie," he said. "I have never said those words to another person in my entire life."

Maggie dismissed that statement with a wave of her hand. "You've wanted to bed me since first you saw me, when you thought me a trollop," she said, sniffling. "You can't deny that."

He held his hands in fists at his sides.

"I did lust after you," he said. "I don't deny that I wanted you at the Inn at Salisbury, and I don't deny that I want you still."

Maggie let out a strangled sob. She hung her head and turned from him.

"I do want you. But I feel so much more than lust for you."

"I am ruined because of you, Philip," she whispered.

"No," he argued. "You are good and pure and sweet."

"Your sweet words will not sway me," she cut in, wiping her tears away. "Leave me, Philip. Please."

Apparently he saw no other argument at last, and he walked slowly to the door. He turned to her once more. "I love you, Maggie," he said fervently. "And if it takes forever to prove it to you, so be it."

He left then, leaving Maggie to stare after him as he had done earlier.

Chapter 10

Philip sat at the table, his plate piled high with eggs and bacon. He picked at his breakfast, his mind not on food at the moment. Maggie had dismissed him last night, as easily as his own father had all those years ago. He gave her his heart and she discounted its worth. Taking up his cup of strong tea, he swallowed down both the brew and his wounded pride. He had vowed to prove his love to Maggie. Pity he had no plan to see that through.

He looked up as Maggie entered, running his eyes slowly over her as he drank in the enticing picture she made in her gold riding habit. The feather trailing from the little hat perched on her head served to bring even more attention to her remarkable eyes.

"Maggie," he said, a smile curving his lips. "You look quite fetching this morning."

"Thank you," Maggie answered stiffly, walking to the sideboard.

Choosing a light meal of sweet rolls and tea, she settled herself at the far end of the dining table.

"Good morning, all," Lady Sarah gushed as she breezed into the room. "Lady Margaret, that outfit is simply adorable!"

"Thank you, Lady Sarah," Maggie returned with a nod.

Lady Sarah served herself and sat beside Philip, who pulled away from her. The three of them ate quietly for a while before Lady Sarah finally broke the silence.

"Are you going riding this morning?" she asked Maggie.

Maggie dabbed her napkin on her lips, taking up her cup of tea. "Yes. Squire Douglas is calling in a short while."

Philip swore under his breath, but not so far under that the two young ladies did not hear him.

"Lord Wilton," the dark-haired girl began, "do you wish to go riding, as well? I would so adore going for a ride with you."

Philip thought of something then, something that lifted his spirits considerably. He turned slowly toward her, a polite smile fixed on his face.

"I would enjoy a ride this morning, yes," he said. "Would you care to join me?"

"Oh, yes!" Lady Sarah exclaimed. "Give me a moment to change into my riding clothes and we shall be off."

He nodded as she rose and left, bound for her guest room. His smile widened as he saw the bemusement on Maggie's face.

"How pleasant our ride will be, Maggie," he said, digging into his meal with renewed vigor. "I believe the four of us will have a most enjoyable time."

Maggie's mouth gaped open. "You are not accompanying us, Philip," she said.

She was interrupted as a servant announced the arrival of the squire. Dabbing her lips once more, she placed her napkin on the table and rose. Philip did likewise, following her into the parlor.

"Lady Margaret," Squire Douglas said with a bow. "I bid you good morning." He noticed Philip's presence then. "Hello, Lord Wilton."

"Douglas," Philip returned with a nod.

The squire turned his attention from Philip back to Maggie, a smile spreading across his face. "Lady Margaret, you look absolutely lovely this morning."

Maggie smiled as she accepted the man's compliment. "Let us be off."

She took the squire's offered arm and the two turned to leave the room.

"If the two of you would but wait a moment," Philip said, drawing them up short. "Lady Sarah and I will be happy to join you."

Maggie fixed a look of pique at him, at which he feigned innocence. She turned back to Douglas.

"Why don't we let them meet up with us at the stables?" she offered.

"Capital," the man returned, leading her from the room.

It was of no consequence. In a few moments he and Lady Sarah would be joining them, putting an end to the possibility of the inane pup's getting Maggie alone.

Nearly thirty minutes later, Philip still paced about the foyer in irritation. Lady Sarah glided down the stairs to greet him.

"What the devil took you so long?" he asked.

Lady Sarah flashed him a coquettish smile as she twirled about in her light blue riding habit.

"I wanted to look my best," she said in explanation. "What do you think of my outfit?"

"You look fine," he said absently, taking her arm. "Now, let's go to the stables."

When they arrived at the stables, Philip wasn't at all surprised to find Maggie and her suitor already gone. He would catch up to them.

"Lord Wilton," Lady Sarah began, her eyelids fluttering, "I daresay I require a bit of assistance into the saddle."

He rolled his eyes and motioned for the groom. The man helped her up as Philip mounted his steed. Waving her ahead of him, they slowly left the stables.

"There's nothing like a good, hard ride in the morning," Philip said with a flick of the reins.

He urged his horse to a gallop, his eyes quickly scanning the landscape for any sign of Maggie. A shrill yell brought him up short. He turned back to find Lady Sarah far behind, her horse barely trotting along. He rode back to her, barely keeping his irritation in check.

"May I ask what is keeping you?"

"It will not do for a lady to overtax herself," she said in explanation. "I won't find myself winded or flushed."

"Ah, for the love of…!" Philip began, irate. He took a deep calming breath and gave her a curt nod. "Let's go," he said without enthusiasm.

The two of them rode side-by-side, with Lady Sarah keeping up a steady stream of irritating chatter as Philip continued to search the grounds for any sign of Maggie and her insipid suitor.

He caught no sight of Maggie or the young squire. He sat stiffly in his saddle as he guided his horse slowly over the green hills. His horse looked at him as if to ask why they weren't galloping freely. He'd already had just about enough of this outing.

He bent down to pat the animal's neck, and then turned back to Lady Sarah. "Why don't we return to the house?"

"Oh, no!" she cried. "We have only just begun our ride."

Philip studied her for a moment, fixing a look of concern on his face.

"I believe your nose is turning a bit pink."

The lady gasped and demanded they return to the stables at once. Hiding his smile, Philip nodded and happily led the way. As they reached the stables, the sound of Maggie's laughter caught his attention. He turned in his saddle to find her and her suitor galloping toward them. They reined in their horses in front of Philip and Lady Sarah, laughing once more.

"I daresay, Lady Margaret," Squire Douglas said, his breath coming fast. "You are an excellent rider."

"Thank you," Maggie returned, sounding a bit winded. "Hello, Lady Sarah. Lord Wilton."

"Hello," Lady Sarah returned.

Philip nodded and ran his eyes over Maggie, noting her flushed cheeks and bright eyes. He barely heard Lady Sarah's going on about their own very pleasant ride, his senses were so filled with Maggie. He wanted to pluck her from her saddle and settle her on his. He wanted to lift her pretty gold skirt and caress her until she melted. He wanted to unbutton his breeches and pull her down on top of himself, letting her softness enfold him. Shifting in his saddle, he tried to ignore the throbbing desire making him most uncomfortable.

"...Lord Wilton?" Lady Sarah's voice broke through to him.

"Hmm?" he asked, turning toward her.

"Wasn't our ride quite wonderful?" she asked.

"Yes," he said shortly. He turned to Maggie once more. "I trust the two of you had an enjoyable ride."

Squire Douglas laughed at that. "Lady Margaret nearly wore me out."

Philip managed a smile at the man's exuberance, and then dismounted. He crossed to where Maggie sat on her mount, thinking to help her down. Douglas got to her first, assisting Maggie as he kept his hands on her slender waist. Maggie lowered her lashes as she stepped out of his grasp. Philip favored her with a dark look. As he watched she turned her attention to her dress, running her hands over her skirt and brushing her hair away from her eyes.

"I must look a fright," she said with a short laugh.

"No," both men answered.

They exchanged a look of surprise. Philip turned away and helped Lady Sarah down from her mount. The woman leaned against him, pressing herself close. He held her away from him and set her on her feet, and then handed the reins to the waiting groom. His ears pricked as Douglas lowered his voice.

"I would like to see you tomorrow, Lady Margaret," the squire said, taking her hand.

Maggie agreed with a nod. Emboldened, the man kissed the back of her hand. Giving him a small smile, Maggie tugged her hand out of his grasp. Philip stepped closer to the couple and the party returned to the house.

***

Over the next two weeks, Maggie managed to avoid being alone with Philip. With just one look, he could set her heart to pounding. Squire Douglas called on her quite frequently and, while she liked the man as a friend, she feared he was eager for a more serious attachment. Thankfully, she still spent her afternoons with Betsy. The child offered her the only opportunity to focus on pleasant if mundane tasks without thoughts of either man intruding.

Upstairs in Maggie's chamber one afternoon, Betsy sat beside her as she readied for tea. As Joan tweaked the curls framing Maggie's face, the child watched her, her eyes huge.

"Mother says that Squire Douglas will ask for your hand." Betsy leaned forward to peer into the mirror. "She says he is captivated with you."

Maggie smiled to hear the child use such a word. She stood and Joan assisted her into a tea gown of light blue.

"I don't believe the squire's feelings are quite as strong as that," she said with a smile.

Joan left them and Betsy took Maggie's seat at the vanity. She picked up Maggie's brush, running it through her own ringlets.

"Mother wants Philip to ask for Lady Sarah's hand," she said offhandedly. "But I don't want him to."

Maggie felt her heart sink as she thought of Philip and that cloying woman together. She shook her head and managed to smile at her young cousin.

"And why is that, sweetheart?"

Betsy shrugged her small shoulders. "I don't like her. She only speaks nicely to me when Philip is near."

Maggie agreed with the child's astute observation.

"Besides," Betsy went on, standing up to brush her hands over her skirt as she had seen Maggie do time and again. "He doesn't love her."

Maggie's heart nearly stopped. "How do you know that?"

Betsy turned to stare at her. "He doesn't look at her the way he looks at you," she said simply. "His eyes get all sparkly when he looks at you."

Maggie felt her heart start beating again. She processed all that the child had told her. Was it true? Did Philip truly love her? Betsy's voice broke through to her again.

"I've been practicing my roses," she said.

"Pardon?" Maggie asked.

"My roses," Betsy repeated. "I still have trouble with the little petals."

Maggie took the child's hand in hers and turned it over. Tell-tale needle-pricks marred her thumb and forefinger. Maggie kissed the tiny injuries and patted her hand. Betsy smiled as she left her, bound for the nursery.

That evening, Maggie was chagrined to note that Lady Sarah apparently hadn't given up on her intent to land Philip for a husband. The woman sat a bit closer to him than was proper, and placed her hand on his arm whenever the opportunity arose. For Philip's part, he didn't seem to be encouraging the woman's attentions. That seemed to confirmed Betsy's innocent observation. He continued his slow perusal of Maggie however, leaving her feeling vulnerable and strangely titillated.

Maggie slept fitfully that night. She recalled the heat in his gaze that evening.

"Oh, Philip," she whispered into the dark.

She hugged her pillow and waited for sleep to claim her.

Chapter 11

Soon after breakfast the next day, a servant announced Squire Douglas' arrival. Nodding to Philip and Lady Sarah, who had joined her in the breakfast room, Maggie adjourned to the parlor.

Maggie found Douglas beside the glass doors, staring out at the gardens.

"Hello, Squire Douglas," she said as she came into the room.

The young man turned and flashed her a bright smile. "Lady Margaret."

She crossed over to where he stood and permitted him to take her hand in his. She smiled nervously as he gently led her to the settee and brought her down to sit beside him. He gazed at her for a long moment, warmth in his eyes. Maggie felt her apprehension grow.

"Squire Douglas," she began, running her hands over the skirt of her violet day dress, "I daresay you seem most intent this morning."

"You are quite right," he said, his eyes bright. "Lady Margaret, I..." He quirked a half-smile at her. "May I call you 'Maggie?'"

Maggie nodded her agreement to the man's request. His smile widened as he slowly stroked her hand with his.

"Maggie," he began anew. "I know that we've only known each other a few short weeks."

Maggie stiffened as she quickly grasped the man's meaning.

"Squire Douglas," Maggie cut in.

"Please," he said, patting her hand. "Allow me to say what I came to say?"

After a moment, Maggie nodded once more, bracing herself for the proposal sure to come.

"What I feel for you, Maggie," he said, leaning closer to her, "I've never felt for another. I'm here this morning to tell you that I wish to speak to your uncle. I'm going to ask for your hand."

She gasped, shaking her head.

"Don't think to give me an answer this day, dear Maggie," he said, stroking his finger gently on her cheek. "I only ask that you think on it."

She faltered. "We hardly know each other, and there is…" She stopped herself before saying Philip's name.

Douglas stood then, taking her with him. "Don't fret," he said, smiling once more. "You'll think on it?"

Maggie nodded, her heart racing. How on earth could she marry Squire Douglas? Her heart belonged to Philip, although the scoundrel had no thoughts toward marriage. Bemused, she permitted the squire to lead her out into the foyer.

"I will speak to your uncle tomorrow," the squire said in the entry.

Maggie could only nod. She took a deep breath and turned, startled to find Philip standing in the foyer. His legs were braced apart, his hands in fists at his side. His sheer masculinity overwhelmed her, sending any lingering thoughts of Squire Douglas fleeing from her mind. How could she think of another man when he stood before her, so strong and magnificent?

Their attachment would come to nothing but she couldn't deny to herself that she loved him. The look on his beloved and handsome face gave her pause, though. Obvious anger caused his eyes to flash green fire.

"Maggie," he said, his voice a low rumble.

She blinked and involuntarily took a step back. He countered with a step forward, and then grasped her elbow firmly.

"Lady Sarah," he said, his eyes not leaving Maggie's face, "would you please excuse us? Lady Margaret and I have a most important matter to discuss."

"Philip," Maggie whispered, digging in her heels.

"A family matter," he clarified, finally looking at the dark-haired girl.

"Certainly," Lady Sarah said easily, turning to go into the parlor.

After the woman left them, Philip strode into the library, pulling Maggie along with him. He all but pushed her into the room, closing the doors before turning to face her. Maggie flinched at his fierce expression.

"Philip," she began, "I don't believe that was very polite."

"Pray, tell me I didn't hear what I think I did," he said through clenched teeth.

Maggie held her hands in front of her, feigning innocence.

"I don't know what it is you believe you heard, Philip," she said. "Perhaps you can enlighten me."

"That pup is going to speak to the earl?"

"Yes."

Philip advanced on her. "About what?" he asked, his eyes narrowed.

She stepped away from him until she felt the wall of bookshelves at her back. She realized her position and consciously straightened, forcing calm in her demeanor.

"He wishes to ask for my hand."

"The hell you say!" Philip growled, reaching out to grab her. "How can you entertain the notion of marrying that boy? My God, you may already be carrying my child!"

Maggie's mouth hung open in shock. "But that's impossible," she stammered. "It was only the one time!"

Philip released her and raked his fingers through his hair in frustration. "Ah, you are so damned innocent."

Maggie's shock gave way to anger. "I am no longer, thanks to you," she returned. "You took my innocence from me."

He grunted at her. "That's not what I meant."

Maggie thought quickly. She'd had her last monthly the past week, as expected. She raised her chin as she met his gaze.

"You need not concern yourself, Lord Wilton," she said coolly. "I'm quite certain that I'm not carrying your child."

As Maggie watched, an inscrutable look crossed his face. If she didn't know better, she would say he looked disappointed. But how could that be?

"Maggie, please tell me you don't think to marry that dolt."

"I gave him no promises, Philip," she said. "He'll speak to my uncle tomorrow."

Philip braced his arms on either side of her, bringing his face to hers. Maggie's breath caught at the intensity in his gaze.

"Promise me that you won't do something we'll both regret?" he pleaded, his lips close to hers. "Please?"

She felt the power he held over her then, his passion causing her love for him to surge anew.

"I promise."

"Maggie," he rasped. "I'll set matters to rights. We'll be together."

He kissed her then, his lips rubbing hers gently. A knock at the library doors brought him quickly away from her.

"Lord Wilton?" Lady Sarah called.

He swore softly. "Yes?" he returned, his eyes on Maggie's parted lips.

"Are you quite finished?"

Philip turned his head, eyeing the door with contempt. Maggie seized the opportunity to duck under his arm and hurry to the door. She pulled it open, smiling at the girl on the other side.

"We are quite finished with our business, Lady Sarah," Maggie smiled. "Do enjoy your day."

"Maggie," Philip said, stepping toward the door.

Maggie turned back. "I promised Betsy that I would teach her some new stitches today, Philip," she rushed out. "Please excuse me."

With that, she left the library, bound for the nursery. There she could puzzle through her feelings for the man without his presence to taunt her.

***

Late that evening, long after dinner, Philip sat alone in his uncle's study, a glass of brandy in his hand. He swirled the amber liquid, his eyes closed as he took a long sip. Maggie's image was before him, as was the case whenever he closed his eyes. She'd managed to avoid him all day, much to his chagrin. He caught a glimpse of her once that afternoon, however, in the parlor. She sat with Betsy, her head bent to the child's as she patiently explained the workings of a particular needlework stitch. The expression on her face was so sweet that his heart had ached. Uncertainty was clear on her face when she happened to glance up at him, though. Draining the last of his brandy, he rose and took himself up to his chambers.

He stripped off his clothes and slid beneath the sheets, a loud sigh escaping his lips. Surely he could convince Maggie to reject the squire's offer. She loved him, not that silly country fool. He'd felt it that afternoon. He'd seen it in the amber depths of her eyes. He closed his eyes at last, a smile teasing his lips.

"Philip," a voice whispered in the dark.

Philip's eyes snapped open, taking a long while to adjust to the gloom in the chamber. "Who's there?"

He saw the nightgown-clad figure and smiled, thinking of Maggie. In the next moment the figure spoke, dispelling that notion.

"It is I, Lady Sarah," Sarah said in a trembling voice.

"What?" he asked, coming to a sitting position in the bed. "What the devil are you doing in here?"

Lady Sarah managed a smile as she stretched out beside him in the big bed. She held herself still, her arms at her side.

"Take me, Lord Wilton," she said, her eyes squeezed tightly shut.

Philip sat there, stunned. He recovered himself and barked out a harsh laugh at the female sacrifice before him.

"Take you?" he asked. "I assure you, miss, were I the least bit tempted, I would greatly object to your lack of enthusiasm."

She opened her eyes then, anger showing in their blue depths. "Then I shall simply tell all that you ruined me," she said, glaring at him. "And then you will be forced to marry me."

Philip leaned over her, anger curling in his belly.

"Don't even think to perpetrate such a ruse," he warned, his face close to hers. "If you do, I'll tell all who will listen that you came here to seduce me."

"No!" She came to her feet beside the bed. "You have my word that no one will know of this."

"Good," he said, sitting back. "Now leave my chamber, please."

Sarah gasped, and then grabbed up her wrapper and moving quickly to the door. Philip settled back down into the covers, his hands folded beneath his head. That was a close thing. He'd seen her disdain for his person, however. There was no chance she would tell anyone she'd been in his room, let alone that she'd attempted an assignation with him.

***

Maggie crept to her door, intent on visiting Philip in his chamber. She had decided she had to reject the squire's offer of marriage, no matter her uncle's opinion on the match. She loved Philip and knew that she would simply have to learn to trust him. He'd promised her he would set matters to rights, and she believed him sincere.

She opened her door and peered out, pulling back inside her darkened doorway as a slight figure hurried past. It was Lady Sarah! The woman wore only her nightgown, and her wrapper dragged on the floor behind her.

"That scoundrel," Maggie muttered.

Tears threatened to spill over her lashes. What a fool she'd been to once more believe his sweet words. Did he use those same words to coax Lady Sarah into his bed? Choking back a sob, she closed her door and returned to her own bed, her tears wetting the pillow as she slowly drifted off to sleep.

Breakfast the next morning was a trying ordeal for all concerned, Maggie presumed. Lady Sarah kept her eyes firmly on the table as she picked at her meal, merely nodding to any questions put to her. She suddenly raised her head to look at Lady Bridgewater.

"I'm returning to town this morning, Lady Bridgewater," Lady Sarah said.

"But you only just arrived, dear," she said.

Lady Sarah stood. "I miss the excitement of London, I fear," she stated with a small smile. "I'm not well-suited to life in the country. I do thank you for your generosity during my visit, however."

"Nonsense," the earl said, his smile wide. "You're welcome at Bridgewater Park anytime, my dear. Do give your father our best."

Lady Sarah smiled and said her farewells, leaving the room to ready her belongings for her trip to London.

Maggie watched the woman go, confused. She happened a glance in Philip's direction. He looked quite relieved, confirming

Maggie's suspicions. Apparently he cast the dark-haired girl aside with even less effort than he had her.

"Maggie, dear," the earl said, "I'm expecting a visit from Squire Douglas this morning."

Maggie nodded, to which the earl raised an eyebrow.

"You know of this?" he asked. "Then I assume you know what this is regarding?"

"Yes, Uncle," Maggie said, ignoring Philip's probing gaze from where he sat beside her. "Squire Douglas informed me of his intentions yesterday."

The earl and his wife exchanged a look.

"You care for him, then?" the earl asked Maggie.

"I'm fond of him, yes."

"And you would be open to such a match?" he asked.

"Yes, Uncle," she said quickly.

The earl nodded, his eyes on his heir. Maggie followed the man's gaze. Philip's face had lost its color as his mouth hung open in surprise.

"I told you, husband," Lady Bridgewater crowed. "Barely a fortnight has passed and Maggie is spoken for. What do you think of this, Philip?"

Philip grunted in answer. Maggie had no desire to know his thoughts on the subject. She excused herself and stood, bound for the relative peace and quiet of the nursery.

Once out in the hall, she stopped to catch her breath. First seeing Lady Sarah and then giving her agreement to a match with Squire Douglas? It was a lot to take in.

"I don't know if they will suit, wife," the earl said from the breakfast room. "There's no need to give her hand to the first man who asks for it."

"She'll do no better," Lady Bridgewater answered. "Surely you see that."

"I refuse to give her to some country fool," the earl went on. "She doesn't even love him!"

"What purpose does love serve, husband?" she asked bitingly.

Maggie froze. What was this about? There was an undercurrent of tension coming from that room but she was in no state of mind to puzzle through this.

She pushed herself off of the wall and headed for the nursery and relative peace and quiet.

Chapter 12

Philip returned to the stables in a much better frame of mind. Surely he could convince Maggie to refuse the squire's attentions, no matter the earl's decision on the matter.

Philip reined in his horse. The animal, a bit lathered from its exertion, turned to eye his rider closely. The horse appeared most pleased to have his old master back, to ride fast and furious as was their custom.

"Take good care of him," he told the groom with a grin. "I worked him furiously today."

Feeling more himself, Philip headed for the house by way of the gardens. As he neared the hedgerows, two figures came into view. He saw they were Squire Douglas and Maggie, standing close to each other. Philip bristled as he watched her permit the man to brush a kiss on her cheek. The squire left her then, obviously bound for the earl's study. Philip took quick strides to where she stood beside the stone wall and came up behind her.

"Maggie."

Maggie gasped and spun around, her eyes round. "Philip!"

"You won't marry that boy, Maggie," he said, grasping her arms gently. "I love you."

Maggie stiffened in his hold. "That's of no consequence," she said, lowering her eyes.

"Of no consequence?" he repeated. "But, why?"

She pulled away from him, flicking her head in a show of nonchalance. "I've already given my word to Squire Douglas."

"You will not marry that whelp!" Philip grabbed her once more. "You don't love him."

"I'm fond of him," Maggie said.

"Does he kiss you like this?"

He crushed his mouth to hers. Maggie opened under his tender assault, permitting his tongue free rein. She sighed into his mouth, pleasure causing her to shiver. Philip, shaken by her response, moaned as he brought his lips to her ear.

"Has he made love to you, Maggie?" he rasped. "Has he felt you come apart in his arms?"

Maggie shook her head in answer.

"What of Lady Sarah?" she managed to ask. "Did she come apart in your arms?"

Philip pulled back. "I've never dallied with Lady Sarah."

Maggie told him all she had seen the previous night. Philip quickly told her of the lady's plans to trap him into marriage.

"Maggie, love," he said. "She sought to trap me into marriage for my inheritance. That's not so unusual among ladies of good breeding. Naturally, I refused the lady's advances."

"Truly?"

"Sweetheart," he said, cupping her cheek with one hand. "How could I be tempted by another woman when I have such perfection before me?"

"Oh, Philip," she sighed, wrapping her arms around his neck.

Philip placed his hands beneath her bottom and lifted her, holding her tightly to him as he carried her to the copse of trees on the other side of the wall.

"Tell me, Maggie," Philip said, his lips on her throat. "Tell me you love me."

Maggie's eyes were closed as she leaned her head back.

"Yes, Philip," Maggie answered breathlessly. "I love you!"

In the dappled shade beneath the trees, Philip shrugged off his jacket as Maggie ran her hands over his chest. He grabbed

164

her hands and placed them around his neck once more, pulling her tightly against him.

"Maggie," he whispered, kissing her ear, her neck. "My Maggie."

Maggie ran her fingers through his hair as his lips caressed her soft skin. Philip managed to unfasten a few of the hooks at the back of her dress, urging the bodice down as he lowered her to the soft grass beneath their feet. He untied the ribbon at the top of her chemise, baring her breasts to him. Maggie shivered as he closed his mouth over one nipple.

"Philip," she sighed, clutching at his shoulders.

Reaching beneath her skirts, Philip deftly removed her drawers and found her damp and ready for him. He caressed her deeply, eliciting whimpers of pleasure from her. He pulled back to unbutton his breeches, coming up to kiss her lips once more.

"There won't be any pain this time, love," he promised in a hoarse whisper. "Only pleasure."

Maggie nodded and rose up to meet him as he entered her with one deep thrust. He drove into her, unable to go slowly. The past weeks of denial caught up to him and he feared he would take his pleasure before she found hers. Miraculously, Maggie soon matched him stroke for stroke, her nails raking his back as she tightened around him. Her climax hit her as Philip came with a shout, pouring himself into her. He fell atop her, a smile curving his lips. With the sun on his back and his angel beneath him, he was certain he'd found heaven.

"I love you, Maggie," he said when he found his voice.

"Oh, Philip," she said, her eyes still closed. "I love you."

After a few moments, they roused themselves. Philip helped her adjust her clothing.

"I'll speak to the earl directly," he said, shrugging on his jacket.

"We'll marry, Philip?"

He saw her uncertainty and sought to dispel it, flashing her a big grin.

"My God, woman," he teased. "You can't expect to take such advantage of me and not give me your hand in matrimony."

She laughed then, the sweet laugh he loved. He hugged her and urged her to go into the house.

"I'll follow shortly, love," he said, unable to resist the urge to kiss her once more.

Philip couldn't hide his grin as he entered the house soon after. He was pleased to see no one about. He hurried up to his chambers to change, thinking to approach her uncle before they all gathered for tea time. Appropriately garbed and his hair combed, Philip paused before Maggie's door. He rapped lightly on the panel.

"Maggie," he whispered at the crack of the door.

Maggie pulled the door open and favored him with the sweetest smile he had ever seen.

"Wish me luck, sweetheart," he said, kissing her lightly. "I'm off to see the earl."

"Good luck, Philip."

He studied her face for a long moment, his eyes settling on her full lips. He cupped the back of her head and brought his lips to hers once more, kissing her thoroughly. When he lifted his head, he was most pleased to find Maggie's eyes closed, her breath quickened. He chuckled, causing her eyes to flutter open at last. With a jaunty bow, he left her.

The Earl of Bridgewater was in his study, as Philip had anticipated. He rapped on the open door, wearing a smile on his face for the man who was more of a father than a cousin to him. The earl returned the expression, waving Philip inside.

"Come in, come in," he urged. "And do close the door, my boy."

Philip arched a brow at the earl's demeanor. He almost seemed as though he fully expected the visit.

"I wish to speak to you, sir," Philip said, closing the door.

"Nothing dour, I hope," the earl teased.

"No, sir. Quite the opposite, actually."

Waving the younger man to take a seat, the earl returned to his chair behind his desk. He folded his hands on the smooth surface and leaned forward, his eyes twinkling.

"I am to assume this is about your betrothal?"

Philip blinked. Recognition settled on him as he realized that the man thought Philip planned to ask for Lady Sarah's hand.

"No," he said, shaking his head. "Well, yes. I... That is, I wish to marry Maggie."

"Capital!" the earl said, coming to his feet once more. "High time you came to realize what a sound match the two of you will make."

"But," Philip said, shaking his head as the earl pulled him to his feet. "How on earth did you know?"

The older man flashed him a bright smile as he clapped him on the shoulder. "I've seen you with her, son. There is also the matter of the young squire's hasty withdrawal of his offer."

"What?" Philip asked.

The earl chuckled as he poured each of them a glass of brandy to celebrate. "Apparently the man discovered that Maggie's affections lay elsewhere," he said, setting the bottle down.

Philip held himself still. "When?"

"This afternoon."

Philip closed his eyes and groaned softly. Surely the young man had not seen him with Maggie in the woods.

"Easy, my boy," the earl laughed. "He was resigned to the matter. Not upset, really."

"That's good, sir," Philip said with a smile. "Now there will be no cause for me to call the man out."

"Or he you."

The two of them laughed as they touched their glasses. Philip drained his glass and set it down, serious once more.

"There is more that I must tell you."

It was the earl's turn to be surprised. "What is it?"

"I know of your relationship to Maggie, sir," Philip said. "I know that you're her father."

The older man sighed, loud and long. "Does Maggie know?"

"No, and I don't intend to tell her."

The earl nodded. "Thank you, son. I have no wish for her to think ill of her mother. Or of me."

"I fear she would be far too upset were she to learn the truth," Philip said. "I would give my life to protect her heart."

The earl eyed him. "You love her, then?"

"Completely."

"Capital," the earl said again, blinking back a tear of joy. "Capital."

***

Maggie sat with Lady Bridgewater in the parlor, her hands twisting nervously in the folds of her yellow tea dress. She looked down into her lap and made a conscious effort to loosen their grip. She smoothed her hands over her hair and smiled nervously at her aunt.

"Goodness, Margaret," Lady Bridgewater said. "What on earth is plaguing you this afternoon?"

Maggie gave her a small smile. "Nothing, I assure you."

The older woman gave a slow nod. "I believe this has to do with your betrothal."

Maggie opened her mouth to respond but movement at the doorway stilling her. The earl breezed into the room, Philip close behind in his wake.

"You are correct in your assumptions, wife," the earl said.

"Oh!" Lady Bridgewater exclaimed, her hands clasped in front of her. "I was certain that Squire Douglas would ask for her hand today."

The earl shared a smile with Philip and shook his head.

"He did," the man told his wife. "And he withdrew his offer almost immediately."

"What?" Lady Bridgewater asked, blinking rapidly. She turned sharply toward Maggie. "Margaret, are you not betrothed?"

Maggie blushed furiously as all eyes fell on her. Philip smiled as he crossed to her, and then turned back to face Lady Bridgewater.

"Maggie is betrothed, madam," he said. "To me."

Lady Bridgewater wore her surprise on her face, her eyes opened wide, her mouth agape. The earl chuckled at his wife's apparent distress.

"I believe we caught her quite by surprise, children." He came to sit beside his wife. "I admit that I was a bit surprised, as well."

Lady Bridgewater recovered herself and gazed at Philip and Maggie. "I should have expected this, Philip." She gave a firm nod. "When Lady Sarah took her leave this morning, I should have known."

Philip took Maggie's hand in his and sat down beside her.

"I believe our match was set when I came to Maggie's rescue at the Inn at Salisbury," he said with a smile.

Lady Bridgewater was quiet for a long moment, worrying Maggie greatly. She suddenly smiled brightly in her direction. Maggie warmed at the expression.

"We must order your dress, Margaret," Lady Bridgewater said. "Philip, I assume that you will procure a special license? Oh, and the flowers will have to be ordered…"

Maggie tried to follow Lady Bridgewater's instructions and suggestions, greatly distracted by Philip's slowly stroking his thumb over her palm. She happened a glance in his direction, and a pleasurable warmth spreading through her as his eyes darkened to the deepest green. She gazed up at him, remembering his sweet kisses and enticing caresses of earlier. He must have caught a glimpse of her thoughts. He grinned and shook his head at her in warning, bringing his lips to her ear.

"If you keep looking at me that way, love," he whispered, "I may have to kiss you right here in front of your aunt and uncle."

Maggie swiftly looked down at her lap. Philip chuckled and turned his attentions back to the earl, who informed him of the procedures involved in obtaining the special license. The license was needed in their case, as Philip's official residence was in London and Maggie was considered a guest in Somersetshire.

Maggie finally looked up, her cheeks cooled sufficiently to comfortably pay attention to her aunt and the many wedding plans the woman already had in mind. She was to marry Philip!

Could she ever have guessed matters would end in such a happy way when they'd crossed paths at that inn?

Chapter 13

The wedding was planned for two weeks hence, with Philip and Maggie marrying from Bridgewater Park. They would return to London the following day for, as Philip happily informed her one afternoon, there were a few major parties left of the Season and he wished to show her off to the *ton*.

"You will captivate them, bride," he said with a grin.

He told her of his London townhouse as well, located in the respectable West End not far from Hyde Park.

"I daresay my home is in dire need of a woman's touch, love," he went on. "Are you up to the challenge?"

She smiled cheekily. "I believe I can persevere, Philip."

Standing on a stool in her chamber one morning soon after their betrothal, Maggie simply nodded her approval as Lady Bridgewater planned the event down to the tiniest detail, mindful of the older woman's expertise in such matters. Maggie withstood the poking and measuring as the seamstress wrapped her in fabric. She created a gorgeous dress of the palest yellow satin for the ceremony, as Lady Bridgewater insisted the particular shade complimented Maggie's own coloring beautifully. Declaring the gown nearly finished, the seamstress took her leave of them.

"You look ravishing, Margaret," Lady Bridgewater said. "Philip will be speechless, I daresay."

"That would certainly be a rarity."

Her aunt nodded. "How do you wish we dress your hair?" She cocked her head to the side. "Of course you will wear it up, and I thought perhaps a bonnet with a veil…"

"Flowers," Maggie said suddenly.

Her aunt thought for a long moment.

"Yes," Lady Bridgewater conceded. "A wreath of roses would suit you nicely."

Maggie shook her head. "Oh, no. Wildflowers, Aunt. Wildflowers of different colors."

"Wildflowers?"

Maggie told her of the meadow and of its vast assortment of beautiful flowers. Finally, the older woman nodded again.

"We'll send the servants to pick them, Margaret," she said. "I believe the wildflowers will look lovely on you."

That afternoon, Maggie and Philip shared tea with the earl and his wife, their discussion turning once again to the upcoming nuptials. Betsy and little Mary each had a fitting that morning after Maggie's, and both children were outfitted with pretty dresses of pale pink.

"Betsy is quite excited, Aunt," Maggie said, sipping her tea. "She nearly fell from the stool during her fitting."

Lady Bridgewater chuckled. "The seamstress had quite a time with her, not to mention the little one."

Maggie smiled as she reached for a fluffy biscuit. "Mary seemed to take it all in her stride," she said. "Although she did look a bit perplexed."

"She surely wonders what all the fuss is about," Philip interjected. "As do I," he teased Maggie. "I would just as easily marry you in my riding clothes, love."

Maggie shook her head at him as the older woman clicked her tongue.

"You will do no such thing, Philip," Lady Bridgewater said. "You'll wear formal black with a crisp white shirt and cravat."

"And shining boots, son," the earl added with a smile.

Philip sighed dramatically, rolling his eyes skyward.

Maggie swatting him playfully on his arm, at which Philip grabbed her hand and brought it to his lips.

"Ah, what I wouldn't do for my Maggie," he said, his eyes sparkling.

Maggie blushed as she gently pulled out of his grasp, running her hands carefully over her skirt. She turned to her uncle then, her brow furrowed. A wonderful notion had occurred to her, although she was a bit nervous to bring the idea to the others' attention.

"Uncle," she began hesitantly, "there is something I wish to ask of you."

The earl nodded and set his cup aside. "You may ask me anything, my dear."

Maggie glanced at Philip and noticed the interest stamped on his face. She gave him a nervous smile and turned back to the earl.

"It would please me greatly if you would give me away at the ceremony," she said.

Silence fell on the parlor as the three others quickly exchanged looks of surprise. Lady Bridgewater gave an almost imperceptible nod to her husband.

The earl blinked rapidly as he took in Maggie's simple statement and his wife's agreement. Maggie suspected her request touched Lord Bridgewater in a way she couldn't imagine. Perhaps he'd come to feel like a father to her over these past weeks. The earl reached over and took Maggie's hands in his.

"Maggie, dear," he said, his voice a bit gruff. "I would be honored."

Maggie smiled sweetly at him and nodded, turning toward Philip at last.

"Capital idea, love," Philip said.

***

Four days later, Bridgewater Park was in a state of anticipation, servants rushing about to perform their last-minute duties. The wedding was set for later that morning, the celebration to commence afterward. Only the family would attend the ceremony itself, with a local clergyman performing the rite. Philip had procured the special license enabling them to marry in Somersetshire, and the parish clerk was expected to attend the service, as well. As to the party following, most of the revelers were friends and long-time acquaintances of Lord and Lady Bridgewater's.

For most of the previous week, Maggie and Lady Bridgewater had painstakingly penned the many invitations. After a moment's hesitation, Squire Douglas was included in the guest list. As Maggie had no friends in Somersetshire, she was more than pleased to have Lady Bridgewater decide who would be graced with an invitation to what she insisted would be the grandest party the county had seen in a very long time.

Most of Philip's contemporaries were still in London and, as he informed Maggie, he did not consider them close enough chums to warrant beseeching them to leave town at the height of the Season. Maggie penned announcements for these acquaintances of his. They planned to move within the social whirl when they returned to town.

At the appointed time, Philip stood in the parlor of Bridgewater Park with Lady Bridgewater nearby. He shifted from one foot to the other and pulled at his cravat, his eyes fixed on the doorway.

"Goodness, Philip," Lady Bridgewater gently chided, readjusting his cravat. "Do calm yourself."

Philip smiled shakily at her and nodded. He glanced over at the others in attendance and quickly read the mild amusement in the clergyman's eyes. The clerk, however, couldn't contain his own smile at the groom's obvious nervousness. Lady Bridgewater soon drew his attention back to her.

"You and Margaret are a sound match, Philip," she said. "She's a wonderful girl."

She clamped her mouth closed on whatever she would have said next. Philip eyed her closely, his mind set. "I know of their relationship, madam," he said softly. "It matters not."

Lady Bridgewater blinked at that, and managed a small smile. "I agree."

Philip turned once more to the doorway. "Where the devil are they?" he muttered.

Lady Bridgewater chuckled.

Movement at the doorway stilled them both. Little Mary took tiny steps into the room, holding a basket of flowers. Philip smiled down at the child, seeing for the first time the marked resemblance between her and Maggie. Mary smiled widely up at him and nearly tripped over her skirts. Lady Bridgewater quickly righted the child and drew her to her side just as Betsy entered the parlor. She wore a dress that matched her little sister's, looking every bit as adorable in it. She looked at Philip and struck an elegant pose, at which he hid his smile at her obvious attempt at worldliness. Betsy joined her mother and sister and turned to face the doorway. Philip followed her gaze, his breath catching in his throat at the sight before him.

Framed in the doorway was the Earl of Bridgewater with Maggie on his arm. Maggie's gown was well-suited to her. The pale yellow hue was very flattering against her flawless skin. Her curls were upswept, with several tendrils left to frame her face and brush her slight shoulders. A wreath of wildflowers—pink, yellow and white—adorned her golden locks, giving her the look of a fairy princess.

Maggie gazed at Philip with the same scrutiny he afforded her. Philip's lips formed her name as the earl drew her to his side. The man's lips touched her cheek as he placed her hand in Philip's. A suspicious sniff issued from him as he joined his wife beside their daughters.

Philip bent his head to hers. "Wildflowers, Maggie?" he asked softly.

Maggie nodded. "From our meadow," she returned just as softly.

His smile widened. Nodding his approval, he turned her to face the clergyman. The couple exchanged their wedding vows and finally they were joined: man and wife, lord and lady, baron and baroness. Philip turned to his new wife and placed his fingers gently under her chin, tilting her face to his.

"My Maggie," he murmured, brushing her lips with the sweetest kiss.

He lifted his head and grinned as the others in the room clapped their approval of the union.

They soon joined the revelers in the grand ballroom. The cavernous space was filled with flowers and candles and music and laughter. Philip and Maggie shared their first dance as husband and wife, twirling about the ballroom amid the applause of their guests.

"Ah, Maggie," Philip said, bringing his lips to her ear. "I can't believe you're finally mine."

Maggie smiled sweetly up at him. "I was already yours."

He smiled and held her closer.

When they concluded their dance, Philip led her to where the Earl of Bridgewater stood. The older gentleman beamed as Maggie placed her hand on his arm. Philip watched with pride as his bride and her father glided out onto the dance floor. Lady Bridgewater's voice drew his attention.

"You love her," she stated.

Philip couldn't suppress his smile. "With all my heart."

Lady Bridgewater turned to watch the earl and Maggie as they danced gracefully together. She wore a soft smile on her face as she turned back to Philip.

"I suppose it's only right," she said with a shrug.

Philip arched a brow at her in question.

"Any woman you married would eventually share in the earl's fortune," she said. "Who better than his daughter?"

Philip regarded her closely, searching for any sign of the bitterness that would have accompanied such a statement mere weeks earlier. Seeing the tenderness in her gaze, it was obvious to him that the woman fully accepted Maggie.

"Who, indeed?" he returned with a grin. "My Dear Lady Bridgewater," he went on. "Would you do me the honor of a dance?"

Lady Bridgewater smiled and shook her head, casting a meaningful glance in Betsy's direction. Philip followed the woman's gaze, smiling himself as he spied the girl. Betsy stood very near the dance floor, her blue eyes large as she watched the couples twirling about. Philip nodded to Lady Bridgewater and crossed to the child.

"Betsy," he said, causing the child to gaze up at him. "Would you care to dance?"

Betsy's eyes widened as she clasped her hands together. "Ooh, Philip!" she gushed. "Do you mean it?"

He nodded, at which Betsy fairly skipped onto the dance floor, dragging Philip along behind her. As he turned her about the room, they chatted about the lovely celebration.

"You dance very well, Betsy," Philip told her.

"Maggie taught me all of the dances, Philip."

Philip smiled, holding the child as she tripped over his booted foot. She flushed as she caught herself.

"Maggie's the most beautiful bride I've ever seen," the little girl said.

"You have my complete agreement on the subject, I assure you. Are you having a nice time?"

"Yes, I suppose," Betsy said with a dramatic sigh. "I do so wish I were older."

Philip couldn't help but chuckle. "Why?"

Betsy looked at him as if he were completely witless. "Because I would then have a suitor of my own."

"Ah," Philip said, hiding his grin. "And do you have anyone in mind for the role of suitor?"

"Hmm," she said, cocking her head to the side. "Perhaps poor Squire Douglas would serve. Maggie did cast him aside, after all."

Philip glanced about the room, his eyes settling on the young man in question. The squire gazed at Maggie as she danced with the earl, a combination of tenderness and resignation on his face. Philip looked down at his young cousin.

"Betsy," Philip gently chided. "Douglas is quite a bit older than you are."

"No matter." Betsy smiled. "In little more than six years I will be out. I imagine Squire Douglas won't seem so very ancient by that time."

Philip shook his head at her, saying a silent prayer that the earl would live a good long time. He had no desire to oversee the coming-out of the spirited girl.

Chapter 14

The party wore on, and the time finally arrived for the guests to adjourn to the supper room. Maggie and Philip wouldn't be joining them, however. A private wedding supper awaited them in Philip's suite of rooms abovestairs. After bidding their guests farewell, the groom and his blushing bride retired to their chambers.

Philip opened the door, waving Maggie in ahead of him. She smiled a bit nervously as she preceded him in to the room. Her eyes widened as she drank in the splendor of his chambers. While her own room was decorated quite elegantly in tones of yellow and white, Philip's rooms were appointed in a more regal fashion.

The room opened into a sitting area and a fireplace dominated the space. Two plumply-upholstered chairs flanked the hearth. The room was decorated in burgundy and gold, and well-suited the man who would one day inherit both the estate and the title.

Maggie looked through a wide arch off of the sitting room, spying the bedroom beyond. The largest bed she'd ever seen sat in the middle of the chamber, its thick posts nearly reaching the high ceiling. She gazed at the bed, picturing her very handsome husband's masculine form reclining upon it. The image caused her breath to quicken. Philip stepped behind her and placed his hands on her bare shoulders.

"Philip," Maggie said, turning to face him. "Your rooms are lovely."

He smiled down at her, brushing his fingers over her cheek.

"Our rooms, Lady Wilton."

"Our rooms."

He lowered his head and caught her lips with his. Maggie leaned into him, opening her mouth to his questing tongue. He tasted deeply of her, wrapping his arms around her. Finally, he dragged his mouth from hers, a deep sigh escaping him.

Maggie took a bit longer to recover, resting her head against his chest. Philip set her away from him. Maggie blinked up at him, slightly befuddled.

"Later," he said, his voice rich with promise. "Why don't you ready yourself, darling, and I'll ring for our supper?"

Maggie nodded and crossed the chamber, bound for the large dressing room. She saw immediately that Joan had seen to all of her effects. The lady's maid had laid out a lovely nightgown with matching wrapper.

The gown was of the thinnest lawn, and a string of embroidered flowers encircling the modest neckline. Maggie carefully removed her wedding dress and set it aside. She slipped the thin straps of her chemise over her shoulders, pushing both it and her petticoat down over her hips. She gazed at the lovely nightgown once more, thinking of her husband's response.

Trembling slightly, she reached for the gossamer confection and slipped it over her head. It fell softly against her skin. Sighing with pleasure, she donned the matching wrapper. It, too, was decorated with tiny flowers. The sleeves of the wrapper ended below her elbows in a froth of wide lace.

Maggie stepped from the dressing room and crossed to the vanity. It was surely a new addition to the room and meant solely for her use. She sat and unpinned her hair, setting aside the wreath of wildflowers she had worn for the wedding. After brushing her hair until it fell in glossy curls, she plucked several still-vibrant flowers from the wreath. Smiling to herself, she adorned her loose curls with the pink and white blossoms. At last satisfied with her appearance, she tied the belt of the wrapper and crossed over to where the bedroom opened into the sitting room.

Philip's attention was focused on the table as he supervised the servants' laying out of their sumptuous meal. While Maggie was gone, he'd obviously seen to his own dress. He wore a dressing gown of deep burgundy, the color nearly matching the rich draperies in the room. It was tied with a gold sash and the cut of the quilted satin accentuated his narrow hips and broad shoulders. Maggie breathed out a sigh as she took in his magnificent form.

Philip heard the soft sound and turned, a smile on his face.

"Those flowers lend you the look of a wood nymph, Maggie. A goddess."

She dipped her head and watched as he dismissed the servants. When they were at last alone, he held his hand out to her. Maggie placed her hand in his and allowed him to seat her before the small table brought in for their meal.

They dined on pheasant, baked in a delicate crust, accompanied by asparagus. For dessert, Cook had prepared a lovely assortment of pastries. Maggie nibbled delicately on a

small berry tart as Philip stood and poured each of them a glass
of sherry.

"Mmm," she sighed, taking up her glass. "Delicious."

He quickly downed his own wine, set his glass aside and
then reached out to grab hers.

"Philip, what are you doing?"

He set the glass down and took her hands in his. "Enough,"
he said as he pulled her to her feet.

He captured her lips with his, plunging his tongue into her
mouth. Maggie caught his passion and wrapped her arms around
his neck. She stroked his tongue with hers, causing him to moan
low in his throat. He ran his hands over her, cupping her round
bottom as he pressed her tightly to him. She could feel his
arousal through the cool satin of his dressing gown and her
breath quickened. Philip's mouth left hers to trail kisses over her
neck, her throat.

She sighed, leaning her head back.

"Ah, Maggie," he breathed, untying the belt of her wrapper.

He cupped her breasts with his hands, caressing her nipples
through her thin nightgown. They hardened to pebbles beneath
his touch.

"Philip!" she gasped, arching toward him.

Her wrapper floated to the floor. Philip swept her into his arms, carrying her swiftly to the bed. Maggie smiled a siren's smile at him, well aware of how she affected him. How could she not? Her own heart pounded as she imagined all that would pass between them this night, their first night together as husband and wife.

Philip reached for her, and then checked his movement. Maggie looked at him in question.

"You'd better remove your nightgown, love," he said, his voice low. "I fear I would rip it in my haste, and I believe I wish to see you in it again."

Maggie nodded and grasped her nightgown, deftly pulling it up and over her head. Philip swore softly, tearing at his own wrap. He grabbed her once more and fell to the bed, stretching out on top of her.

"My heart is fairly pounding." He tunneled his fingers in her curls and stared down at her. "If I don't contain myself, our wedding night will be over before it begins."

Maggie placed her hand on his cheek. "I love you, Philip."

He sharply drew in a breath and brought his lips to hers. His tongue slowly penetrated her mouth, setting the two of them on fire anew. Maggie ran her fingers through his thick hair, whimpering low in her throat. He trailed kisses over her throat, her breasts. He flicked his tongue over one taut nipple and she arched wildly.

"My wife," he said in awe, closing his mouth over the sensitive bud.

He gently teethed her nipple as his fingers unerringly found the dampening curls between her legs. Maggie closed her eyes, reveling in his expert attention. She whimpered in protest as his mouth left her breast to trail kisses over her stomach. He parted her legs as he flicked his tongue in her navel. Before she knew what he was about, he placed his mouth on her.

She tensed her legs. "Oh, my!"

He lifted his head, his fingers slowly caressing her. "Does that feel good?"

Maggie lost her shock as warmth spread upward through her body. She closed her eyes once more.

"Oh, yes," she sighed, letting her legs fall to the mattress. "Oh, my."

He lowered his head once more and flicked his tongue over her flesh. Maggie clutched at the sheets as his rasping tongue found her tiny nub of pleasure. Her climax rushed through her as she screamed with delight. When she quieted, Philip came over her, entering her with one deep thrust. She quivered around his shaft, welcoming him. He moaned her name as he drove swiftly toward his own climax. She was astounded as she began to tighten around him again. She found her second release as he found his, crying out once more.

Philip breathed out a heavy sigh, deep satisfaction in his every motion. Maggie shifted beneath him and he rolled off of her. She stared at him, her eyes wide.

"Philip," she began in a small voice, "That was unexpected."

He leaned up on one elbow, tracing his finger over her flushed cheek.

"We're married, Maggie," he said. "Your body belongs to me as mine belongs to you. Didn't you enjoy that?"

She lowered her lashes. "I did."

"Good. You were meant to."

She raised her eyes to his. "Would you enjoy that, Philip?"

"More than you can imagine."

Maggie kissed him, and then nudged him onto his back. Her fingers trailed over his flat stomach to capture him. He was already hard in her hand.

"How can you be recovered?"

"You, love," he said, closing his eyes. "It's you."

Emboldened, Maggie bent her head and kissed the tip of his arousal. He nearly bowed off the bed. When she stroked the length of him with her tongue, he shuddered beneath her.

"Maggie," he groaned, twining his fingers in her thick curls. "Ah, God!"

She took him fully in her mouth and gently suckled. He suddenly grabbed her up to him, crushing his mouth to hers. He rolled her onto her back and drove into her, again and again. Maggie gasped as pleasure began to course through her anew. He shook with the power of his orgasm, bringing her to her own release.

His breathing slowed as he rained kisses on her face. Her satisfied smile caught his attention and he arched a brow at her.

"I believe you enjoyed that, husband," she teased.

He managed a strangled laugh at that. "Minx," he said, kissing the tip of her nose.

Maggie sighed as Philip rolled onto his back, taking her with him. She cuddled against his side and closed her eyes. Philip dropped a kiss on her curls, hugging her tightly to him.

"Good night, Maggie," he said softly.

"Good night," she yawned, letting sleep claim her.

***

The sunlight woke Maggie as Philip pulled aside the heavy draperies. She yawned and stretched languorously, cuddling once more into the covers. Philip chuckled and crossed to the bed, pulling the sheets aside as well.

"Come, slugabed," he teased. "I wish to arrive in town by tea time."

Maggie brushed her tousled curls back from her face and turned to regard him closely. Philip smiled as she favored him with the look that never ceased to please him. When her eyes held such love in them, he felt as if he were the most noble of men. He bent to kiss her lightly on her parted lips.

She smiled up at him. "Good morning, Philip."

"Good morning, wife," he said, straightening. "I'll ring for your bath, love."

When Philip emerged from the dressing room later, clad in his traveling clothes, Maggie sat in the hip tub, fragrant clouds of steam rising from the hot water. Her glorious curls were pinned atop her head. Her back was to him and her creamy shoulders and the slender curve of her neck were visible. Sensing his presence, she turned and smiled over her shoulder.

"Philip," she said softly, her eyes glittering.

He blinked at her, desire beginning to tighten its hold on him. He grinned wickedly at her. "Don't look at me in that manner, wife," he warned. "I'll be forced to join you in that ridiculously small tub and delay our leaving for London."

Maggie's eyes widened. He crossed to her and gazed down at the flush spreading from the swell of her breasts to the roots of her hair.

"Shy blushes, Maggie?" he teased. "For your husband?"

She recovered herself and splashed some of the rose-scented water on his jacket and trousers. He jumped back, laughing. He shook his head at her and dropped a quick kiss on her lips.

"I'll be in the breakfast room, love," he said, reluctantly taking himself from the very pleasing picture she made in the tub.

Lord and Lady Bridgewater were seated at the table when Philip entered the breakfast room.

"Good morning," Philip said with a grin.

Whistling, he crossed to the sideboard and helped himself to a large serving of the hearty breakfast fare. Philip joined them.

"Did you sleep well, son?" the earl asked, taking up his tea cup.

Philip beamed a smile. "Very," he said in answer, digging into his meal with relish.

Maggie joined them not much later, wearing a traveling dress of white dotted with yellow blooms, and a very lovely blush on her cheeks. She bade good morning to her aunt and uncle, and then favored her husband with a very bright smile. She served herself some eggs and ham, and joined them at the table.

They spoke of their trip to London, and Philip beseeched the earl and his wife to join them in town before the Season concluded. The older couple happily relented, saying that they would perhaps be able to get to town sometime in July.

Soon after breakfast, Philip and Maggie readied to depart from Bridgewater Park for their stay in London.

Chapter 15

They arrived in town a bit before tea time, Philip wearing a grin of satisfaction on his face. Maggie clicked her tongue at him as she brushed the wrinkles out of her skirt.

"Did I rumple you, Maggie?"

She tucked a few more loose curls into her braid and shrugged. "I found I couldn't resist your delightful idea to share our pleasure in this carriage."

"You couldn't resist my passions, you mean."

She laughed and waved a hand at him.

The carriage rolled to a stop in front of the townhouse. Maggie gazed up at the structure. The townhouse was quite handsome. It was built of tan bricks and the front door was painted a deep green. Shutters of the same glossy green framed the large windows on the facade. Wide steps led to the front door.

Philip alighted the carriage and assisted Maggie down. Before another moment could pass, he swept her up into his arms and carried her swiftly up the steps to the front door. Maggie clutched at his shoulders, laughing gaily as he pushed open the door and carried her into the foyer. The butler, a man not much older than Philip, stood beside the door, a look of surprise on his face. He quickly recovered himself.

"My lord," the butler said, bowing to his master.

"Hello, Grimes," Philip returned, setting Maggie on her feet. "This is the new Baroness Wilton."

"Lady Wilton," Grimes returned with a small smile of his own.

"Tell me, Grimes," Philip said. "Isn't she the most beautiful woman to ever be called 'Lady Wilton?'"

The butler, well-used to his master's jesting nature, hid his grin.

"Yes, my lord," Grimes said solemnly in answer. "Your lady is a welcome addition to your household."

Maggie, flushed from both their energetic entrance and Philip's question, could only stare as the butler bowed low to her.

"A wise man is our Grimes," Philip laughed. "We'll take tea in the parlor shortly."

Grimes bowed once more and took his leave. Philip smiled down at Maggie, taking her hands in his.

"Why don't you go up to our chamber and ready for tea, love?" he asked. "I'll sort through our correspondence and see you in the parlor."

Maggie nodded and turned to climb the staircase. When she reached the landing she took note of the pleasant sunny spot, thinking it would serve nicely as an afternoon retreat with the addition of a chair or perhaps a settee. She had no trouble locating the master's chamber. Turning left down the short hall, she found the chamber door resting open in anticipation of their arrival. Removing her bonnet, Maggie stepped into the room.

It was a large room, encompassing both a sitting area with a fireplace and a sleeping chamber. The bed within was nearly as large as that at Bridgewater Park. Maggie found the room most pleasant, thinking the decor of green and gold quite relaxing. Crossing the chamber, she entered the dressing room. She wasn't surprised to find evidence of Joan's handiwork. The lady's maid had all of Maggie's effects in order, even having readied two gowns from which Maggie could chose for the ball they would attend the next evening. Smiling to herself, she rang for the girl.

"Hello, Joan," Maggie greeted her. "How did you fare on your journey to town?"

Joan paled, and Maggie knew she'd felt ill enroute. "I survived, my lady," she sighed.

Maggie nodded and stepped out of her traveling dress.

"And how do you find London?" Maggie went on as she sat herself at the vanity placed not far from the large bed.

"Everyone is most kind here in the house, my lady," Joan said, gently pulling the pins from Maggie's hair. "Very pleasant indeed, save for that butler."

"What?" Maggie asked, surprised. "You don't like Grimes?"

Joan's eyes narrowed as she shook her head. "He is likable, I suppose," Joan said. "Just a bit too free with his jests and much too full of himself, if you ask me."

Maggie sensed something else in Joan's voice. Was she smitten with Grimes?

"Did he tease you when you were ill?" Maggie asked.

Joan's pursed lips were all the answer Maggie needed. She hid her grin as the maid brushed and styled her hair. Maggie stood and donned a tea gown of light blue and then dismissed the maid. Hurrying downstairs, Maggie found her husband in the parlor.

"Maggie," he said, coming to stand in front of her.

He kissed her lightly and led her to a blue settee beside the hearth. Maggie looked about the room as the tea tray was brought in and set on a table beside them. The room was pleasant, if sparsely furnished. The furnishings present were of good quality, but little decoration adorned the space. Perhaps some flowers on the mantle and a few plump pillows.

Philip handed her a cup of tea. "I trust you found our chamber to your liking?"

Maggie smiled. "Oh, yes," she said, sipping delicately from the cup. "The room is very handsome, indeed."

"And what of the parlor?"

Maggie set her cup down and tilted her head to the side. "It's a pleasant space, if a bit spartan."

"Ah," he chuckled. "Missing a woman's touch, is it? Perhaps we can add some of your lovely needlepoint."

Maggie agreed, mentally adorning the walls with her work.

"I'll write my aunt directly and beg her to send several pieces," she said. "There are some very pretty ones Betsy and I did together."

Philip nodded absently as he helped himself to a biscuit.

"I believe I miss her," Maggie went on. "I've grown quite accustomed to her chattering. I think of her as a sister."

Philip stilled for a moment, and then he smiled.

"We'll return to Somersetshire at the end of the Season, love," he told her. "That's in just a few weeks. Betsy will undoubtedly have much to tell you on our return."

She laughed. "After two months' time she'll be full to bursting!"

Philip's laughter joined hers.

Talk soon turned to their plans for the coming day. Philip spoke of his wish to ride in the morning, and perhaps make a few calls on Lord and Lady Bridgewater's friends who had been unable to attend the wedding ceremony. Then of course, he went on, they could expect many callers in the afternoon. Maggie nodded, endeavoring to keep her growing apprehension about meeting so many new people to herself. Apparently Philip didn't miss the change in demeanor.

Late that night, in the big four-poster in their chamber, Maggie sighed in contentment. She cuddled against her husband, whose deep even breathing told her he was sated. He had taken her twice before letting sleep claim him, bringing her easily to climax with his sweet words and caresses. She rested her chin on his chest and gazed up at his handsome visage.

His fair lashes rested against his cheeks and a faint smile curving his well-formed lips. Maggie reached up a traced her fingers over his cheek. She sighed again, causing Philip's eyes to snap open.

"Maggie?" he murmured.

"Hmm?"

"What is it?" He smiled sleepily at her. "Surely you can't be dissatisfied."

"Hardly," she laughed softly, dropping a kiss on his chest.

Philip shifted in the bed, propping himself up on one elbow. "Is something troubling you?"

Maggie thought of the many people she would meet the next day, and of the callers that were sure to come to the townhouse. "I admit I'm nervous about tomorrow."

"Nervous?" he asked. "About what?"

"You've traveled within the *ton*, husband," she said. "I've scarcely ever been out of Sussex."

He cupped her cheek with his hand. "Maggie," he said, brushing his thumb over her cheek. "You possess more beauty and grace than any other woman I've ever encountered in so-called Society. You, my love, shouldn't be nervous."

Maggie smiled at him, loving him for the sweet words.

"And you are prejudiced."

"I love you." He shrugged. "Still, it's true. Now, let's get some sleep."

Maggie nodded and settled down once more beneath the covers. Philip dropped a kiss on the top of her head and held her close, falling back to sleep in mere moments. Maggie sighed again, her fears lessened but far from dispelled. She feared that the women she would encounter on the morrow would be much like Lady Sarah: manipulative and cold.

No matter. She had Philip and he loved her regardless of her inexperience with Society.

***

Philip was quite attentive to Maggie the following morning. Although she didn't mention her apprehensions again, he suspected they still plagued her. There was no call for false praise on his side, however. When she joined him in the breakfast room, clad in a lovely day dress of rose, all of his compliments came from his heart.

"How would you like to ride through Hyde Park this morning?" he asked her, serving himself from the sideboard.

Her face brightened. "Oh, I would so love to see it! I've heard it's lovely."

"It is," he said, taking his seat. "It doesn't compare to the grounds at Bridgewater Park, though."

Maggie waved her hand and took up her plate. She helped herself to a plate of eggs and ham. "Where shall we ride?"

"Along Rotten Row," he said. "It's the most-preferred track. This way, I'm assured that my beautiful wife will be seen by the most people possible."

Maggie clicked her tongue at him as she took her seat beside him. He noted that her brow was slightly furrowed. Philip broke the silence, thinking to turn her thoughts.

"I thought we would take my curricle," he said.

His words had their desired effect. Maggie smiled brightly once more. His light carriage was two-wheeled and open to the weather. It was pulled by a matched pair of horses and was considered the perfect thing for a summer morning's ride through the park.

"That sounds wonderful, Philip."

After they finished their breakfast Maggie donned a straw bonnet, tying the wide white ribbon beneath her chin as Philip called for the carriage. He assisted her into the curricle and climbed up to sit beside her. He gave her a quick kiss and flicked the reins, easily maneuvering the carriage through the morning traffic on the thoroughfare.

"The park is quite pretty in the summer sunshine," she said.

"I've never found the park so pretty as I do this fine morning, Maggie."

Maggie blushed at his compliment. They were soon met with several acquaintances, primarily matrons accompanied by their unattached daughters. Philip introduced Maggie with his voice full of pride, making it most obvious to all but the very cynical that he was a man very much in love with his new bride.

As they rode on, Maggie remarked that so few young men were present.

"Where are these chums of yours, Philip?" she asked.

Philip laughed lightly at her question, causing Maggie to raise a brow. He thought to enlighten her.

"I'd be very surprised indeed if my friends were out and about this early, love," he said. "They stay very late at the pubs as a rule. Most of them do not rise much before midday."

"Truly? And what is it that keeps your friends at the pubs so late that they sleep half the day away?"

Philip winked at her in answer. She gasped at what he was intimating, causing him to chuckle. He shook his head, leaned over to kiss her lightly and they continued on their ride.

"Why don't we turn back for home?" he asked after a while. "It'll soon be time for luncheon."

Maggie nodded her agreement, and he suspected she wanted to get away from the prying eyes and wagging tongues they'd encountered along the track.

***

Philip and Maggie returned to the townhouse and shared their nooning meal, dining on baked fish accompanied by roasted potatoes. Grimes soon announced their first callers of the day, Lord and Lady Gladdings. Escorting Maggie into the parlor, Philip explained that they were friends of Lord and Lady Bridgewater. Taking a deep breath to steady her nerves, Maggie preceded her husband into the parlor.

To Maggie's great surprise and relief, their visitors were most solicitous. They inquired after the earl and his wife, and voiced their regrets over missing the wedding more than once. They were the first of many callers that afternoon, and did much to allay Maggie's apprehensions.

An apparent lull in activity occurred as the afternoon wore on.

"Why don't you go ready yourself for tea, Maggie?" he asked. "I believe our respite won't last overlong. I have some matters that need attention in my study."

Maggie smiled and then accepted a sweet kiss. She went upstairs to change as Philip took himself into his study.

Maggie left their chambers shortly thereafter, bound for the parlor to await any additional callers. Passing the salver in the entryway, she noted that the number of cards the callers had left confirmed her suspicions regarding the high number of people she'd met this day. The little silver tray was fairly full to overflowing. She brushed her hands over the skirt of her lovely yellow tea dress and smoothed down her hair. Joan had loosened a few of her curls, allowing the tendrils to float about Maggie's face and shoulders.

She checked her appearance once more in the mirror hung in the hallway outside the parlor doors, and then entered. She came to an abrupt halt as she spied the very regal woman gracing the space within. The woman, a bit older than the Earl of Bridgewater, eyed Maggie closely as she walked fully into the room.

"Pray forgive me if I kept you waiting," Maggie began with a nervous smile. "I wasn't aware of your presence."

"Lady Hunsford," the older woman said. Her eyes still held that measuring look.

Maggie curtseyed in greeting and then took a seat opposite the woman. Silence fell on the room as Lady Hunsford continued to regard Maggie closely. Under the woman's close scrutiny, Maggie began to lose the composure her previous visitors had afforded her. She fidgeted in her seat, brushing her hands over her skirt once more. Lady Hunsford finally broke the silence.

"You are a pretty girl, I will allow," she sniffed.

"Thank you."

"Not that I expected the baron to settle on a homely wife."

Maggie's brows arched at that supposition. Several more minutes of silence passed after its utterance. Maggie felt her apprehension grow.

"Would you care for some tea?" she offered, eager to find something with which to occupy the lady's visit.

"No, thank you," came the stiff reply. "Who was your mother?" Lady Hunsford asked sharply.

Maggie blinked at the tersely-asked inquiry. She squared her shoulders and smiled sweetly at the woman.

"Lady Cecilia Penworth," Maggie said.

"Penworth," the woman repeated, her mind apparently searching for some recognition. "Penworth. And your father? Who was he?"

Maggie began to lose her patience with the cold woman. True, she had no real information of her sire. But that should have no bearing on her worthiness as a wife to Philip. Or should it? Taking a breath to calm herself, she answered.

"My father was—"

"Her father was Baron Penworth," Philip replied from the doorway.

Maggie looked up at him, relief flooding through her. Philip smiled, crossing over to her and brushing a kiss on her cheek before turning to face their visitor.

"Lady Hunsford," he said, his charm evident. "How good of you to call."

"Lord Wilton," she nodded.

Philip bowed low to her. "How are you, madam?"

"Very well," she returned, flushing under Philip's kind attention.

"And your daughters?" he went on. "Are they also well?"

Lady Hunsford nodded in answer.

"Maggie," Philip said, sitting beside his wife, "can you believe that Lady Hunsford is of an age to have not one but two daughters married and settled these past three years?"

Maggie watched Lady Hunsford, amazed as the matron's flush deepened. Philip and their visitor discussed her daughters as well as the friends she had in common with Lord and Lady Bridgewater. Philip made every effort to draw Maggie into the conversation, and his easy manner did much to lessen her apprehensions.

At the end of her visit, apparently having seen the regard Philip had for his wife, Lady Hunsford expressed her delight over their marriage. Maggie accepted the good wishes as they were intended: a compliment to her fine husband if not a true acceptance of herself.

Chapter 16

After the woman left Philip settled himself closely beside her, taking her hand in his. She gave him a grateful smile.

"Were you in dire need of rescuing, love?" he teased.

"Oh, yes," Maggie sighed. "I feared she would eat me alive before your timely arrival."

He laughed. "You carried yourself with grace and ease," he kissed her. "Of course, I knew you would."

"You flatter me, husband."

He pulled back and ran his gaze over her. "I do so love your hair down around her face," he said, running his fingers lightly over the curls. "You look like an angel."

Maggie saw the spark of desire burning in the emerald depths of his eyes. Her breath quickened as he brushed the hair off of her shoulder, his fingers gently caressing her neck.

"Maggie," he breathed, nuzzling her ear. "I want you."

"Philip...," she sighed, closing her eyes.

"I want you here," he went on, nibbling her ear. "Now."

She gasped, her eyes open wide. "Here?"

"Mmm," he replied, placing his hands on her waist and drawing her closer. "I want to lift the skirt of this pretty yellow dress and come into you."

"Oh, my," she breathed, her pulse pounding in her ears.

Philip kissed her again, nibbling her lips, tasting her tongue. The sound of Grimes' clearing his throat brought him swiftly away from her. Maggie gasped at his abrupt withdrawal, her eyes snapping open.

"My lord," the butler said, keeping to the hallway outside the parlor. "My lady."

"Yes, what is it, Grimes?" Philip answered with obvious regret in his voice.

"Lord Rawlings has called, my lord," Grimes answered.

Philip sighed and came to his feet. "Send him in."

Maggie stood, brushing her hands over her skirt. Their visitor soon entered the parlor.

"Wilton!" Lord Rawlings said, striding into the room. "How are you, old man?"

Philip grinned and shook the man's hand. "Quite well, thank you."

Maggie managed a small smile, still a bit flustered by Philip's words and actions before Lord Rawlings's untimely arrival.

"And this must be your lady," Rawlings said with a smile, his gaze finally settling on Maggie.

"Maggie," Philip said, grasping her hands. "Allow me to introduce Viscount Rawlings. Rawlings, this is Lady Margaret Wilton."

Rawlings let his eyes run over her figure. He took her hand in his and bowed low. "Lady Margaret." Rawlings brought her hand to his lips. "I take great pleasure in making your acquaintance."

He let his lips linger on her skin a bit longer than was proper. Maggie trembled as his eyes, dark as midnight, bore into hers. She must be misreading the intent in them. He was frightfully handsome and no doubt forthright in his interest.

Rawlings schooled his expression then, making Maggie all the more certain that she had been mistaken. She sat and the two gentlemen following suit.

"Would you care for some tea, Lord Rawlings?" Maggie asked.

"Tea would be lovely, Lady Margaret," Rawlings said. "Thank you."

Maggie rose, bringing the men swiftly to their feet. She thought of something and quirked a half-smile at her husband. She turned back to their guest.

"And perhaps some finger sandwiches?" she offered. "I assume that you were out very late at the pubs as were Philip's other friends, and are quite famished."

Rawlings reddened a bit. "Yes, I…"

Philip laughed at Rawlings's distress as Maggie left the room, bound for the kitchen.

***

The men settled themselves down once more. Rawlings let out a low whistle.

"My God, man," he said. "She is incredible. And she's the earl's niece?"

"Yes."

"You met her at Bridgewater Park upon your return?" Rawlings asked. "She was right there under your nose?"

Philip thought for a moment, recalling their conversation in the pub. He thought it best not to remind Rawlings of it, preferring to let the man think he first encountered Maggie in Somersetshire. He simply nodded, at which Rawlings chuckled.

"Wilton, I have always said that you are one lucky son-of-a..."

"I'm the lucky one, Lord Rawlings," Maggie said, breezing back into the room.

Maggie smiled and perched herself beside her husband.

"You consider yourself lucky to be married to this rogue?" Rawlings teased.

"Oh, yes," she returned, her eyes on Philip. "Philip is everything a young lady could want in a husband."

Philip beamed a smile at her and kissed her hand. For the first time since making Rawlings's acquaintance nearly five years earlier, he saw a flash of envy on the man's face. He appeared to recover his good humor as the tray was brought in, laden with fragrant tea, fluffy biscuits, and the aforementioned finger sandwiches. Philip put his friend's odd expression out of his mind as the three of them set about their afternoon repast.

"I do admit, Lady Margaret," Rawlings said after a while, "that when I received the formal wedding announcement penned in your delicate hand I was quite astonished."

Maggie merely smiled.

"Although now that I have met you," Rawlings went on, "I can well see the inducements that drew Wilton from his comfortable bachelorhood."

"Ah, my fate was sealed when we met at Bridgewater Park, Rawlings," Philip said to that. "You see, she seduced me."

"Philip!" Maggie cried.

He laughed and took her hand once more. "She stole my heart," he went on with a grin. "When I saw that golden hair, those incredible eyes, I was captivated." He turned back to his friend. "She smiled her siren's smile at me and my heart was lost forever."

"Lady Margaret," Rawlings began. "I assume this scoundrel will be escorting you to the bashes this evening?"

"Philip has promised me so, Lord Rawlings."

Rawlings grinned broadly, his eyes darkening once more. "Then I must beseech you to save a dance for me."

"Certainly," she allowed.

After agreeing to see them later that evening, Lord Rawlings took his leave of the couple. Philip saw him to the doorway, telling Grimes before closing the double doors that they would receive no more callers that afternoon. He turned back to Maggie and leaned against the wooden panels. Maggie caught his eye and arched a graceful brow at him. He grinned as he removed his jacket.

"Philip?" she asked suspiciously. "What are you about?"

He loosened his cravat and unbuttoned his waistcoat. Maggie's eyes widened in response.

"Ah, wife," he said, coming to sit beside her on the settee. "I was simply thinking to take up where we left off before Rawlings's untimely arrival."

Her mouth was an O of surprise.

"Surely you can't be serious. Not here in the parlor!"

He nodded slowly as he ran his fingers over her cheek, her throat.

"I want you, Maggie," he said. "And I can't bear to wait."

He deftly slipped his hand into the bodice of her dress, cupping her breast. Maggie closed her eyes as his thumb brushed over her nipple, causing it to harden.

"Ah, Maggie," he rasped, gently pushing her down on the settee. "You want me too, don't you, love?"

"Yes," she sighed.

Philip tugged on the bodice of her dress, freeing her breasts for him to touch, to taste. He circled one nipple with his tongue, driving her mad. She pulled at his hair, whimpering. Chuckling softly, Philip gave her what she craved. He drew the sensitive bud into his mouth and gently suckled. Maggie arched wildly beneath his ministrations.

"Touch me, Maggie," he said, taking her hand and placing it on himself. "Feel how much I want you."

Maggie stroked him through his breeches, causing him to moan low in his throat. She unbuttoned his breeches, freeing him to her touch. She grasped him, squeezing gently. He moved against her hand, nearly filled to bursting. He grabbed her hands in the next moment, placing them behind his neck. Flipping her skirts out of the way, he quickly removed her drawers. He caressed her, arousing her further. Philip's control threatened to leave him as she moaned his name, close to her release.

"Now, Maggie?" he asked raggedly, kissing her lips, her cheek. "Now?"

"Yes, Philip," Maggie breathed. "Now."

He lifted her hips and entered her with one deep thrust. Her body arched as Philip kissed her once more, catching her cries of pleasure in his mouth as his own climax tore through him. He continued to move inside her until the tremors left her body, amazed at the intensity of the pleasure they brought to each other.

"My God," he said at last, his breath slowing. "That was a close thing."

Maggie simply sighed in contentment. Philip kissed her tenderly, telling her of his love for her, whispering the sweet words in her ear. They roused themselves after a while, retiring to their chamber to ready for the coming evening.

Philip entered their rooms sometime later, freezing in the doorway as his wife's beauty struck him speechless.

Her curls caught the light as she turned her head, and several tendrils floated freely to frame her face and brush her shoulders. She'd chosen a gown of golden silk and quite daring in cut. The tiniest sleeves draped off of her shoulders, the bodice dipping to a V between her breasts.

After a long moment, he found his voice. "Maggie."

"Philip," she said with a half-smile. "You look so handsome I fear I may swoon."

He arched a brow at her and crossed to where she stood. "I can't believe you would do any such thing."

He studied her once more, finally giving a slow shake of his head. "That gown, Maggie," he murmured, taking in the expanse of creamy flesh visible above the bodice. "I believe part of it is missing."

Maggie's smile widened. "I'll have you know that this gown in considered the height of fashion."

"It's indecent." He growled playfully. "I daresay I'll have to beat the men away from you. I vow to remain by your side this evening, love."

"I prefer you to stay by my side," Maggie said with a shrug.

He grinned at that admission. He suddenly remembered the box he held in his hands.

"I fear that dress is missing more than a top," he said, cocking his head to the side.

Maggie blinked at him, befuddled. Philip held the black jewelers' box before him.

"Philip, what is this?"

"For you, my love," he said, opening the box with a flourish.

Maggie gasped as she spied the beautiful pearl necklace within. The pearls were perfect, seeming to glow with life against the black velvet.

"There are earrings to match."

She reached out one finger to stroke the orbs. "They're exquisite."

"And well-suited to you, wife."

Philip removed the necklace from the box and draped the pearls over her. Maggie turned as he fastened the clasp behind her neck. She fastened the earrings on her lobes, frowning a bit as she stared into the mirror.

"What is it?" Philip asked her.

"I was thinking about something our steward said," she told him.

"Tallman?" Philip asked, confused.

Maggie shook her head. "Not at Bridgewater Park. Our steward in Sussex," she provided in answer. "He spoke of a treasure, and alluded to jewels belonging to my mother. I found no jewels when I packed her personal effects, however. Or any great amount of money, for that matter."

"What could the steward know of her belongings?"

Maggie suddenly shivered as she recalled the last time she saw the despicable Mr. Lavery. "I don't wish to speak of that horrid man, Philip," she said. "He said terrible things about my mother. Things I dare not repeat."

Philip shared Maggie's unease over the topic. Did the man know about Maggie's mother's involvement with the earl and possibly alluded to as much? But, what of the jewels? He decided to let the matter drop for the time being, preferring to focus instead on his wife.

He placed his hands on her shoulders, turning her to face him once more to study his gift to her. The pearls rested at the swell of her breasts. He traced his fingers around them, caressing her silken skin.

"They glow against your skin," he said, his voice husky.

Maggie caught his hand with hers, her eyes sparkling. "Thank you, Philip," she said simply. "I love them."

Philip pulled her into his embrace, brushing her lips with his. The gentle contact was not enough for him. He slanted his mouth over hers, his desire growing. When he lifted his head, he was most pleased to see the answering heat in Maggie's eyes.

"Come," he said, taking her hand. "Let's go to the blasted parties and be done with them."

Maggie picked up her long satin gloves on their way out of the room. "I'm looking forward to the bashes, Philip," she said, trailing down the stairs after him. "You make them sound like an ordeal to be gotten through."

He stopped at the bottom of the stairs, barking out a short laugh. "I do, don't I? I'm sorry, love. I promise to let you dance your fill."

Maggie smiled widely as she pulled on her gloves.

"And then," he added, assisting her into the waiting carriage, "I'll drag you home and peel that indecent gown off of you."

Her eyes widened at that provocative notion. Philip chuckled as he settled himself next to her for the short ride to the first party of the evening.

Chapter 17

They soon arrived at the Winston bash, held at the Earl of Winston's grand townhouse. Their carriage rocked to a stop behind the many vehicles which lined the drive before the home and guests were crowding the steps leading to the entryway. Philip and Maggie alighted directly into the hubbub.

Upon entering the house they were greeted by the hostess, an older woman with warm eyes and an easy smile. They expressed their delight in attending the lovely affair, at which the woman fairly beamed. That duty complete, Philip led Maggie into the main salon.

The ballroom was large, beautifully-appointed and lit by many candles. The orchestra played tunefully from the far end of the room, and Maggie unconsciously began swaying in time to the music.

"Ooh, Philip," Maggie said happily. "Everything is so lovely."

He nodded, apparently catching her enthusiasm. The room was quite full, and Philip grasped her elbow as he began to lead her through the throng of party-goers. He was soon waylaid by several of his friends.

"Wilton!" one man exclaimed, a grin on his face. "Can it be true?"

"Porter," Philip said in greeting.

"Are you truly married, Wilton?" another man asked.

Philip couldn't hide his grin as his friends slapped him on the back. The gentlemen continued their easy jibes at Philip's expense. Maggie wore a half-smile as she looked on. She soon found herself the object of attention, however, with several of the men present openly gawking at her. Philip quickly introduced the men, at which they bowed to her in their turns. They didn't bother to hide their impressions of the new Lady Wilton, giving Philip open looks of approval. Lord Porter, the first to approach the couple upon their arrival, took Maggie's hand and lightly kissed it.

"It's a great pleasure to meet you, Lady Margaret," the blond gentleman said, his brown eyes warm. He grinned at Philip before looking back at Maggie. "I do admit, however, that when Lord Rawlings described you, I believed him to be exaggerating."

Philip arched a brow at Porter's statement. "Pray, what precisely did Rawlings say?"

Porter opened his mouth to respond.

"Wilton!" Rawlings cut in, shouldering his way through the men. "Lady Margaret," he said, immediately taking her hand in his.

Maggie was overwhelmed by the attention. Lord Rawlings's eyes again held the inappropriate warmth she had sensed that afternoon. She pulled her hand quickly from his, causing him to blink in surprise. He grinned then, stepping back to greet his friend properly.

"It's high time you arrived, Wilton," he chided. "Your lovely wife has promised me a dance, and I aim to hold her to her word."

"I think not, Rawlings," Philip said, taking Maggie's hand, "I believe my wife wishes to dance with me."

Maggie's spirit brightened as she looked up at her husband. "Oh, yes, Philip. Please."

Philip beamed a smile, bringing her hand to his lips. He led her out onto the dance floor, leaving his friends to stare after them.

On the dance floor, Maggie gazed up at her handsome husband as the number ended, a bit out of breath. Philip smiled and held her close to him, kissing her cheek.

"I'm sorry about my friends' behavior, love." He led her to one of the many chairs which lined the ballroom. "They are unused to being in the company of a lady possessing your breathtaking beauty."

Maggie swatted his arm and asked for a glass of refreshment. Philip bowed to her and left to do her bidding, a crooked smile on his face. She watched him go, admiring his easy grace as he crossed the room. A voice to the side of her broke through her reverie.

"Hello, Lady Margaret," Lady Sarah Addington said.

Maggie turned, startled to find the young woman seated beside her. She quickly recovered herself and smiled.

"Hello, Lady Sarah," she said. "How nice it is to see you again."

Lady Sarah nodded as she ran her eyes over Maggie, a look of displeasure on her face. She smiled stiffly.

"I daresay I was surprised by the announcement of your wedding." She brushed her hands over the skirt of her blue evening gown. "Although, I suppose I shouldn't have been."

The woman's meaning was quite clear, causing Maggie's cheeks to burn.

"Lady Sarah," she began softly, "I assure you that Philip and I never meant to—"

Lady Sarah held up one delicate hand to still her. Maggie closed her mouth with a snap.

"Please don't trouble yourself," she said coolly. "I realized at Bridgewater Park that your husband was ill-suited to me."

Maggie kept her anger in check, though barely. "I don't know what you mean, Lady Sarah."

"I prefer a more refined gentleman," Lady Sarah went on, her eyes settling on several dandies in attendance. "Although, a girl raised in the country as you were would undoubtedly find his manners quite suitable."

Maggie held her hands in fists in her lap. "My husband is a gentleman," she said, her voice firm. "Perhaps a girl raised in town would not be able to recognize him as such."

Lady Sarah looked at her then, an ugly sneer curling her lips. Maggie recoiled, surprised by the anger coming from the young woman.

"It was very clever of you, I admit," Sarah whispered. "Discarding a simple country squire for a future earl was very clever indeed."

With that the young woman stood, dismissing Maggie as she crossed the floor to join several ladies at the refreshment table. She bumped into Philip, causing him to nearly drop the two glasses of punch he held in his hand.

They exchanged a few words and Philip glanced in Maggie's direction. He must have seen the expression she was having trouble hiding, for he made his quick way back to her.

"Maggie, what is it?" he asked.

Maggie shook her head, unconsciously looking toward Lady Sarah. Philip followed her gaze, turning back to arch a brow at her in question.

"That woman." She took a deep breath in an attempt to rein in her anger. "She said some very hateful words, Philip."

Philip's eyes narrowed on the dark-haired girl.

"Just what did she say?" he asked, beginning to rise out of his chair.

Maggie's hand on his sleeve stilled him. "It's all right." She straightened her shoulders. "I won't allow that cold, insolent girl to ruin our evening."

Philip smiled and leaned toward her, his forehead touching hers. "There's my Maggie." He kissed her brow. "Come," he said, setting the glasses aside. "Another dance?"

Maggie nodded and placed her hand in his, laughing as he pulled her swiftly out of her seat and into his arms.

***

Later, when they had eaten their fill of the sumptuous fare in the supper room, Philip and Maggie returned to the ballroom. Lord Rawlings spied them at once, and hurried over to greet them. He nodded to Philip, quickly turning his attention to Maggie.

"Lady Margaret," he said with a crooked smile. "I believe you still owe me a dance."

Maggie glanced quickly at Philip, who shrugged his broad shoulders in answer.

"Take her, Rawlings," Philip smiled. "Pray, don't forget that she's mine."

Rawlings laughed lightly at that, taking Maggie's gloved hand and leading her out onto the floor. Philip watched them for a moment, recalling the glint he had spied in Rawlings's eye earlier in the evening. He was well aware of the man's appetite for women, having spent much time in his company at the public houses. Philip shook his head. No. Rawlings had no designs on Maggie. She was an incredibly beautiful woman, and the man was simply reacting to her. But let him think to touch her… Lord Porter's voice broke through his reverie.

"Your wife is astounding, Wilton," he said. "Simply beautiful."

Philip smiled at his friend. "She is beautiful, Porter," he agreed. "And not only on the outside."

"Pray, elaborate," Porter teased.

"Maggie's a wonderful girl." Philip turned to watch her on the dance floor. "She's the sweetest, kindest… Ah, she is beyond words." He glanced at his friend and spied a wide smile on the man's face. "And why are you grinning, friend?"

"You're obviously a man in love with his wife," he said with astonishment.

"Guilty as charged."

He waved down a server and took two glasses of wine from the man's tray, handing one to Porter. Porter nodded his thanks.

"And you met her at Bridgewater's?" Porter asked.

Philip nodded. "Yes," he answered. "Although I daresay my pursuit of her wasn't without its obstacles."

"One such obstacle taking the form of Lady Sarah Addington?" Porter asked.

Philip's eyes widened in surprise. "What do you know of that?"

"She let it be known that you would soon ask her to marry you," the other man said. "Was such an occurrence ever possible?"

"Not bloody likely," he spat. "That little—"

"Easy, friend," Porter chuckled.

Philip leaned toward Porter. "The silly chit attempted a seduction."

Porter's stunned silence was soon broken by booming laughter. "That cold witch?"

Philip simply nodded. Porter let out a low whistle, shaking his head.

"Unbelievable," Porter said. "There at Bridgewater Park?"

"Believe it," he said. "I found it quite easy to refuse the lady."

Porter chuckled at that.

The gentlemen continued to watch the dancers, both of them unconsciously showing great attention to the dark-haired man leading Lady Wilton through the dance.

***

Maggie held herself ramrod-straight in Lord Rawlings's arms, keeping her eyes downcast. She was loathe to see the desire in his eyes again. She'd noted it on more than one occasion this evening.

Rawlings held her a bit closer than was proper, but certainly not as close as Philip had. He led her through the steps as Maggie kept her gaze fastened to the front of his jacket. She followed him woodenly, unable to lose her stiffness.

"Lady Margaret," Rawlings said, causing her to lift her head.

She looked at him warily. "Yes?"

"Are you enjoying your evening?"

Maggie quickly saw that his eyes sparkled with good humor, that no sign of any inappropriate intent was present. She relaxed a bit.

"Very much so," she smiled. "The affair is just lovely."

Rawlings nodded, encouraging her ease.

"Pray, tell me," he began. "You met Wilton at Bridgewater Park?"

"Yes," Maggie said. "When he came to stay with the earl."

"A most fortunate occurrence for Wilton," he said. "And you had never made his acquaintance before that occasion?"

Maggie suddenly thought of something then and laughed gaily, causing him to raise a brow. Maggie saw his reaction and held her hand to her lips. He smiled winningly at her.

"Have I said something to amuse you?" he teased.

Maggie shook her head and smiled. "No," she assured him. "It is just that Philip and I… Well, before I arrived at Somersetshire—"

"I knew it!" Rawlings cut in. "You knew of him before his arrival at Bridgewater Park, yes?"

"Yes," she answered. "We met a few weeks before that."

Rawlings nodded his dark head. "You were here in town, weren't you?" he asked with confidence. "But how is it that I never saw you? For I assure you, Lady Margaret, I would certainly remember making your acquaintance."

Maggie shook her head. "I've never before been in town, Lord Rawlings."

"But, then where did Wilton meet you?"

"Philip and I met when I was traveling to my uncle's," she told him. "At the Inn at Salisbury."

Lord Rawlings's eyes rounded for a moment, and then he flashed a smile and led her to where Philip was waiting. He left them with a bow and Maggie and Philip went out onto the terrace.

Out on the terrace, Maggie and Philip stood beside the railing and stared out at the night sky. The terrace was large, and there were no other couples visible from their private corner of it. He wrapped his arms around her as she leaned back against him, smiling as she sighed contentedly.

"Are you having a nice time, love?" he asked, rubbing his cheek against her hair.

Maggie simply nodded and cuddled closer. He brushed his lips over her cheek.

"Ah, sweetheart," he said softly. "You feel so good in my arms."

She turned and placed her hands on his chest. "Is it time to depart for the next bash, Philip?"

Philip shrugged. "I suppose," he said. "Are you in a hurry?"

"Oh, no," she laughed lightly. "Quite the opposite, actually."

He arched a brow at her. "Pray, elaborate."

Maggie fingered the buttons of his waistcoat, keeping her eyes downcast.

"Would our presence be missed if we didn't attend any more parties this evening?" she asked, finally looking up at him.

"I don't believe so. Why do you ask? Is there something you would rather do?"

Her lips curved in a smile as she gazed up at him. Philip grasped her meaning immediately and grinned.

"I believe I would much rather you take me home, husband," she whispered.

Chapter 18

Philip and Maggie easily adapted to life in town, and were soon accustomed to the social whirl that was part of circulating among the *ton*. Philip found the seemingly-endless parties and engagements quite tolerable with his lovely wife at his side. Their life in London fell into a pleasant pattern of diversions.

They rode through the park nearly every morning, and then paid calls or received callers of their own in the afternoons. Maggie made Lady Marianne's acquaintance, and she apparently found the pretty girl as pleasant as her brother, Lord Porter.

Lord Rawlings was a frequent visitor as well, much to Philip's consternation. While he enjoyed his friend's company, he couldn't rid himself of the feeling that the viscount was quite taken with Maggie.

Early one afternoon, after they had been in town for nearly a month, Philip and Maggie paid a call on Porter and Lady Marianne. Lord Rawlings was also in attendance. The man wore a big grin to see Maggie enter the parlor on her husband's arm. Philip eyed him closely as he crossed to where his wife stood and grasped her hand in a most familiar fashion.

"Lady Margaret," he began with a bright smile. "How lovely you look this afternoon."

Maggie thanked him softly and discreetly tugged at her hand in an attempt to free it from his grasp. After what seemed like forever to Philip, the man pressed his lips to her skin and released her. He turned to greet Philip with a nod.

"Wilton," he said. "How does this day find you?"

Philip studied him for a long moment, his brow slightly furrowed. He'd seen the interest in the man's eyes.

"Very well," he answered at last.

Philip's smile returned as he greeted Porter and Marianne. Marianne was delighted to see Maggie and told her as much. She took Maggie's hands in hers and led her to the settee. The two ladies sat closely together. Philip turned from Porter to find Rawlings once more staring most intently at Maggie. He squared his shoulders and came to stand behind his wife.

The five of them spoke of the parties they most recently attended and Rawlings expressed his great delight in twirling Maggie about on the dance floor.

"You dance like an angel, Lady Margaret," he said with a grin. "I cannot recall when I have so enjoyed having a woman in my arms."

Philip bristled at that. He placed his hand on Maggie's shoulder in a show of possessiveness. Maggie must have felt the tension in his grip for she reached up and touched his hand, sending his anger fleeing. His grip loosened and his fingers absently stroked her skin as the conversation continued.

Talk soon turned to business matters, at least where the gentlemen were concerned. Philip asked Porter his opinion on some investments he was considering. The man was quite savvy in such matters, and Philip thought to make use of the man's expertise.

"I have an appointment with my solicitors this afternoon," Philip told him. "I'd hoped I could persuade you to accompany me?"

"Certainly," Porter returned easily. "When must we depart?"

"Shortly, I'm afraid," he said. "We can bring Maggie home on our way."

Maggie stood in response to her husband's words.

"Oh, no!" Lady Marianne cried. She looked beseechingly at Maggie. "I had thought that you would stay for tea."

Maggie looked from her friend to Philip, who opened his mouth to voice his very reasonable opinion that they could simply have tea together on the morrow when Lord Rawlings spoke out.

"See here, Wilton," he said with a crooked grin. "Let the ladies have their visit. I'll see your lovely wife home safely."

Maggie's eyes grew round at that suggestion. Philip hadn't missed the startled look on Maggie's face when the man made his gallant offer. The very last thing he wanted was for the viscount to be alone with Maggie. But he also knew that the man possessed a modicum of honor where proper young ladies were concerned.

"If you wish to stay, Maggie?"

"Oh, of course she wishes to stay," Marianne said with a giggle. "You and my brother may go see about your stuffy old business and the three of us will have a lovely time without you."

Maggie nodded her head, and then reached up on tiptoe to give her husband and brief yet sweet kiss. Philip looked pointedly once more at Rawlings before taking his leave, searching his friend's face for any sign of the desire he spied earlier. Although Rawlings's easy smile did little to reassure him, he followed Lord Porter out of the room.

***

Maggie felt Lord Rawlings's eyes on her as Marianne rang for tea. His attentions made her uneasy. She was most grateful when the tea arrived, accompanied by light and fluffy biscuits. As they shared their repast, Maggie's apprehensions began to lessen.

Rawlings had quite a few stories to impart, humorous stories regarding certain members of the House of Lords that surely had no truth in them whatsoever. Maggie and Marianne laughed gaily as he told his tales. Maggie was also pleased to note that the dark-haired man paid at least as much attention to Marianne as he did to her. His easy smiles and winning charm were doled out in both equal and generous amounts. Therefore, it was with very little unease that she anticipated his escort home when tea had been concluded.

"Thank you, Lady Marianne." She stood and embraced her hostess warmly. "I've enjoyed our visit."

"You must come again, Lady Margaret," Marianne said. "At such a time as my poor brother and your beleaguered husband can stay for longer than a minute or two."

Maggie laughed lightly and told her she would be delighted to pay a call on them again. After assuring Marianne that very little time would pass before they were once more in each other's company, she allowed Lord Rawlings to lead her from the room to his waiting carriage.

Maggie settled herself on the cushioned seat, bestowing a small smile on her escort as he took the seat opposite. She turned to gaze out the window as they pulled away from the curb, her mind occupied on her happy anticipation of seeing Philip very shortly. Her thoughts then turned to the imminent arrival in town of the Earl of Bridgewater and his wife. Philip and Maggie had just that morning received a missive to that respect. Pleasure at the thought of seeing her relatives caused her smile to widen. Lord Rawlings's voice, low in tone, suddenly broke through her reverie.

"Maggie," he said, causing her to start. "You are the most beautiful creature I have every encountered."

Maggie's mind reeled from his very familiar use of her given name. She swiftly recovered her composure. "Lord Rawlings, you must not address me so."

"Although," he went on, "I can't help wondering if Wilton realizes how bloody lucky he is to have you in his bed."

She gasped at his words, her cheeks burning. "Y-you should n-not speak to me so!" she stammered. "It's not proper!"

He chuckled then, leaning forward so that his legs brushed against hers in the close quarters.

"You speak to me of propriety?" he asked with a grin. "That is truly diverting."

Maggie blinked, utterly confounded. She could only stare at him as he joined her on the seat, frozen as he brushed her hair back from her face.

He leaned closer to her. "I want you, Maggie," he said, his lips nearly touching her ear. "I believe I've wanted you from the moment I first saw you."

Maggie recovered herself and pulled away from him. "How dare you say such words? I'm a married woman. Married to your good friend!"

Rawlings shrugged. "That's of little consequence to me," he intoned, sliding closer. "I'm very rich, Maggie." He lifted a lock of her hair and twined it around his finger. "Oh, not as rich as Wilton will be when finally he comes into his inheritance. But I can give you possessions. Gifts to make our attachment all the more attractive to you."

"I don't care of your riches." Maggie shook with her anger. "You will unhand me this instant, you rogue."

He smiled widely. "You play the part of the outraged maiden quite effectively, my love." He laughed. "Although we both know it's but a show for my benefit."

She gasped.

Rawlings grasped her arms then, obviously intent on stealing a kiss. Maggie struggled in his grasp, anger giving her strength as she twisted away from him. Her actions only served to increase his ardor.

"My God," he murmured. "I would wager that you're a wildcat in bed."

She managed to free one hand and delivered a stinging slap to his cheek. Rawlings released her then. Maggie took the opportunity to quickly move to the seat opposite, as far away from him as she could manage in the tight interior of the carriage. Her breath came fast as she struggled to make sense of all that was happening.

He rubbed his cheek absently as he ran his eyes over her, eyes which still held the gleam of wanting. "There's no need for such bravado, Maggie. I know of your meeting with Wilton at the Inn at Salisbury."

Maggie squared her shoulders and faced him fully. "I'm well aware of that fact, Lord Rawlings," she said firmly. "It was I who told you of it."

He shook her head at her. "You misunderstand me," he said. "Wilton told me of his meeting you shortly after the event took place."

"What?" Maggie asked, confused. "When did he speak to you of it?"

"He was quite taken with you." His eyes gleamed. "Though who could blame him? Such a comely doxie, and so in need of assistance."

Maggie opened her mouth in defense, but Rawlings had warmed to his topic and would not be interrupted.

He held up one hand to still her as he continued. "How very cunning of you to rebuff his advances," he said. "You piqued his interest. That is certain. Wilton is ill-used to refusals from women. As ill-used as myself. Do you know that he asked all in town about you?"

Maggie shook her head in disbelief.

"Yes," he continued. "He was in great need to learn the name of the man who was keeping you. You see, he was intent on gaining you for himself."

"But I was never being kept."

"He must have been quite pleased to locate you in Somersetshire," Rawlings said. "Although you weren't quite finished with your games, were you?"

Maggie shook her head as if to clear it, his words befuddling to her. "I assure you I played no games."

Rawlings chuckled once more. "Lady Sarah would certainly say differently."

"Lady Sarah?"

He nodded sagely. "She told all who cared to listen of a certain naive country squire who was quite taken with you as well. Obviously, Wilton couldn't stand the thought of yet another having you before he could sample your charms."

Maggie's head spun as she took in his words. Philip had indeed been quite jealous of Squire Douglas. Why, the first time he made love to her was immediately after the dance at which the young man paid her such attention! And afterwards, after Douglas' courting became an offer of matrimony, Philip decided that he would at last take her as his wife. Were jealousy and lust the true reasons Philip married her? No. He loved her.

"One matter puzzles me, however," Rawlings said in conclusion.

Maggie could only stare at him, her mind trying frantically to make some sense of all the man told her.

"Why did he wed you when he could have simply bedded you?" he asked, fully expecting no answer. "That is," he added, coming to sit beside her, "unless you would only bestow your considerable charms on him were such an offer made." He reached for her once more. "I must sample those charms," he rasped. "I must see for myself if you are as hot as you appear to be."

Maggie shrank from him, her eyes wide and darting desperately about the carriage for some means of escape. She was saved from his ravishment by the sudden jerking stop of the carriage.

Reluctantly, Rawlings pulled away from her. "Damn," he said without anger, looking out the window at the townhouse she shared with Philip. He placed his hand on her cheek. "Another time, my love." He opened the door and took her hand.

Maggie allowed him to assist her down from the carriage, taking her hand swiftly from his as she hurried up the steps. Grimes opened the door for them, a smile on his face for his mistress. He soon lost his smile as he took in the look of distress on her face along with the very predatory glint in her escort's eyes. Maggie absently noted that the butler left their company swiftly.

"We must take another ride together very soon, love," Rawlings said when they were once more alone.

Maggie could only shake her head as he pressed close to her, her back against the wall of the entry. He laughed softly as he stroked her cheek with one finger. She pulled back from the contact, glaring at him in impotent anger.

"You will take your hand from me, Lord Rawlings." She spoke softly but her voice was firm with conviction. "You will leave me alone."

Rawlings shook his head. Maggie shook her own in response, eager to get away from the lustful glare in his dark eyes.

"Leave you alone?" he asked, turning her face toward his. "I'm afraid that's impossible."

Chapter 19

Grimes rapped sharply on the study door, opening it without waiting for his master's voice to come from within.

"Lady Wilton has returned, my lord," he said without preamble.

Philip looked up from the pile of papers on his desk to smile at the man. He arched a brow at the butler's obvious anxiety.

"Why, you seem quite put out, Grimes," he teased. "Is everything all right? Is Lady Wilton's little maid running you in circles again?"

Grimes gave a quick shake of his head. "Lady Wilton is not alone, my lord," he said quickly. "Lord Rawlings is with her."

Philip stood, a bit puzzled. "I was well aware that he would be," he said. His puzzlement increased as the butler's agitation became more evident. "What the devil is wrong, man?"

Grimes shook his head once more. Philip felt inexplicable alarm shoot through him. He hurried from the room, bound for the entryway. He came upon Maggie and Rawlings in a most suspicious circumstance. She was pressed against the wall and Rawlings held her arms, his face close to hers.

"What the devil is going on here?" Philip asked, his voice low.

Lord Rawlings stepped quickly away from her. Maggie choked back a sob as she straightened away from the wall.

"Philip," she said in a small voice.

Philip saw her distress and felt his alarm turn to rage. Maggie ran from the two men and flew up the stairs.

"Maggie!" Philip called. He spun on his heel to face Rawlings once more. "What have you done to my wife?"

Rawlings managed a smile. "I assure you, old man, that I have done nothing to harm your lovely wife."

Philip raked his eyes over him, not believing the smooth words for one moment. "Then why the devil was she so upset?"

Rawlings shrugged his shoulders. "We were merely speaking of the past."

"What?" Philip asked sharply.

"I know her little secret," Rawlings said easily.

Philip stared at his friend, anger and fear warring within his heart. "In my study, Rawlings," he said curtly, spinning on his heel.

Rawlings followed. Philip watched him as he entered the study and closed the door. He leaned back against his desk, crossing his arms over his chest.

"Just what is it you believe you know?" he asked Rawlings.

Rawlings shrugged his shoulders. "I know that your wife isn't quite what you profess her to be," the man answered. "That her origin is a bit murky."

Philip closed his eyes and groaned softly. His stomach clenched violently.

"How did you learn of this?" he had to know.

"It wasn't difficult for me to ascertain, Wilton," he answered. "Although your wife feigns her innocence very well."

Philip raked his fingers through his hair and cursed softly. "Maggie is innocent," he said. "Who else knows of this?"

"Wilton," Rawlings said, his hand over his chest. "I'm cut to the quick that you believe that I would ever divulge such a matter."

Philip eyed him closely. "You've told no one?"

"Of course not," Rawlings answered. "Although I do wonder how you convinced Bridgewater to go along with such a ruse."

"You'll leave the earl out of this," Philip growled. "He loves Maggie as his own."

Rawlings's eyes widened. Philip realized in that moment that the man had no inkling of the earl's particular involvement.

"Never mind," Philip said, reining in his anger. "You'll tell no one of this, do you understand me?"

"You have my word," Rawlings said. "I don't wish to see Maggie hurt."

Philip's eyes narrowed at the man's familiar use of her name. "What did you call her?"

Rawlings shrugged. "I meant nothing by it."

Philip studied him for a long moment, his hands in fists at his side. He finally dismissed the viscount with a wave of his hand. Rawlings nodded as he turned to exit the room.

"Don't let me catch you alone with her again, Rawlings."

Rawlings turned back to him and nodded.

Philip watched the study door close behind the man. He slammed his fist down on his desk. Just how did that rogue learn of Maggie's illegitimacy? And what would he do with such information? Rawlings didn't know that the earl was her father, and for that Philip was grateful. And while he believed Rawlings sincere in his promise to keep the story to himself, he didn't believe for a moment that the man would stay away from Maggie. He all but panted after her like a lovesick pup.

He left the study in search of his wife, intent on seeing to her ease and comfort as best he could.

***

Philip entered their chamber, a brooding look on his face. Maggie turned from where she sat at her vanity to look searchingly at him. Would she glimpse the anger and jealousy she'd seen in the entry? She hadn't seen it since those afternoons when Squire Douglas came calling.

"Philip," she said, standing to face him.

Maggie saw the strange and befuddling mix of emotions etched on his handsome face, and crossed to him.

"Are you all right?" Philip asked brusquely.

She took a breath as she brushed her hair back from her face. "Yes, I'm all right."

"Maggie," he said, grasping her arms. "What precisely did Rawlings say to you?"

Maggie stiffened as all of Lord Rawlings's inappropriate words rushed back to her. How could she tell him all that the man had said? His stating his desires, his alluding to her performance in bed... And what of Philip's only wanting her out of jealousy? She could only shake her head, her eyes on the front of his jacket. Philip gently grasped her chin and lifted her face to his.

"Tell me, Maggie."

She stared into his emerald eyes. "He said that you wanted me."

"What?" he asked. "But, whatever does that have to do with his advances?"

"He said that he wanted me, too."

His grip on her tightened as the tenuous hold on his anger snapped. "The hell you say," he bit out. "How dare he say such words to my wife?"

Maggie withdrew at his outburst, stepping out of his grasp. "Philip—"

"Maggie, you're mine, do you hear me?" he said. "No one will ever say such words to you again."

Maggie's own anger soon matched his. "I'm yours?" she challenged. "Is that all I am to you? A possession?"

"A what?" Philip blinked at her words. "Surely you don't believe that."

"Lord Rawlings seems to believe that you only married me because you wanted me." She found her voice faded along with her anger. "He said that I'm not whom I appear to be."

"You are what you appear to be and more," he said. "You are my wife."

Maggie shook her head. "He said that I... That you said I was..." She couldn't bring herself to say all the man had told her.

"How on earth could you believe anything that scoundrel told you? Unless you were as receptive to his words as you were to his advances."

Maggie's mouth fell open in shock. "I would never welcome another man's attentions."

Philip raked his fingers through his hair. "Ah, I know that." He stared into her eyes, his gaze intense. "But, when I saw him with you, with his hands on you..."

"Oh, Philip," Maggie said, clutching at his jacket. "Tell me you love me for myself! Tell me it's not mere jealousy, or possessiveness, or... or... lust that keeps you with me."

Maggie watched as his mouth dropped open.

"What is this?" Philip grabbed her shoulders. "I love you, Maggie. I've never said those words to another, and I feel them as strongly as when I first uttered them."

She sobbed as her grip on his jacket loosened, leaning against his chest. Philip soothed her with sweet words

"How on earth could you doubt my love? You were made expressly for me."

Maggie's throat was thick.

"Maggie," he said softly, stroking her hair. "I love your kind heart and your sharp mind," he said, kissing her brow. "I love your golden hair and your beautiful eyes," he added, cupping her cheek with his hand. "I love your passion, and the way you love me. I love all of you."

Maggie stared up at him. "Truly?" she asked in a small voice. "You love me?

Philip smiled at her then. "Utterly and completely," he said, brushing her lips with his.

"Oh, Philip." She sighed and opened her mouth to him.

He kissed her deeply, his tongue teasing and stroking hers until she clung to him. His mouth left hers to nuzzle the sensitive skin on her neck.

"You're mine, Maggie. And I'm yours. Forever."

Maggie leaned back to stare up at him in question.

He lowered his head and continued his subtle assault on her senses until she was as weak as a kitten in his arms.

"My God," he said at last, brushing her curls back from her face. "How could you ever doubt me?"

Maggie shrugged. "I knew that you wanted me. But I was unsure."

"I'll always want you, wife," he said, dropping a kiss on her brow. "Because I love you. You have my heart, along with the rest of me," he finished with a grin.

She caught his smile and returned it with one of her own.

"The rest of you?" she teased. "Oh, that."

"Never mind," he growled playfully.

Maggie laughed sweetly, wrapping her arms around his neck.

"Oh, Philip," she said. "I love you!"

Her declaration after so puzzling an exchange pleased him immensely. He cupped her cheek once more.

"My Maggie," he said reverently. "It will always be this way, love," he said, caressing her cheek. "I'll always want you. I'll always love you."

Maggie stared into his eyes for a long moment, and she saw she did indeed have his love as well as his passion.

She brought her hand to his face. "I'll always love you."

"Maggie," he began. "What else did that scoundrel say to you?"

"What else?" she repeated, her brow slightly furrowed.

He needed to know precisely what the man said regarding her illegitimacy, but was loath to bring up the subject.

"What precisely did he say about the past?"

Maggie gave a slight shudder and dropped her gaze to the floor. "He said that you wanted me at the Inn at Salisbury," she said. "You told him that I was a…" She couldn't finish her thought.

"How could he think so, Philip?" Maggie asked worriedly, finally looking at him. "I wasn't being kept by anyone, and yet you told him so."

"Shh, love," he said. "I'll set Rawlings straight on the matter." His grin widened and he nodded. "When I first told him of you, I was indeed misinformed. If you recall your circumstances were a bit, um, unusual."

"If you recall," she amended, "your misconceptions followed you into Somersetshire."

He laughed and shook his head. "I promise I'll set Rawlings straight," he said again. "He'll know you are indeed the lady you appear to be."

***

Lord and Lady Bridgewater were expected to arrive in town on the morrow, and Philip was certain they would call in the afternoon. He wished to rid Lord Rawlings of any lingering confusions regarding Maggie's character prior to their visit. In addition, they would undoubtedly accompany Maggie and himself to the bashes, and Philip didn't want the slightest shadow of a scandal tainting their visit. He quickly penned a note requesting an audience with Rawlings in the morning. His note was curt and to the point, and he was certain that the viscount would be hard-pressed to deny him.

How could Rawlings say such words to her? And to put his hands on her? Philip folded the single sheet of paper and pressed his seal upon it. He addressed it and arose from his seat.

"Grimes," he called, pulling the study door wide open.

The butler responded immediately to his master's summons. "Yes, my lord?"

Philip handed him the note. Grimes read the name neatly penned across the missive and couldn't contain his astonishment, his eyes opened wide as he stared at Philip. He quickly schooled his expression as he took in his master's stern demeanor.

"See to it," Philip ordered.

The servant nodded and saw immediately to the note's delivery.

Philip returned to his chair. He leaned his elbows upon the polished surface, tenting his fingers beneath his chin. His mind worked as he sought to decide how much information he would have to give Rawlings. He would certainly strive to dispel any notions the scoundrel had that Maggie was anything other than the proper young lady she appeared to be. He would tell him of his own misconceptions at the Inn at Salisbury but say nothing of her illegitimacy.

The man would simply have to believe that Maggie's father was truly the imaginary Baron Penworth.

Chapter 20

Maggie found her husband in his study, his head bowed in deep thought.

"Philip," Maggie said softly.

He lifted his head and gave her a small smile. "Hello, love," he said, his eyes sparkling.

Maggie's eyes ran over his face, searching for any signs of the brooding look his face had worn when first she came to the study. Apparently having put aside whatever had been troubling him, Philip's expression was as warm and open as she had grown to both expect and love.

"Are you planning to ready for dinner, husband?" she asked, her head tilted to one side.

Philip nodded in response, a smile teasing the corner of his mouth. He rose once more from his chair and let his wife lead him from the room. He left her in the parlor, hurriedly readied for dinner, and soon joined her there. He escorted her into the dining room. They shared a fine meal—punctuated by much animated conversation—and adjourned to the parlor. Grimes brought in a tray of tarts, accompanied by a bottle of sherry.

As Maggie sipped delicately from the glass her husband poured for her, Philip took a few moments to gaze about the room. Many of Maggie's prettiest pieces of needlework now adorned the walls and, taken with the floral-patterned pillows resting comfortably on the settees, the room was a most pleasant place to spend their time.

"I daresay, love," he said, taking up his own glass. "This room has benefited greatly from your very feminine touch."

"Thank you, husband," Maggie returned. "I do believe Lady Bridgewater will find the room quite lovely."

Her comment brought the other residents of Bridgewater Park to mind, and talk soon turned to the children.

"Has Betsy written recently?" he asked her.

Maggie nodded in answer, unable to keep a laugh from bubbling from her lips. Philip arched a brow at her.

"I don't know how she managed it," she said in answer to his unasked question, "but reading her letter was quite like hearing the child chattering in my ear."

Philip smiled to hear the affection in her voice.

"I'm so pleased she's accompanying your aunt and uncle," he said with a crooked smile.

Maggie laughed. "I daresay even I won't be able to contain her in the confines of the townhouse, husband."

"She'll run you fairly ragged, wife," he agreed with a grin.

They sat and played a few games of cards. Maggie expressed her fatigue at the long and confounding day, asking her husband very sweetly to escort her to their chambers. Philip was more than happy to honor his wife's request.

He laid awake in the big bed long after Maggie had fallen into slumber. While their lovemaking had been satisfying both physically and emotionally, he couldn't seem to fall asleep.

Rawlings's words still rang through his head, the picture of Maggie in the man's arms still haunted him. He would make him aware of Maggie's true character. Rawlings would know what she truly was and treat her accordingly. And if he persisted in his blatant admiration… Philip couldn't finish the thought. He dropped a kiss on Maggie's brow and closed his eyes, willing sleep to find him.

The next morning Philip soon strode from the dressing room, stopping to favor his wife with a wide smile.

"Good morning, love," he said, tying his cravat. "It is high time you rose to greet the day."

Maggie shook her head even as her mouth opened wide in a yawn.

"I am quite certain the sun has barely risen, husband," she said, brushing her hair back from her face. "May I inquire as to what you are about so early this morning?"

"The answer to your query is quite a simple, really," he said, coming to stand over her beside the bed. "You see, I have the great need to set a certain matter to rights."

She puzzled over that for a moment and Philip laughed at her obvious confusion. He placed a finger beneath her chin as he tilted her face up to him.

"I need to be assured that a certain gentleman realizes the true nature of my very proper, very beautiful wife," he said, kissing her lightly.

"Oh!" she suddenly cried, causing Philip to turn. "What if Lord Rawlings does not believe you?"

Philip took in her appearance with a sly grin. Her hair was a cloud of curls, her face flushed from sleep. She held the sheets close to her bosom, her naked figure all but visible beneath the thin fabric. She looked like a most delectable chit, he thought.

"I daresay if the man saw you at this very moment," he teased, "he would find it bloody difficult to believe me."

Maggie gasped aloud, at which he couldn't contain his laughter.

"I'm jesting, sweetheart," he said.

She clicked her tongue, narrowing her eyes at him. "You may jest, husband," she chided. "It's not your reputation that was sullied."

Philip hid his grin and crossed to her once more.

"Your reputation was not sullied, Maggie," he assured her. "Rawlings assured me that he told no one of his opinions. And we both know that those opinions resulted from misinformation he received from…"

"From you?" Maggie finished for him.

"Well yes," he grinned sheepishly. "I'll set the matter to rights, and all will be well again."

Maggie smiled sweetly at him.

"The scoundrel will make a full apology to you, love," he said. "I will see to it."

She shook her head wildly, her eyes round in alarm.

"Oh no, Philip!" she said quickly. "I don't want him to apologize to me. I cannot face him. I would be far too embarrassed."

"As you wish, love," he said, kissing her brow. "I suggest you rise," he went on. "Lady Bridgewater will undoubtedly write you this morning upon their arrival."

His words had the desired effect, changing her mind swiftly from the distasteful subject of Rawlings and his horrid misconceptions.

"Oh, yes," Maggie said, swinging her legs over the side of the bed. "I must see to matters, for I would so love for them to call this afternoon."

Philip left her to her morning toilette, taking his breakfast alone as he anxiously awaited an answer from Rawlings. Grimes soon brought him a missive from the viscount, stating Rawlings's agreeing most graciously to a meeting that very morning.

Philip's face was set as his carriage rolled over the cobblestone streets, bound for Rawlings's townhouse. Although it was not a great distance from his own home, he was more than pleased when the carriage finally rocked to a stop. He alighted and walked to the front door, rapping his knuckles sharply on the thick wood panel.

Rawlings's butler bowed to Philip and escorted him to his master's study. Philip narrowed his eyes on his friend, pleased to see the nervous smile as he swiftly came to his feet.

"Good morning, Wilton," he said easily.

"I want to know all that you said to my wife," Philip said without preamble.

Rawlings pulled back at the intensity in Philip's gaze, confusion clear on his face.

"I thought this matter was settled yesterday," he said, taking a seat behind his desk. "What more could you want to know?"

Philip's lips thinned to a hard line as he sat in the chair facing his friend.

"Maggie told me of your brazen comments, Rawlings," he said stiffly. "The only reason my hands aren't around your throat at this very moment is that I believe you mistook my wife for someone of questionable character."

Rawlings blinked rapidly as he sought to think of some excuse for his behavior.

"Wilton," he began, "I don't know what it is your wife told you, but I assure you that she misunderstood my meaning."

Philip's hands clutched at the arms of the chair until his knuckles showed white.

"You told her that you want her," Philip ground out. "One cannot be any more clear."

"I…," Rawlings choked.

The man's obvious befuddlement confirmed Philip's suspicions.

"She isn't the person you believe she is, Rawlings," he said at last.

The other man stared blankly at him. Philip laughed without humor.

"I take a share of the blame," Philip said. "Because of my comments last Spring, you came to the same conclusion I did." The viscount's brow furrowed at Philip's words. "I was wrong, Rawlings," Philip went on. "Maggie was not a doxy under another's protection. She was—and is—what she appears to be. A lady."

Rawlings's eyes were round in surprise.

"But," the man began, "when you spoke of her in the pub, you said that—"

Philip held up a hand to still him, his anger simmering. He would make the scoundrel well-aware of Maggie's true character. And if the man persisted in his ill opinion, he would use his fists instead of his words to drive his point home.

"I was wrong," he added in a firm voice. "I was captivated by her, Rawlings. But my wife was both pure and unspoiled." He stood and braced his hands on the desk, his eyes narrowed as they bore into Rawlings's blue ones. "And I'm the one man who can be certain of that fact," he stated firmly.

Philip's meaning was not lost on Rawlings. He sprang to his feet and placed his hand on his chest, sincerity in his stance.

"My God, Wilton," he said. "What must your wife think of me? I never meant to upset her."

Philip studied Rawlings closely.

"Your obvious surprise at my disclosure is the only fact preventing me from calling you out," Philip said through clenched teeth.

Rawlings nodded, aware that were he in Philip's place, he would be hard-pressed to deny himself the pleasure of a duel at dawn. It was unspoken that the two of them were extremely well-matched. However, neither gentleman had the slightest desire to be either killer or killed.

"You have my word that I will never say anything disrespectful to Mag—to Lady Wilton again," he said fervently.

Philip gave him a slow nod, straightening once more.

"I'll tell Maggie as much," he said, turning toward the door.

"Wilton," Rawlings said fervently. "You must allow me to apologize to her."

Philip shook his head, mindful of Maggie's expressed wishes of the morning.

"She was most upset, Rawlings," he said. "I don't believe such an action is wise."

"Please," the man said. "I must be allowed to make amends."

Philip acquiesced, albeit with great reluctance.

"I won't see her upset again," he qualified. He paused for a moment. "You may come to the townhouse this afternoon."

"Splendid," Rawlings said, his shoulders slumping with relief. "Thank you, Wilton."

Philip nodded and took his leave. He raked his fingers through his hair as he climbed aboard his carriage, nearly growling with frustration. The urge to choke the life out of his good friend was still pounding in his veins. Regardless of the man's heartfelt apology, Philip rightly sensed the man's strong regard for Maggie. Would Rawlings stay true to his word? he mused. Or would he continue his brazen pursuit of her?

"The hell he will," Philip grumbled.

***

Maggie happily greeted Lord and Lady Bridgewater as Grimes showed them into the parlor. Before she could give voice to her greeting Betsy scampered into the room, launching herself at Maggie.

"Oh, Maggie!" the child cried. "How I have missed you!"

Maggie laughed gaily as she bent down to return the girl's embrace.

"I've missed you too, sweetheart," she said. "Hello, Aunt," she said, straightening. "Hello, Uncle."

"Hello, Margaret," Lady Bridgewater said with a nod. "Betsy," she gently admonished. "Do let loose your hold on Margaret before she swoons."

"Yes, Mother," Betsy said, stepping back to strike a pose obviously meant to replicate Maggie's ladylike posture.

The two ladies shared a smile.

"Hello, Maggie," Lord Bridgewater said, his eyes warm. "And where is your husband, may I inquire?"

"Philip had an appointment, Uncle," she said in answer. "He should return momentarily, I imagine."

Lady Bridgewater nodded again, taking a long moment to look about the room. Her practiced eye saw immediately the feminine and gracious changes Maggie had made to the residence since her coming to London.

"I daresay, Margaret," she intoned, seating herself on one of the settees, "this room is vastly improved since last we saw it. Isn't that so, husband?"

"Hmm?" Bridgewater murmured. "Yes, dear. I suppose we could place the blame for the house's previous condition squarely on Philip's shoulders, bachelor that he was," he elaborated with a grin.

"It was quite dull and drab," Lady Bridgewater added.

"I've never before seen Philip's townhouse, Maggie," Betsy pouted. "Was it quite as dreary as Mother says?"

"Not quite," Maggie laughed. "Although it was sorely lacking in decoration."

"Philip never did give much thought to adding beauty to the place," Lady Bridgewater went on. "Apparently, it mattered little to him."

"On the contrary," Philip intoned from the doorway.

"Philip!" Maggie cried happily, crossing to him.

He ran his gaze lovingly over her face.

"This house is filled with more beauty than any man could want," he said.

Maggie blushed prettily at his compliment, lost in his emerald gaze. Lord Bridgewater chuckled deeply, drawing Philip's attention from his wife's visage.

"Did you wish to say something, sir?" he asked, hiding his smile.

"Marriage obviously agrees with you, my boy," the older man returned with a grin.

Philip could only answer the man's grin with one of his own. He turned his attention to Betsy, who was watching the newlyweds' exchange with starry eyes.

"How was your trip from Somersetshire, Betsy?" he asked.

Betsy went on to extol the virtues of the inn at which they had taken their nooning meal. She spoke of the bumpy ride out of Somersetshire, and of the pretty flowers lining the lanes toward town and the bustling carriages and horses as they arrived. For his part, Philip managed to follow her meandering chatter, nodding wherever he deemed necessary while Maggie looked on with a smile.

Grimes interrupted their discourse, announcing Lord Rawlings's arrival. Maggie's eyes flew to Philip's in alarm. Philip leaned close to her, cupping her cheek with his hand.

"I granted him an audience, love," he explained in a low voice. "I told him that he may apologize to you."

"But," she began in a nervous whisper, "you told me that I didn't have to speak with him."

"The man was quite adamant in his appeal. Don't fret. I will be with you."

After a long pause, Maggie nodded. Philip smiled in reassurance and straightened.

"Send him to my study, Grimes," he instructed the butler.

Philip told the others that he and Maggie had need to speak with Rawlings and assured them that they would not tarry long.

Philip led Maggie from the room, leaving Lord and Lady Bridgewater to exchange speculative glances. No doubt Betsy's chatter would soon sent any thought of possible reasons for their absence fleeing from their minds.

Maggie preceded her husband into the study, walking only far enough into the room to allow him to close the door. Rawlings stood with his back to them, staring out the window. The sound of the door clicking into place caused him to turn. His eyes met Maggie's for a brief moment, remorse clear in their blue depths. Maggie quickly averted her gaze, her lashes shielding her from his eyes. She couldn't bear to look at him, his actions of the previous afternoon fresh in her mind.

"Lady Margaret," Rawlings began, taking a step toward the couple.

Philip crossed his arms, censure clear in his demeanor as well as on his face. Rawlings managed a small smile.

"Wilton," he said with a bow. "Thank you for allowing me to come here this afternoon."

Philip accepted the man's thanks with a curt nod, his face set. Maggie, her eyes once more focused on her clasped hands in front of her, held her breath. She could feel his gaze on her and bristled. She heard him take a deep breath and braced herself.

"Lady Margaret," he said. "Please allow me to tell you how dreadfully sorry I am for my words and actions of yesterday." At Maggie's small nod he continued. "I was rude, boorish and disrespectful. On my word, I shall never again say such words to you."

Maggie could only nod once more, her cheeks hot with her acute embarrassment despite Philip's calming presence at her back.

"Lady Margaret," Rawlings beseeched. "Please say that you forgive me?"

Silence fell over the room, the three of them standing stock still. Philip, obviously well-satisfied with the man's heartfelt apology, placed his hand on Maggie's shoulder. She took her strength from him and finally lifted her head to stare unblinkingly at Lord Rawlings.

"Yes, Lord Rawlings," she said softly. "I forgive you."

Swallowing audibly, he took her hand in his. "Thank you," he said. "You are indeed a lady of incredible grace and generosity."

Maggie blinked at the tenderness in his gaze for, while it was very different from the lust that had been evident the previous day, she couldn't help but find it all the more unsettling. Thankfully, Philip once more put an end to the tension that had fallen over the room.

"Well done, Rawlings," he said, satisfaction in his voice.

Chapter 21

The afternoon passed in a much more pleasing fashion than either Maggie or Philip had anticipated at the time of Lord Rawlings's arrival. That gentleman—while he seemed to be watching Maggie closely anytime she happened a glance in his direction—did not approach her for conversation. Philip kept close to her side of course, ever-mindful of the dark-haired gentleman's close scrutiny of his wife.

Lord Bridgewater succeeded in gaining Philip's attention at last, and the two of them were soon in deep conversation. Maggie and her aunt discussed the coming evening's festivities, causing Lord Rawlings to cross the room to join them where they sat beside the hearth.

"Are you attending the bashes this evening, Lady Bridgewater?" he asked.

"Why, yes, Lord Rawlings," the woman replied. "Do you still find amusement in such events?"

Rawlings laughed at her jest.

"I daresay I find nothing more pleasant than being in the company of genteel young ladies," he assured her, his eyes falling on Maggie. "They make the most wonderful dance partners."

Maggie suddenly jumped from her seat, reddening.

"I'll see to the tea," she rushed out. "Betsy," she added, addressing the child. "Perhaps you would like to sample some of our cook's biscuits? I believe you'll find them quite scrumptious."

Betsy smiled widely as she skipped from the room to follow Maggie to the kitchen. Philip didn't miss Maggie's hasty departure or her obvious discomfort. He watched as Rawlings took the seat she had vacated, leaning close to speak with Lady Bridgewater.

"What think you of Philip's marriage, Lord Rawlings?" Lady Bridgewater asked the viscount.

Rawlings smiled crookedly.

"I believe Wilton is a lucky man, madam," he said in truth. "Lady Margaret is incredible."

Philip simply listened to his friend, ever-mindful of his tone.

"She is a wonderful girl," the woman agreed. "We're all quite fond of her."

"May I ask how Lady Margaret came to reside at Bridgewater Park?" Rawlings asked.

"Certainly," the lady replied. "My husband sent for her after her mother passed away."

"What of her father?" he asked.

Lady Bridgewater fidgeted, losing her smile. Philip held his breath as he also waited for the lady's answer.

"Margaret lived alone with her mother."

"And she's the earl's niece, yes?" he asked.

"Margaret's mother was sister to the earl's first wife," she said stiffly.

"And where did she reside?" Rawlings pressed. "Near the earl's estate?"

"No," Lady Bridgewater said shortly. "Sussex. Not far from the sea shore."

"Ah," Rawlings said with another nod. "Sussex. Quite a pleasant county." He turned his eyes to the door once more. "And what town was…?"

"Ah, Maggie," Philip cut in as she reentered the room at that moment.

The earl crossed to his wife and Rawlings stood to allow him to sit. Philip ran his eyes over Maggie's face, concerned. She appeared strained to him, and a bit flushed. He covered her hand with his.

"Is everything all right, love?" he asked softly. "Rawlings hasn't said or done anything to make you feel uncomfortable?"

"No, Philip," she said quickly. "Lord Rawlings has carried himself like a gentleman."

Philip nodded. "And what of Betsy?" he asked. "Is she driving our cook quite mad?"

Maggie laughed sweetly, drawing unwanted attention from Rawlings standing beside the hearth.

"Betsy's quite happy to find a person she can regale with her stories of her eventful trip to town," she answered.

Philip chuckled. As they spoke—leaning their heads close to each other's—Rawlings watched, his eyes dark. Philip didn't miss the man's vigilance, but he managed to restrain his ire.

Lord and Lady Bridgewater departed soon after tea time, but only after Betsy extracted a promise from Maggie that she would see her on the morrow. Lord Rawlings took his leave as well, once more professing his appreciation to Maggie for her generous acceptance of his apology.

When they were once more alone, Philip drew Maggie into the circle of his arms.

"You're indeed a generous woman, Maggie," he told her, kissing her temple. "Rawlings's apology satisfied me."

"Oh, Philip," she said wearily. "I don't wish to speak of it again."

"As you wish," he said, kissing her cheek. "I can think of much more interesting tasks to do."

He brushed her lips with his as Maggie leaned into him. All the uneasiness of the afternoon seem to leave her as she reveled in his tender kiss. He lifted his head and held her closer. Maggie tucked her head under his chin and sighed softly.

"Do you wish to forego the bashes this evening, love?" Philip asked, rubbing her back.

She shook her head. "My aunt and uncle will be expecting us, Philip."

"Hmm," he mused aloud. "You're aware that my friends will each request a dance with you. They have become accustomed to it, although I can't say that I blame them."

Maggie lifted her head, her expression thoughtful. She gave him a nod. "I will not dance with them," she said firmly. "I will only dance with my husband this night."

He smiled crookedly down at her. "Three dances and no more?"

She smiled cheekily at him. "You, dear husband, may have all the dances you wish."

"Pray, tell me wife," he began, "you're not going to wear that sinful golden gown, are you?"

She cocked to her head in thought. "I believe I have one or two gowns you haven't seen," she said. "Perhaps I'll surprise you."

"And will you wear the pearls?"

"Yes," she said with a smile.

"Good," he said. "And perhaps later you'll wear them just for me."

Maggie's brow furrowed in slight confusion. Philip brought his lips to her ear.

"Perhaps you'll wear the pearls and only the pearls," he whispered.

She gasped, heat soon replacing the surprise in her gaze.

"Philip," she said, her eyes glittering. "That's absolutely wicked."

Philip gave a slow nod to that, his eyes mirroring the passion in hers. He thought to ravish her there in the parlor, seeing her in his mind's eye in nothing but the pearls right at that very moment. Instead, with a show of control that struck him, he shook his head and led her upstairs to their chamber, leaving her to ready for the evening as he took himself into the dressing room to see to his own preparations.

***

Maggie had not missed the heat in his gaze, marveling at the way he could still make her pulse race though they had made love more times than she could count. She hoped it would always be so. She shook her head at her fancy, ringing for Joan's assistance.

Together they decided upon a gown of blush rose, modest in cut. It would nonetheless hug her curves, as did all of the dresses Lady Bridgewater helped her choose, but she was quite certain that Lord Rawlings would not find her so much to his liking.

Leaving the gown to hang in readiness Maggie sat at the vanity, her mind drifting as Joan fashioned her hair into an artful pile of curls atop her head, twining rose-colored ribbons through the shining mass. She thought once more of Lord Rawlings's apology, unable now to deny the affection evident in his eyes when she had finally met his gaze. What would Philip think if he ever caught a glimpse of it?

Her heart was true. She had no desire to court another man's attentions as did some of the women she had met in town. Perhaps they were woefully unhappy in their marriages, she reasoned. No matter. If Lord Rawlings ever approached her again—with either lust or love on his mind—she would make certain he finally understood that her heart, her soul, belonged to Philip. Forever.

Joan spoke at last, bringing Maggie swiftly out of her reverie.

"What do you think, my lady?" she asked, proud of the intricate hairstyle he had fashioned.

Maggie smiled brightly as she turned her head from side to side.

"Why, Joan," she said. "It looks marvelous!"

Joan glowed under her mistress' praise. Maggie noticed then that the maid had surely been practicing her art on her own hair, as she wore a fancier style than was her custom. Maggie believed she knew the cause for Joan's taking new pains with her own appearance.

"Joan," Maggie began, "I believe you look quite fetching this evening, as well. Am I wrong to assume that this is due to a certain man in our employ?"

Joan's blush was all the answer Maggie needed.

"Has Grimes been more sensitive to you of late?" she asked the lady's maid.

"Oh, yes," Joan nodded in answer. "He is most solicitous now, my lady."

Maggie smiled at the affection brightening the girl's face. Joan suddenly flushed, nervously shaking her head. Maggie quickly put an end to any further discussion of the topic, more than pleased for the girl who was companion as well as servant.

Joan assisted Maggie into the beautiful gown, deftly fastening the few hooks at the back. She stepped back as Maggie checked her appearance in the cheval mirror.

"Thank you, Joan," she said at last. "Do enjoy your own evening."

Joan blushed again, bidding her mistress farewell. Maggie returned to the vanity and pulled open one of the drawers, withdrawing the velvet box cradling her pearls. She fastened the earrings to her lobes and gingerly lifted the necklace in her hands. She crossed to the mirror and draped the pearls around her neck, liking the weighty feel of them as they settled against her breast. She ran her fingers over them, thinking once more of her husband's words in the parlor. She suddenly imagined herself wearing only the pearls, with nothing else against her skin save for Philip's hands, his mouth. Her heart fluttered as her face flushed in response to her thoughts.

Philip found her there, gazing into the mirror as she ran her fingers over the pearls.

"Pray, tell me what you are thinking, wife," he drawled, breaking her trance.

Maggie met his gaze in the mirror. "I…," she began. "That is…"

He arched a brow at her, hiding a grin.

"Never mind," she rushed out, pulling on long gloves as she kept her eyes downcast.

Philip chuckled then, causing her to finally raise her eyes. She placed her hands on her hips, slowly drinking in the dashing figure he cut in his formal black. A waistcoat of burgundy and crisp white shirt and cravat were the perfect finishing touches to his dress. She crossed to him.

"You look marvelous, husband," she said, placing her hands on his chest. "I'm so pleased you'll dance all the dances with only me."

He covered her hands with his. "And why is that?"

"I fear you would steal all of the ladies' hearts."

"Ah, wife," he said, touching his forehead to hers. "There's only one lady's heart I want. And I believe I already have it in my possession."

Maggie smiled as she nodded her agreement.

"Let's be off," he said, dropping a kiss on her brow.

They went downstairs to his waiting carriage, hands clasped as they settled close to each other on the cushioned seat.

***

295

Before much time had passed, they arrived at the first party, held at Lord and Lady Bulword's townhouse. Philip alighted, assisting Maggie out of the carriage and into the house. The Bulword's townhouse—while as elegant as Lord Winston's whose bash Philip and Maggie had attended when first in town— was much smaller in size. Apparently Lady Bulword saw this as a great deficiency to be overcome, for the place was filled to bursting with guests, flowers, candles and musicians. The orchestra was larger than the space should have indicated, the music scarcely allowing for conversation. As a result of all of this, the ballroom was warm, crowded and noisy.

Philip and Maggie greeted their hostess and made their way into the ballroom. He leaned close to Maggie's ear.

"I see your aunt and uncle, love," he said, gesturing toward the other side of the room.

Maggie followed with her eyes, filled with pleasure as she too saw her relatives. As the two of them began to cross the crowded room, Maggie lost hold of Philip's hand in the crush. She called out to him, her voice carrying little in the din. She hurried to catch up to him, relief flowing though her when she spied broad shoulders she guessed were Philip's. Maggie grabbed on to the black jacket covering those shoulders, causing the man to turn sharply. She gasped as she stared up into dark blue eyes.

"Lord Rawlings!" she cried, her hand flying to her throat.

Rawlings flashed a bright smile. "Lady Margaret," he said with a bow. "Good evening."

Maggie quickly recovered her composure and curtseyed. "Good evening," she returned. "I seem to have lost my husband."

He inclined his head to her. "And you thought to seek out a substitute?"

Maggie shook her head firmly. "If you would excuse me," she said, keeping her tone light. "I believe I see Philip now."

She hurried to where Philip stood with Lord and Lady Bridgewater.

"Philip," she breathed when finally she reached his side.

"I thought I'd lost you," he said to her at last, his voice low.

"You'll never lose me, husband," she answered, puzzling over his odd expression.

Philip seemed to recover his good humor at last, standing aside as Maggie greeted Lord and Lady Bridgewater. It was soon time to adjourn to the supper room, which they were not surprised to find crowded as well. The food was abundant, however, and more than adequate. When they finished their repast, Maggie and Philip returned to the ballroom.

Philip led his wife onto the dance floor, smiling down at her. They twirled about in as large a circle as the crowded floor would allow. Maggie followed him through the dances, her breath coming fast. As promised, they danced nearly every dance, the closeness and heat of the room soon causing her to flush. She begged for a respite at last, laughing as he pulled her even closer.

"Do you need to rest, love?" he teased. "Am I wearing you out?"

"I believe I can do with a bit of fresh air, Philip," she said. "It's frightfully hot in here."

He nodded his agreement and led her to the doors opening onto the terrace. Maggie breathed deeply of the fresh air, sweet after the confines of the ballroom.

"Would you like a glass of refreshment?" Philip asked her, brushing a stray curl from her cheek.

"Oh, yes," she smiled. "That would be lovely."

He bowed to her and then strode across the room, his big frame easily cutting a path through the crowd. Maggie watched him go, her back to the open door. She found the slight breeze quite heavenly on her neck and shoulders, letting out a sigh of pleasure as she closed her eyes. A familiar voice soon broke the tranquility of the moment.

"It was your beauty," Rawlings said softly from behind her, causing her to gasp in surprise.

Maggie spun to face him. He stood in the dim light of the lanterns encircling the terrace, as if he had materialized out of the night. She could only stare at him.

"It was your beauty and your grace," he went on. "Taken with what I presumed to be your vast experience with…," he trailed, shrugging. "I found the combination undeniably attractive."

"Lord Rawlings," she said at last, her voice weak. She stepped back from him. "You mustn't speak of this anymore."

Rawlings held his hands in front of him, his brow furrowed.

"I didn't mean to upset you yet again."

"Don't speak of this anymore," Maggie whispered again, shaking her head.

He could only stare at her, his eyes dark. Maggie's own eyes widened at the warmth evident in his.

She turned swiftly and hurried to where she had last seen Philip, near the refreshments.

Chapter 22

Philip turned from the refreshment table as Maggie reached his side. He began to smile, rapidly losing his easy grin as he sensed her distress.

"What is it, love?" he asked worriedly.

"I couldn't wait any longer, husband," she said. "I daresay I very nearly perished from thirst."

Philip chuckled at her words, lifting his head to scan the room. He sought out the dark-haired gentleman whose presence was a trial on his patience this evening. He noted with satisfaction that Rawlings and Porter were speaking with the Bulwords, obviously making their excuses for their hurried departure.

He looked down at Maggie once more, taking her nearly empty glass from her hand. Setting the glasses aside, he turned back to find her looking up at him in question.

"Another dance, wife?" he asked, taking her hands in his.

She smiled her answer, permitting him to lead her back out onto the dance floor. They danced long into the night, well-pleased at the absence of a certain handsome viscount.

***

In their bedchamber at the townhouse, Philip watched as Maggie slowly undressed, leaving only her lustrous pearls as a compliment to her flawless skin. He stripped out of his formal wear and grabbed her to him.

"You're incredible, sweetheart," he said, kissing her gently. "I can hardly believe you are mine."

"Philip," she said, pressing tightly against him. "I love you. Only you."

"I'm the luckiest man on earth," he murmured, leading her over to the bed.

He stretched out on his back, holding her on top of him. Maggie's hair fell in shining curls around the two of them. She placed her hands on his face and kissed him with all the love in her heart, all the passion in her body. He ran his hands over her bare skin, cupping her bottom. He urged her upward, trailing kisses over her throat. Maggie's body arched as his mouth found her breast.

"Philip," she whispered.

Philip circled her hardened nipple with the tip of his tongue, finally drawing it into his mouth to suck greedily. Maggie closed her eyes and ran her fingers through his hair, letting the sensations wash over her as her legs fell on either side of him. She instinctively rubbed against him.

He shuddered as he felt her heat against his hardened flesh.

His fingers moved between her legs, caressing her deeply.

Maggie writhed against him as he set her to burning. Her response drove him mad for release. He took his mouth from her breast, causing her to whimper her disappointment.

"Maggie," he rasped, his control slipping. "Maggie, love, take me inside."

His words seemed to confuse her. She opened her eyes to stare at him in befuddlement. Philip would have laughed if he could have managed it, desire causing him to ache to be inside of her.

"Please, sweetheart," he said, placing her hands on his chest. "Ride me. Take me inside of you."

Philip instructed her to lean back. Maggie suddenly understood and straddled him, taking him deep inside of her. She threw her head back as she began to move over him. Philip let her set the pace for a few moments, the pressure growing steadily inside of him. He stared up at her in wonder, at the passion making her skin glow as richly as the pearls draped over her. He cupped her breasts with his hands, rubbing her nipples as his control slowly ebbed away. Maggie nearly screamed at the added torment.

"Oh!" she gasped, close to her release. "Oh, Philip!"

He could be passive no longer. He grabbed her hips and drove up into her, stroking up and down as he sent her over the edge into a stunning climax. He joined her in fulfillment, arching off the bed as he exploded within her. Maggie collapsed on top of him, dropping little kisses on his chest as he ran his hands over her back.

"My God," he said at last, brushing her damp curls away from her face. "The way you love me."

Maggie brought her lips to his to place a gentle kiss there. Philip sighed with intense satisfaction, hugging her tightly. She slipped off of him to cuddle against his side, her face resting on his chest.

"I never knew that we could," she began, her lashes brushing her cheeks.

"There are many different ways for a man and woman to come together, love," he told her.

"Truly?" Maggie raised round eyes to stare at him. "How many different ways?"

Philip barked out a laugh. "I would be more than happy to show you at this very moment," he drawled, "if you had not nearly killed me once already this evening."

Maggie clicked her tongue at him, a smile teasing the corner of her mouth.

"I suppose it will have to wait, then," she sighed dramatically.

"Go to sleep, minx," he growled.

Maggie pulled the sheets up to cover them both, and was asleep in mere moments. He kissed her brow and held her closer, joining her in slumber.

Philip awoke the next morning well before his wife, content to hold her, to gaze at her as she lightly snored in her slumber. The strange conversation the previous evening in their bed came back to him, both her embarrassment and avid interest causing him to grin. Lord, he was a lucky man to have found such a warm, loving, passionate woman. Someone to love him as he had dared not hope before. A wave of possessiveness seized him, so sharp it caused him to groan.

He hadn't missed the affection in Lord Rawlings's eyes, the man's regard obviously as strong as before his apology. Philip suddenly saw Rawlings in his mind's eye, holding Maggie—kissing and caressing her—as clearly as if it were happening before him. He was filled with such anguish at the prospect of losing her that his arms tightened convulsively around her. She instantly awoke, crying out in surprise. He swore softly, loosening his hold.

"Philip?" she asked, rubbing the sleep from her eyes. "What's happening?"

"Shh," he soothed, kissing her brow. "I'm sorry I woke you."

Maggie leaned up to study him in the pale morning light.

"Is something wrong?" she asked, worry etched on her face.

He flashed her an easy grin, putting aside his dark thoughts for the moment.

"On the contrary," he answered, turning to stretch out on top of her. "Everything is quite right."

He kissed her lips, her cheek. He lowered his head to nuzzle her neck. Maggie sighed, closing her eyes once more.

"Mmm," she murmured. "That feels wonderful, husband."

He lifted his head to glare at her, the vision of her and Rawlings fresh in his mind. Although she was warm and pliant in his arms, he couldn't shake the premonition of her betrayal.

"You're mine, Maggie," he suddenly said, squeezing her shoulders. "You'll never belong to another."

She shook her head in obvious confusion.

"You'll never leave me," he went on.

Maggie placed her hand on his cheek. "I'll never leave you," she said firmly. "You're my husband. I love you."

Philip stared at her, unsure. Her gaze—soft and loving—finally penetrated the hard shell he had erected since waking.

"My Maggie," he whispered reverently, kissing her gently.

He slowly aroused her passion to match her affection, taking the two of them to sweet release in the soft morning light flooding the chamber.

***

Philip then left her to ready for her day. As Maggie soaked in a tub of warm water set near the hearth in their chamber, Philip's very strange behavior of the morning plagued her. While he'd been quite passionate—and most thorough—during their

307

lovemaking, she couldn't help but feel as if he were preoccupied, that it was something other than simple passion driving him. His eyes were shuttered soon after his release, she recalled, and while he had kissed her sweetly before leaving to see to his own toilette, she felt his distance from her.

Shaking her head to rid it of such troubling thoughts, she finished her bath and rang for Joan. The lady's maid, as if sensing her mistress' odd mood, styled Maggie's hair simply and left her to her day.

As Maggie had fully expected, Betsy arrived soon after breakfast. Philip greeted the child and took himself off to his study, his having quite a bit of paperwork to see to that morning. Maggie watched him go. She sensed his withdrawal, both physically and emotionally, and sorely wished she had the opportunity to explore it further. Betsy's happy chatter soon drew her attention, brightening her spirits considerably.

"What will we do this day, Maggie?" she asked excitedly. "Perhaps some needlework, or painting?"

"Hmm," Maggie mused aloud. "What do you say to working a bit on your lettering?"

Betsy nodded slowly, a frown replacing her happy smile. She reluctantly followed on Maggie's heels to the front sitting room.

"I know my letters, Maggie," she pouted, sitting in the chair Maggie pulled beside the writing desk. "My tutor instructs me daily."

"I know that, sweetheart," Maggie agreed, sitting beside her. "I thought you would like to try your hand at some fancy lettering."

Betsy shrugged her tiny shoulders. Maggie opened one of the drawers and withdrew a book of poetry and laid it on the surface.

"Why don't we try our hand at copying some of the flowery verse in this book, dear?" she suggested. "You may choose which one."

"Oh, yes!" Betsy cried happily. "I'll pick one about a beautiful summer day, like this one," she said, thumbing through the pages.

Maggie smiled as they worked beside each other, their heads bent over the desk as letter after painstaking letter was written on the crisp papers.

"Betsy," Maggie said after a while. "I simply must show Philip the lovely job you've done."

"Philip!" Maggie called, rushing into his study. "You must see Betsy's lettering. It has— Oh! Excuse me," she said, dropping into a graceful curtsey. "I didn't realize that you were here, Lord Porter."

"Good day, Lady Margaret," Porter smiled, coming to his feet. "How nice it is to see you."

Maggie smiled brightly at the blond-haired gentleman.

"And how is Lady Marianne?" she asked.

"Very well, thank you," he answered.

Philip stood and crossed to her. "Porter has come to invite us to dine with them, love," he told her. "Two days hence. It promises to be most enjoyable."

Maggie's smile faltered, her mind working. Surely Lord Rawlings would be among those in attendance, she worried. How could she possibly avoid his company at an affair attended by such a small number of guests? She blinked her worries away, smiling once more.

"We would love to come to dinner, Lord Porter," she assured him. "Thank you for the invitation."

Porter bowed to her in answer. Philip took notice of the ink-stained paper in Maggie's hand then, nodding his approval of the fancy letters sprinkled among the ink splotches.

"The child improves, love," he said, taking her hand in his. "Although, I daresay your hands have nearly as much ink on them as the paper."

Maggie laughed lightly.

"You should have a look at Betsy's. The poor child had some of trouble with the ink well."

"A bit unsteady, was it?" Philip teased.

Maggie nodded vigorously, a cheeky grin on her face. Porter smiled at their easy exchange. He soon bade farewell to Maggie and Philip and took his leave. Maggie took Philip's hand and led him from the study, bound for the front sitting room and the little girl happily sitting within.

Chapter 23

Maggie prepared for bed that night, unease still nagging at her mind. The day had passed in pleasantness. Betsy's visit came to an end after luncheon, which the child was thrilled to share with Philip and Maggie. Philip's strange behavior of the morning was never far from Maggie's mind however, causing her to study him throughout the day for any signs of the distance she had sensed earlier.

As if this was not enough to trouble her, there was the matter of the dinner party at Lord Porter's and her certainty that Lord Rawlings would attend. Maggie sighed in irritation, roughly pulling her brush through her curls.

Philip entered the chamber then, stripped down to his breeches. His fair hair was damp from his bath and fell across his brow, shielding his eyes.

"Are you ready for bed, love?" he asked, settling his big frame onto the four-poster.

"In a moment," Maggie answered, setting her brush aside and arranging her curls to fall about her shoulders.

When she turned to face him, she saw a dark frown on his face once more.

"My God, husband," she said softly. "Whatever is troubling you?"

He turned his eyes to hers then, blinking. "What?"

"Is something wrong?" she asked, perching on the edge of the bed.

Philip brushed his hair back from his eyes and shook his head. "I have a bit of work on my mind," he said. "Estate business. Nothing serious, I assure you."

Maggie didn't believe his answer for one moment. She knew that, while he cared little for his business, he had proven to have a natural affinity for it. As a result, matters were quite steady in that regard. She feared his heart was causing such dark looks. She hadn't seen such in his eyes since they were at Bridgewater Park, before their reconciliation.

"Philip," she began, folding her hands in her lap. "You told me once that you felt you could speak freely to me."

Philip cleared his throat. "I...," he began haltingly. "I still feel that way."

"Pray, tell me what is wrong," she implored. "You look so troubled."

Philip pulled himself to a sitting position to better face her. "I assure you, darling," he said, covering her hands with his. "I'm not troubled. A bit preoccupied is all."

Maggie studied his face. Although he now wore a smile, his eyes still seemed haunted. Did he know of Rawlings's approach toward her at the Bulword's? Surely he didn't believe she welcomed the man's attention.

"Come to bed, Maggie," he said, pulling the covers aside for her.

"But, I wish to know."

"What is it you wish to know?" he asked, holding her gently in his arms.

Maggie rested her chin on his chest to better see his face.

"I wish to know what's in your heart," she said softly.

Philip couldn't bear the intensity of her gaze for but a moment, she saw with regret.

"The answer to your question is quite simple," he said, stroking her cheek with one finger. "You're in my heart."

Maggie set the matter aside, loath to spoil the evening with an argument. She turned her face and kissed his fingertip.

"I love you, Philip," she said simply. "You do know that? You do know that I'll always love you?"

He gazed at her for a long moment.

"Yes," he murmured, brushing her lips with his. "Always."

He unbuttoned her nightgown and stoked her breast. He brushed his hand over her nipple, causing it to harden to a point.

"And what of you?" she asked on a sigh.

"I love you, Maggie," he said, kissing her throat. "Always."

She surrendered to him, coming apart in his strong arms as he stroked her deeply, chanting her name.

***

Two days later, Maggie woke to find herself alone in their big bed. Still groggy from a fitful night's sleep, she sat up slowly. A wave of nausea gripped her, causing her to cling to the thick bedpost. Her heart pounded as a cold sweat broke out on her forehead. Almost as quickly as it assailed her, the ill feeling passed. She stood carefully and made her way to the washstand to splash her face with the cool water in the bowl atop.

Feeling more herself, she rang for Joan to assist her with her dressing. The lady's maid was alarmed by her mistress' paleness and wrung her hands worriedly.

"Are you quite all right, my lady?" she asked.

"I…" Maggie paused, taking a breath of air. "I felt a bit queasy upon waking, Joan. The feeling has passed."

"Perhaps it was something you ate last evening," Joan suggested, withdrawing a pretty day dress from the dressing room.

Maggie shrugged her shoulders, pulling on her petticoat and chemise.

"I do hope you won't be ill this evening," Joan added. "We've settled on a lovely dress for you to wear to Lord Porter's dinner party."

Maggie gasped as a realization settled on her. She'd slept little the previous night, the prospect of the coming evening's festivities weighing heavily on her. Her apprehensions caused her lightheadedness, she thought with certainty.

"I believe an upset in my mind is affecting my stomach," Maggie said with a small smile. "I'll set any dour thoughts aside, I promise."

Joan returned her smile as she ran the brush gently through her hair. Maggie smiled absently as the girl braided her hair and bade her good day. She went downstairs to search for her husband, disappointed when he was not within the breakfast room as expected. Wearing a small frown, she served herself from the sideboard and sat. She chewed mechanically, sorely wishing that she could remove the specter of Lord Rawlings from her mind.

***

Philip found her there, confident that she would at last have come downstairs. She looked lovely, if a bit strained. Her dress—ivory and dotted with red roses—complemented her fair coloring. Her hair, lustrous in the morning light flooding the sunny breakfast room, made him itch to tunnel his fingers through it, to rid it of its confinement in the braid. He noted her frown with displeasure, guilty as he guessed the cause of it.

She'd sensed his aloofness of the past few days, his dark mood worsening as she tried to ascertain its cause. How on earth could he tell her he felt certain that she would betray him? While she'd given him no cause for such vile thoughts, he was more than certain Rawlings was plotting a seduction. The man had been curiously absent from the bashes of late, making no calls on them or on their friends, as Philip was able to learn. What the devil was he about?

317

He forced a smile on his face as he strode into the room.

"Good morning, love," he said, brushing a kiss on her upturned cheek. "I trust you slept well?"

Maggie shook her head. "Not very well, I'm afraid," she answered, taking up her tea cup.

"Is everything all right?" he asked, sitting beside her. "You looked so tired this morning I couldn't bear to wake you when I arose."

Maggie grew thoughtful for a moment. Secretive, perhaps?

"Everything is fine," she said with a small smile. "I merely had troubling getting to sleep till very late last night."

Philip studied her for a long moment. He had once more kissed her questions away in their bed, choosing to overwhelm her senses as he sought to clear his own mind. After delaying his release for as long as possible, his climax had struck him full force. He'd fallen asleep almost immediately, smiling as he held her close. Apparently, his wife hadn't been as fortunate in her quest for slumber.

"Was I too rough with you last evening?" he asked softly.

Maggie's eyes widened. She smiled even as a blush covered her smooth cheeks.

"No, Philip," she said quickly. "You were ever so gentle."

Philip stole a piece of bacon from her plate and took a bite, chewing thoughtfully. "Perhaps I left you unsatisfied?" he asked, his eyes sparkling.

Maggie slanted him a look. "You loved me thoroughly, husband," she assured him. "I simply couldn't get to sleep afterwards."

He nodded, satisfied with her answer. He stood then, leaving her to finish her meal.

"I'm pleased we are going to Porter's this evening, love," he said, kissing her once more. "I believe it will be much more enjoyable than those tedious bashes with their music and dancing."

Maggie smiled at his jest, knowing he was aware of how much she enjoyed the crowded affairs.

"I suppose I'll persevere," she teased. "If you promise to keep me close to your side."

Darkness stole into his thoughts again. "Try to leave it," he said, smiling once more.

As it turned out, both husband and wife's apprehensions proved unfounded. When they arrived at Lord Porter's townhouse and were shown to the parlor, both quickly took note that Lord Rawlings was not in attendance. There were nine guests, counting Maggie and Philip, and they were the only married couple present.

The gathering was composed of free and unfettered gentlemen and young ladies of Marianne's acquaintance. Lady Sarah Addington wasn't there for, although she had once set her cap on Philip, she didn't travel within their circle of friends. The guests were as familiar to Maggie as to Philip, for she'd come to know them from their attendance at the parties and such. Relieved, Philip escorted Maggie further into the room, searching out their host and hostess.

Soon after, the guests were shown to the dining room. Dinner was marvelous, consisting of roast game hen and late-summer vegetables. Animated conversation and pleasant jests abounded at the table. Philip leaned toward her more than once, whispering comments and drawing her into the different discussions going on around the table.

After dinner, the ladies retired to the parlor and the gentleman to Porter's study. Philip brooded as the gentlemen around him discussed several topics: issues pending in

Parliament, the newest and fastest curricles, and the like. He folded his arms in front of him, leaning against the wall.

"Wilton, old man," one of Philip's friends said jovially. "How is married life treating you?"

Philip smiled crookedly at the man, a long-time acquaintance.

"Marriage is a most desirable state, I assure you," he grinned.

The man returned his grin with one of his own.

"Not bloody surprising given the wife with whom you have been blessed," the man intoned.

Another came to join in the conversation.

"My God, Wilton," the gentleman offered. "You surely have plucked an angel from Heaven."

"I agree," Philip said. "Although I'm quite certain that Maggie would disabuse you of such a notion, friend," he said. "She doesn't know her own worth."

"I fear I'll never find a woman of my own," the first man said.

"Your trouble," another laughed, "is in finding too many!"

More ribald comments soon filled their corner of the room as the gentlemen recounted several experiences they had at the pubs of late. Philip shook his head and crossed to where Porter stood, waiting patiently until his host finished his discussion with another man. With a nod to Philip, that man joined the spirited conversation on the other side of the room.

"I fully expected Rawlings's attendance, Porter," Philip said in a low voice.

He was shocked as a look of disgust crossed Porter's usually-pleasant countenance.

"That bloody fool," Porter grumbled. "He gave me his word he would be here."

"What on earth could be keeping him?" Philip asked, fearing the answer.

Porter opened his mouth to reply, quickly closing it with a snap.

"It's all right," Philip said with a frown. "I would wager that I know precisely what's keeping him from my company."

"Wilton," Porter began hesitantly, "I don't know to what you are referring."

"I know of the scoundrel's infatuation with my wife," Philip said in a low voice. "I fear it must be far more serious than I believed to cause him to stay away from as benign a function as this."

Porter shook his head. "I haven't seen him nor spoken to him since leaving his townhouse three days ago, Wilton," he said. "He wasn't at home when I called on him yesterday."

"What is that rogue about?" Philip asked. "If he so much as thinks to approach my wife again, I will—"

"Again?" Porter asked. "No."

Philip nodded. "If he comes near her again," he went on, "it will be his very last deed on this earth."

Porter nodded in return.

"What say we rejoin the ladies?" he suggested, loud enough for the others to hear.

In agreement, the gentlemen all filed out of the study to join the ladies in the parlor.

Chapter 24

One afternoon, two weeks after the party at Lord Porter's, Maggie stood in the front sitting room, perusing the leather-bound books on the shelves lining one wall. Having grown tired of the firescreen she'd been painting, she decided to indulge in some light reading to pass the afternoon. Philip was paying a call on Lord Bridgewater, as the two of them had need to discuss some of their mutual interests in Somersetshire, so Maggie was in search of something to occupy her mind instead of her fingers.

She chose a book of sonnets, much like the one she and Betsy had used for the child's fancy-writing lesson. She smiled at the memory as she took a seat in a plump chair beside the window. Her strange illness of the morning two weeks past had revisited her nearly each morning since. She was almost certain she was expecting, though she hadn't said anything of it to Philip. Perhaps Lady Bridgewater would be able to confirm her suspicions.

Lord Rawlings had not been to call. In fact, she hadn't seen him since the night of the Bulword bash. Therefore, she was more than confident that the man had set aside his strange affection for her. Tiring of the book of prose, she stood and crossed to the shelves once more, intent on making another selection. Her stomach rumbled, putting her in mind to have Grimes see to a bit of refreshment to sustain her until tea time. She heard the sound of footsteps near the doorway and turned, expecting the servant's arrival. She gaped in surprise as she saw Lord Rawlings walk into the room.

"Lord Rawlings!"

He smiled slyly and closed the door, causing her alarm to increase tenfold.

"Have you missed me these past weeks, my love?"

"What on earth are you doing here?"

"Ah, Maggie," he said, crossing to her. "I believe you know precisely why I'm here."

She held her hands in fists at her side, anger causing her cheeks to flame. "You gave me your word that you would cease this," she said. "You promised me that you wouldn't speak to me so again."

He shrugged his shoulders, his smile widening. "That was before," he said, running his eyes over her. "Before I knew the truth."

"What truth?" she asked, her eyes wide.

He stroked her cheek with one finger, causing her to recoil. He sighed and placed his hand on his chest.

"You've been like a fever in my blood, Maggie," he said. "I tried to forget you, but it proved impossible. I had to know all about you."

Maggie shook her head. "You had to know what?" she began. "I don't understand."

"I've been to Sussex, my love," he said. "Your steward had a few interesting facts to impart to me."

"Mr. Lavery?" She was appalled. "What on earth could that horrible man have to say to you?"

"He's a strange man," Rawlings said. "A bit crazed as well. But he's quite knowledgeable." He leaned closer to Maggie. "At least where your mother is concerned."

Maggie recalled all the horrid words the steward had said to her about her mother: some mysterious treasure, a fancy man's keeping her.

"My mother?" Maggie managed to ask. "But what could he have told you about my mother?"

"What do you know of your father, Maggie?" he asked.

"My father?" she stammered. "I didn't know my father. He died before I was born."

"A Baron Penworth, I believe?" Rawlings asked.

"Yes," she answered. "What could Mr. Lavery know of my father?"

Rawlings suddenly threw his head and laughed heartily. Maggie placed her hands on her hips, irritated with the viscount's strange behavior. He saw the motion and bit back his laughter.

"My dear Maggie," he said, smiling crookedly. "There was no Baron Penworth."

"No Baron Penworth?" Maggie asked softly. "What do you mean?"

"Your mother was never married to your father," he told her. "Never married to any man, for that matter."

Maggie's heart raced as her mind sought to make sense of Rawlings's words. No, her mind whispered. It could not be true.

"She was kept by a gentleman," he went on. "Lavery didn't know the man's identity, but he assured me that they never married."

She stared up at Rawlings, reading his thoughts clearly despite the horrific content.

"But that would mean I am a… a…," she began softly.

"A bastard?" he provided in answer. "Yes," he said, grasping her arms. "A bloody beautiful bastard."

She shook her head, numb to his caress as he brushed a loosened curl from her cheek.

"You're the most beautiful, most desirable woman I've ever encountered," he rasped, brushing his lips over her ear. "Legitimate or not, I still want you."

She heard his words as if from far away. Fat tears rolled down her cheeks as she realized what this revelation would mean to Philip. And what of Lord and Lady Bridgewater? Surely they wouldn't want Betsy to have contact with a… She couldn't bear to even think the word.

"What will Philip say?" she asked in a whisper.

Rawlings heard her nonetheless and shrugged.

"Wilton won't want you, Maggie," he said with certainty. "Oh, perhaps as a mistress, but never as a wife."

"No," she sobbed, shaking her head. "That's not true!"

"Wilton will be an earl one day," he went on, wrapping her in his arms. "Bridgewater's holdings are quite extensive. Wilton won't want heirs from a woman with such a murky history."

Maggie squeezed her eyes shut, thinking of the baby she might be carrying. Would Philip despise it as well as he would her? Her shoulders shook as her sobs increased.

"Ah, Maggie my love," he said, kissing her wet cheek. "Don't fret so. Give yourself to me. I'll have you any way you wish," he said, nearing her lips. "As mistress or wife, it doesn't matter."

He placed his lips on hers, bringing her rapidly to her senses. Her eyes snapped open, widening as she spotted Philip looming in the doorway.

"Take your hands from her, Rawlings!" Philip shouted.

Rawlings turned, unhanding Maggie but not leaving her side. He wore a smug smile on his face, seemingly undaunted by the rage on her husband's face that frightened her so.

"Wilton," Rawlings said with a nod. "You weren't expected back so soon."

Maggie barely heard the man's words. She could only stare at Philip, thinking in that moment of his casting her aside, of a life without him to hold her.

"Philip," she gasped, her tears increasing.

"Maggie," he ground out, his hands in fists. "Pray, what have I interrupted?

She shook her head, her lips moving silently. Philip cursed and turned to Rawlings, who had the audacity to place his hand on her arm in a show of possessiveness. Maggie couldn't muster the energy to pull away.

"Come, Maggie," Rawlings said, causing Maggie to shake her head once more.

Philip's anger flared to full force in an instant.

"Let go of her, you bastard!" he growled, punching Rawlings square in the jaw.

Maggie didn't see the man go down, the horrid word mouthed by Philip with such contempt echoing in her brain.

"No!" she suddenly screamed, clutching her belly.

Philip froze, his eyes flying to her stricken form.

"What the bloody hell is going on here?"

Maggie couldn't answer, couldn't tell him that she was illegitimate. That the terrible epithet belonged to her, not Lord Rawlings.

Rawlings stood, rubbing his jaw. He placed himself in front of Maggie.

"You won't speak to her in this manner," he said to Philip.

Philip grabbed the man by the throat. "And you won't tell me what I can and cannot do with my own wife," he ground out. "Leave my home, you scoundrel, or I'll throttle you here and now."

Rawlings shook free of Philip's hold and turned to Maggie.

"Remember all I have said, Maggie," he said.

Maggie stared past him, at the anger pouring out from Philip's eyes. Rawlings hastily took his leave, leaving the couple to sort through the mess left in his wake.

"Tell me what's going on here, wife," Philip said, grabbing her arm. "Tell me why that son-of-a-bitch was holding you?"

Maggie couldn't make sense of his words. She only knew that she was illegitimate, a fact she had only just begun to digest.

"What?" she asked, her eyes a bit unfocused. "What are you asking me?"

Philip flexed his fists. "Tell me why that bastard—"

Maggie burst into fresh tears at his use of the word.

"Damn it to hell, Maggie!" he spat. "What the devil is going on?"

"I can't say," she whispered hoarsely. "Please don't make me."

She watched as an ugly look twisted her husband's beloved face into a mask of disgust.

"What can't you tell me, dear wife?" he taunted. "Have you dallied with that rogue?"

"God, no," she whispered, shutting her eyes tightly. "How can you even think that?"

"Maggie," Philip said in a low voice. "You'll tell me now, or I'll believe you've cuckolded me in my own home."

Maggie opened her eyes, recoiling at the hatred on her husband's face.

"No," she whispered again. "No!" she cried, running from the room.

Maggie ran up the stairs and threw herself on the bed, sobs racking her. She was illegitimate! What would Philip do if he found out the truth? Would it be as Lord Rawlings said? And what of the baby growing within her?

"Oh, Philip," she sobbed. "What will you think of me?"

***

Philip watched her go, stunned. He placed his hands on the writing desk, his head hung low. He thought of what Rawlings had said, of Philip's not being expected back so soon. He recalled Maggie's appearance then. Her cheeks had been flushed, her hair in disarray. Had he interrupted an assignation? And when he had struck Rawlings… Philip felt a stab of pain settle in his heart at what he perceived as her defense of her lover.

She'd cried copious tears when he'd tried to extract an explanation from her. Was she truly upset? Or was she simply unwilling to admit her indiscretion? He suddenly swept the desk clean, spitting out a curse that shook the books on their very shelves.

He went into his study and poured himself a glass of brandy, muttering curses as he drained the glass and slammed it on the top of the desk. He reviewed the scene he had come upon in the sitting room, his stomach churning. It was as he had imagined these past few weeks. He poured another glass and settled into his chair. The bastard still wanted her, and had the audacity to accost her in Philip's own home! But was she a victim? Or a willing participant, welcoming the man's kisses and caresses?

"Ah, Maggie," he groaned, burying his face in his hands.

After a long while, a knock at the study door roused him.

"Yes?" he called, his voice hoarse from restrained tears.

Grimes entered the room, his eyes widening at his master's rumpled condition. He cleared his throat and held his arms stiffly at his side.

"Dinner is served in the dining room, my lord," he said.

Philip nodded and slowly rose to his feet. "Please tell Lady Wilton to join me there," he said.

"I'm sorry, my lord," Grimes said nervously. "Lady Wilton has requested her dinner be served abovestairs in your chamber."

Philip froze for a moment, finally nodding.

"Very well," he said wearily. "Please do as she asks."

Philip sorely missed his wife's presence at the table. He consumed his food but barely tasted it, his mind occupied fully with the events of the afternoon. Why couldn't she tell him what was going on?

Before this day she had told him all, even when the man had approached her in the past. Had matters changed? Did she now want, even seek, Rawlings's attentions?

Shoving his plate from him, he rose and returned to the study. He poured himself another brandy, loath to join his wife until he had a better grasp on matters.

Philip found Maggie on the bed in their chamber an hour later, clad in her chemise and petticoat. He saw the discarded dinner tray, still bearing most of its meal. He saw the crumpled dress tossed on the floor beside the bed. He crossed quietly to the bed, uncertainty flitting through him as he glimpsed her tear-streaked face. Tears clung to her thick lashes, sparkling like diamonds. Was he wrong about her and Rawlings? Could she be the innocent in all of this?

He shook his head and stepped into the dressing room to ready for bed. He emerged, naked save for his breeches, steeled for a confrontation. He would learn the truth this very night.

"Maggie, wake up," he said sharply.

Maggie whimpered in her sleep, burying her face in the coverlet. Philip grabbed her arm then, urging her to a sitting position.

"Wake up, wife," he ground out.

She opened her eyes then, pulling back from him in surprise.

"Philip?" she asked, her voice husky from sleep. "What is this about?"

"You'll tell me," he returned, releasing her arm. "I won't be denied, Maggie. You'll tell me the truth."

"No, Philip," she sobbed. "Don't make me say the words."

Her refusal cut him to the quick.

"It's true, then," he concluded aloud. "You've given yourself to Rawlings."

"No!" Maggie shouted, coming to her feet. "You couldn't be more wrong!"

"Tell me, then," he countered. "Tell me what that bastard was doing here."

Maggie held her hands in front of herself as if fending off an attack.

"He said that I…," she began. "No!" she shouted again. "I can't tell you!"

Philip felt his mind snap, his pulse pounding in his ears as he grabbed her once more.

"You will yield to me, wife!" he roared, pulling her hard against him. "You'll withhold nothing from me!"

"No, no!" she cried, writhing in his arms. "I won't!"

"You will," he vowed. "Here and now."

He grabbed the front of her chemise and ripped it from her, leaving her nearly naked. His eyes raked over her, his breath harsh in the silence of the room.

"You're mine, Maggie," he said. "Yield to me."

"No, Philip," she sobbed. "Not this way."

He dropped his hands from her, chastened. "As you wish."

"How can you think so ill of me?" she asked, tears spilling over her lashes. "I've never given you reason to doubt me."

"Tell me, then," he countered. "Tell me all that happened."

She jerked her arm free of his hold, holding the pieces of the torn garment together as she hurried into the dressing room. Philip raked his fingers through his hair in acute frustration, his eyes following her when she emerged wearing her nightgown and wrapper. To his amazement, she walked toward the door of the chamber.

"Where do you think you're going?" he asked.

Maggie flung her hair back from her face, striving to hold on to her composure. She lost the battle, breaking into fresh sobs.

"I won't stay one more moment with a man who would think the very worst of me," she said brokenly.

"Maggie," he growled, coming to his feet.

"Good night," she rushed out, bound for the guest room down the hall.

Philip cursed as he crossed to the door. He slammed it shut and sat down at the edge of the bed. How could he say such words to her? he thought with a cringe. Yet, why didn't she deny the affair?

Feeling like the lowest creature on God's earth, he closed his eyes and prayed for sleep to take him.

Chapter 25

Maggie sat alone in the breakfast room, but Philip soon joined her.

"Good morning," he said stiffly, crossing to the sideboard.

She nodded in response, picking at her eggs. Her stomach was still unsteady, having given her much discomfort upon waking. She'd barely made it to the chamber pot before bringing up the little she'd consumed last evening. Her sickness only served to confirm her suspicions of her condition, causing her to dread the inevitability of Philip's learning her secrets.

Should she tell him of the child? she worried, watching him as he sat down to face her. No, she decided in an instant. It wouldn't be right to cause him such distress, not when he would soon learn of her illegitimacy.

During the long sleepless night, she had come to the conclusion that Lord Rawlings was correct. Philip wouldn't want an heir from a woman with essentially no past, with absolutely no familial ties to the titled gentry. Her heart nearly broke at the thought of leaving him, despite his hurtful words last night. She thought to tell him that he was wrong in his assumptions, that she wasn't involved with Lord Rawlings in any way. But she would have to tell him all of it, she thought sadly. And that she couldn't do. As selfish as it might seem even to herself, she wouldn't give him up until absolutely necessary.

Perhaps when their child made its presence more obviously-known, she reasoned. Then she would have no choice but to give him the complete truth. Philip's voice reached her as if from far away.

"How are you this morning?"

She raised her head to stare at him. He must assume that she had been upset over their argument, she thought at the concern she glimpse on his face. How concerned would he be were he to learn of the true reason for her illness? Would he show the least concern for the child of a woman of presumably low birth? She wouldn't tell him of the child. Not when she was so certain that he wouldn't want any part of it.

"I'm all right," she said stiffly. "A bit tired, but all right."

He studied her for a long moment, finally turning his attention to the food on his plate. They ate in silence for a while, Maggie the first to push her plate aside. There was little missing from the plate.

"Is that all you're eating?" he asked, a brow raised.

She simply nodded and left the room.

Matters didn't improve over the next few days. Maggie continued to sleep in the guest room, loath to give Philip the opportunity to speak to her again in anger. And knowing herself as she did, she was aware that she would more than likely allow him to make love to her were he to bestow but one kiss on her. After repeatedly asking—begging, cajoling, commanding—her to tell him precisely what had occurred between herself and Lord Rawlings, Philip ceased trying to ascertain the truth.

He'd told her that if it was so important for her to keep her secret buried deep in her breast, then surely she was involved in an assignation. They both knew he had no evidence to prove his certainty, but that didn't stop her from erecting a wall around herself from both his interrogations and her own worries.

Lord and Lady Bridgewater called on them before returning to Somersetshire with Betsy, the two of them receiving them with reluctance. Maggie excused her strange mood by admitting only that she had been ill of late. Philip, however, had made no excuse for his stony silence, leaving the earl and his wife to guess at its cause.

Maggie sat in the parlor one afternoon a few days later, a piece of needlework in her lap. Her hands appeared nearly as pale as the muslin she held. Grimes approached her, a look of worry fixed on his face.

"My Lady," he said softly from the doorway.

"Yes, Grimes?" she returned, lifting her head.

"You have a caller, my lady," he said. "Lord Rawlings wishes to see you."

Maggie felt no apprehension over the butler's announcement, but the simple apathy that had invaded her heart and mind over the past week. She gave a slight shrug of her shoulders, setting her needlework aside.

"Send him in," she said tonelessly.

Lord Rawlings entered the room, a cocky grin on his face. He rapidly lost his smile, her condition causing him to frown.

"Maggie," he said, coming to sit beside her. "What's wrong? Are you ill?"

"Not precisely," she answered in a flat voice.

He studied her face. "What has Wilton done to you?"

Maggie smiled wanly as she shook her head. "Philip hasn't done anything to me, Lord Rawlings."

He shook his head as he took her hand in his. "My God. Your hand is as cold as ice."

She pulled out of his grasp with a gentle tug. He squared his shoulders, determination on his face.

"You'll come with me now," he said firmly.

"No," she said softly.

"But, you're miserable here. That's plain to see," he argued. "Does he know of your…?"

"I haven't told him of the accident of my birth," she said in that same flat tone. "He assumes that you and I are lovers, and I can't disabuse him of that notion."

He noted the paleness, the dark smudges under her beautiful eyes. "Has he hurt you?" he asked.

Maggie gave another shake of her head. "Only my heart."

"Come with me, Maggie," Rawlings beseeched. "You mustn't stay here. The man obviously cares little for you if he believes you're the kind of woman who would betray him."

Maggie managed the shadow of a smile at the irony of the man's statement, for he himself had wanted her when he thought her a trollop who would lay with any man.

"What Philip believes is of no consequence, Lord Rawlings," she said wearily. "I love him."

"I love you, Maggie," Rawlings said fervently, kissing her cheek. "So cold," he mused aloud, placing his cheek against hers. "Come with me. You'll learn to love me, I vow."

Maggie shook her head once more, a tear slowly coursing down her face. "I can never love another," she said. "Not ever."

"But, why?" he asked, his brow furrowed. "If Wilton doesn't want you, why must you stay?"

"There's a very good reason I must stay," she began in a voice so low it scratched her throat. "I'm carrying his child."

Rawlings's eyes widened as he sharply drew in a breath.

"No," he rasped. "What have I done?"

Rawlings kissed her cheek once more and left her. She picked up her needlework, oblivious to the tears soaking the satin roses she half-heartedly embroidered onto the muslin. A while later, she rose to dress for tea, doing so more out of habit than out of anticipation of another afternoon spent with her husband's anger and distrust.

***

Philip returned to the townhouse, calling out to Grimes as he strode into the foyer.

"Yes, my lord?" Grimes answered.

"Where is Lady Wilton?"

"She is abovestairs, my lord," the butler answered.

Philip thought for a moment. He would take it upon himself to put an end to this business once and for all, he vowed. He turned and began climbing the stairs.

"Were there any callers?" he asked over his shoulder.

"Yes," Grimes said with regret. "One."

Philip froze at the hesitancy in the man's voice. He faced the servant fully.

"Who?" he asked, certain that he already knew the answer.

"Lord Rawlings," came the butler's reply.

Philip cursed, bounding up the steps and tearing open the door to their chamber. Maggie looked up from where she sat at the vanity. She briefly met his gaze in the mirror, quickly lowering her head.

"Your lover's insolence astounds me," he said, slamming the door with a bang.

She shrugged her shoulders, apparently having neither the strength nor the desire to argue her innocence again. Philip felt his heart clench at her dismissal, in his mind a clear admission of her guilt.

"Will you go to him?" he asked, his voice betraying his pain.

"No," she whispered.

He reined in his emotions and crossed to face her in the mirror, placing his hands on her bare shoulders. The silky skin beneath his fingers tantalized him. And she had permitted Rawlings to touch her? Anger won the battle in his mind in that moment.

"Why not?" he growled. "Surely your lover hasn't grown tired of you so soon."

The shadow of a smile curved her lips as she shook her head.

"My lover no longer wants me," she said.

Philip snorted in disbelief. "I don't believe that," he said, gripping her shoulders tightly. He brought his lips to her ear. "I've tasted you, Maggie. A man can only want more after having you."

Maggie winced. He lifted her to her feet and spun her to face him, denying the emptiness in her amber eyes. He ran his own eyes hungrily over her scantily-clad form, lust and anger raging through his body in a rush of raw sensation. He saw the fear in her gaze then, and welcomed it when compared to that vast emptiness.

"I still want you, Maggie," he rasped, pulling her close. "I don't care if that man had you this very afternoon. I'll take you until you can think only of me. Until I tire of you myself."

"No," she whispered, stiffening in his arms. "You won't."

"Yes!" he said angrily, tossing her down on the bed. "You're still my wife," he said, tearing at his own clothes. "I'll take you whenever I choose."

He joined her on the bed, groaning as he fell upon her. Any guilt he might have felt he simply pushed to the back of his mind, thinking only of easing himself with her supple body.

Maggie squeezed her eyes shut as he stretched out on top of her, nearly crushing her with his weight. His brought his mouth to hers, pulling back as he felt the chill of her lips beneath his.

347

"Kiss me, damn you," he growled, taking her mouth once more.

Maggie went limp as he plundered her mouth, still as a stone as he ripped her chemise open to the waist. He ran his lips over her neck, her throat, trying in vain to force a response from her cold flesh.

"Maggie," he commanded, flicking his tongue over her breast. "Give yourself to me."

She was stone-cold and as still as a corpse. He spat out a curse, lifting his head to glare at her.

"Has your lover doused the passion in you?" he taunted. "You were always such an insatiable wench I hadn't believe such was possible."

She closed her eyes. "Leave me."

"Very well," he ground out, standing beside the bed to stare down at her. "I'll avail myself of another woman's flesh, as my wife no longer welcomes me."

When she shrugged again he roughly pulled on his clothes. He watched as she turned onto her side, ignoring the tears that coursed freely down her smooth, cold cheeks. He left the chamber then, his mind set on a trip to the pubs to find a willing woman to ease his lust and rage.

In the wee hours of the morning Philip staggered out of his carriage, besotted from the overconsumption of cheap ale. What the devil was wrong with him?

Maggie. He couldn't betray her despite his belief that she'd done so to him.

As he climbed the stairs to the bedchamber, he thought again of Maggie's cold response earlier. Was her mind so occupied with that bastard that any thought of pleasing her husband was abhorrent to her? Once more finding the big bed empty, he removed his jacket and walked into the guest chamber.

Maggie was curled up on the bed within, her pale face composed in the moonlight streaming through the lone window. She looked like a fragile flower to him: soft and delicate and lovely beyond anything he had ever encountered. He leaned over her. Was she even now dreaming of her lover? As if to put his mind at ease, she murmured her husband's name in her sleep, the sound as soft as a whisper.

Philip leaned closer, certain the ale addled his hearing.

"Philip," she sighed again, cuddling into the covers.

He drew back, stunned. He turned away. Stumbling into their chamber, he fell upon the bed as dreams of his wife flitting through his fevered mind.

***

Maggie found him sleeping in their chamber when she entered the next morning. She'd waited for what she was certain was sufficient time for him to have risen and readied for his day, chagrined to find him within. She now saw the effects of his ill-spent night clear on his face. His cheeks were ruddy, his hair and clothes rumpled. She leaned over him and brushed a thick lock of hair back from his forehead. The smell of ale assailed her, causing her stomach to churn in protest. She pulled her hand back from him as if the touch of his skin burned her. Had he taken another woman to bed? she worried, tears welling up in her eyes. Sniffling, she went into the dressing room and saw to her morning toilette.

When she emerged, Philip was sitting at the edge of the bed, his head held in his hands. She froze, thinking to withdraw into the dressing room once more. He heard her nonetheless, the soft swish of her skirts in the quiet chamber. He lifted his eyes to hers. She saw it then, the guilt in his emerald eyes. It was true, she thought with a heavy heart. He'd gone to another woman to assuage his lust. Suddenly she felt faint as the room appeared to spin. She closed her eyes and struggled to keep her composure, her hand pressed to her stomach.

"Maggie," he began, straightening.

She breathed in deeply, recovering herself. Before he could come to his feet, she ran from the room.

Later that day, Maggie found herself alone as was the norm in the afternoons. The day was quite temperate, so she decided to sit in the courtyard behind the townhouse. She found it a pleasant space, with lush, green ivy trailing over the stone walls that enclosed the small garden.

Maggie walked to one of the wrought-iron benches set about the garden and sat. She took comfort in the knowledge that she and Philip had spent little time in the courtyard together, for today she was able to sit there without a constant flow of memories to torment her. She allowed herself a few moments to think of the child growing within her: whether it would be a boy or a girl, whether it would have Philip's beautiful eyes and dazzling smile.

How soon before the babe made its presence known to one and all? With whom would she share this incredible new life? Joan would remain loyal to her. That was certain. But her connection to the Bridgewaters would cease once the truth of her birth became known. The only family she'd known since losing her beloved mother would no longer welcome her. An errant tear slipped from one eye, and she swiped at it with resolve.

Pushing any unpleasantness from her mind, she closed her eyes and tilted her face to the sun, willing the warmth to ease the chill in her heart as she stubbornly imagined Philip's warm welcome of their child.

"Ya' look fetchin' sittin' there, girl," a voice said, jarring her form her reverie.

The steward from Sussex, Mr. Lavery, stood in the courtyard, an ugly grin on his face. Maggie blinked rapidly, certain she was imagining the man there beside the carriage house at the back of the yard.

"Mr. Lavery?" she asked, confused. "What on earth are you doing here?"

Lavery didn't answer her question. He closed the back gate and strolled over to where she sat, gazing up at the townhouse.

"Ya' did well fer yerself, girl," he sneered. "Better than yer mother, I'd wager."

Maggie broke out of her befuddlement, her mind suddenly sharper than it had been in days. She stood to face him, her hands on her hips.

"Don't speak of my mother!"

Lavery laughed at her, an ugly grating sound.

"At least ya' got yer fancy man to marry ya'," he said. "But, what of the other?"

Maggie shook her head in confusion. "What are you saying?"

"The gentleman what came to Sussex," he shrugged in answer. "Seems he had to know everything about ya'."

Maggie's mind raced as she recalled Rawlings's revelation of the previous week. Had he informed the steward of her place of residence?

"Ya' must have more of yer mother in ya' than just her face," Lavery said, sliding his eyes over her form.

Ridding her mind of Lord Rawlings, Maggie faced the thin, unkempt man before her.

"Get out," she said in a low voice.

"No," he said, stepping closer. "Ya' must be as talented as yer mother to have two fine gentlemen panting after ya'."

"Stop it!" she cried, her hands pressed to her ears.

Lavery grabbed her then, placing his hand over her mouth.

"Look, missy," he hissed in her ear. "I tore that cottage apart and could find nothin' of that bitch's treasure. You'll come to Sussex with me."

"N-no," she mumbled against his hand.

"Yes," he said squeezing her hard around the waist. "And know this. If you can't find it for me, I'll enjoy taking my pleasure with ya' until such time as ya' grow tiresome."

Maggie's eyes watered as her fear increased. Shaking her head wildly, she fought him. Lavery proved stronger, dragging her out of the courtyard toward the alleyway behind the carriage house. He threw her roughly into a hired hack.

Her heart pounded when he instructed the driver to set out for Sussex.

Chapter 26

Philip saw to the execution of several tasks for Lord Bridgewater, happy to have business to occupy his mind. The hurt he'd glimpse on Maggie's face cut him to the quick. He returned to the townhouse by tea time and strode directly to the parlor. He would tell her he didn't dally with another. Whatever he thought of her behavior with Rawlings, he couldn't bear for her to go on believing he would betray her. He was surprised to find the room empty.

"Maggie?" he called, walking into the front sitting room. "Where the devil is she?" he murmured. "Grimes!" he called.

"Yes, my lord?" the servant answered, quickly coming to his master's aid.

"Where is Lady Wilton?"

The butler's brow knit. "Isn't she in the parlor, my lord?"

"No, she isn't," Philip returned sharply. He took a breath to cool his anger. "When did you last see her?"

"At luncheon, my lord," Grimes answered. "I assumed she was in the parlor."

"Were there any callers?" Philip cut in.

"No, my lord," Grimes rushed out, shaking his head. "None."

Philip dismissed the man and hurried up the stairs to their chamber. He found her missing from the room they'd shared just a few days ago, but that didn't come as a surprise to him. When he found the guest chamber empty, however, a sense of dread settled over him.

"She went to him," he muttered. "She went to Rawlings."

He rushed down the stairs, intent on going directly to Rawlings's townhouse and retrieving his wife. When he reached the front door, he suddenly came to a dead stop.

"No," he said to himself. "If she wishes to be with her lover, then so be it."

With a sick, dark ache in his belly, he went into his study and slammed the door.

***

Maggie stared out the small window of the hack as it wound through the streets of London on its way toward Sussex. She happened a glance at Mr. Lavery, noting with alarm the predatory glint in his dark eyes.

"You've grown quite comely, girl," he leered, his eyes on her bosom. "Very womanly, I daresay."

Maggie shrank back from his piercing gaze, trying in vain to hide herself in one dark corner of the carriage. Lavery leaned back, rubbing his hands together in anticipation of what Maggie could only imagine.

"I'd wager these gentlemen of yers have taught ya' a trick or two about pleasing a man," he said. "Perhaps even if you do find me your mother's treasure…"

He let his words hang in the air, leaving Maggie to contemplate his meaning. She did, closing her eyes as a shudder of revulsion crept through her. Lavery laughed deep in his throat.

He stopped the hack at a small inn just outside of Sussex for a quick meal, which Lavery procured and tossed to her. She couldn't eat much of the crusty bread or smelly cheese, and only prayed that the bit she consumed would stay within her for the baby's sake.

Maggie thought desperately of Philip, her throat burning with unshed tears. She prayed that he would find her, that he would put aside his anger and distrust and sense the great danger she was in. And the danger to the child, she mentally added, her hand covering her still-flat stomach. After casting a careful glance at Lavery—who seemed sated with his meal and the ale accompanying it—she turned her eyes out the window at the darkening sky.

***

Lord Porter called on Philip early that evening. Philip barely roused an acknowledgment of his friend. While he wasn't drunk, he was in so low a mood as to feel like he was in a stupor. His jacket was flung over the back of his chair, his cravat pulled loose over his rumpled shirt.

"Wilton," Porter said after Grimes had left them. "What the devil ails you?"

Philip ran his fingers through his hair and gazed up at his friend. "Hello, Porter," he said tonelessly.

"Are you ill?"

Philip's lips curled sardonically as he shook his head.

"She left me, Porter," he said, his voice low.

"No," Porter said. "It can't be so. I don't believe it."

"Believe it, friend," Philip said, coming to his feet. "She's with him even now."

"With whom?" Porter asked in befuddlement.

"Rawlings, the bastard," Philip sneered in answer. "He has won her to him. Even now he's holding her, kissing her." He couldn't finish, groaning as the image of Maggie and her lover seared his brain.

He turned his back to Porter and stared out the window, seeing neither the darkened street nor the haggard face staring back at him from the smooth glass pane. Porter's voice reached him as if from afar.

"She isn't with Rawlings, Wilton," he said.

"What?" Philip asked, spinning toward him. "What do you mean?"

"Your wife isn't with Rawlings," the man said firmly.

Philip felt a tiny spark of hope flare to life in his heart.

"How do you know this?" he asked Porter, his voice shaking.

"I've just come from his house," Porter said in explanation. "He's alone, Wilton. And nearly as miserable as yourself."

"Then, where the devil could she be?"

Porter shrugged. "I don't know," he said. "But perhaps Rawlings can help you."

Conviction filled Philip. "He'll tell me everything he knows," he said, straightening his shirt and shrugging into his jacket. "If I have to beat the truth out of him, he'll tell me everything."

Porter followed his friend out, bound for Rawlings's townhouse and the confrontation that had been a long time coming. Philip stormed into Rawlings's study, leaving Porter to follow in his wake. He braced his hands on Rawlings's desk.

"Tell me all you know," Philip said sharply.

The viscount looked up at Philip in surprise. "Wilton," he said, blinking. "What the devil are you doing here?"

Philip grabbed the man by his jacket and pulled him to his feet. "Where's my wife, you scoundrel?" he demanded to know, giving him a hard shake.

Porter grabbed hold of Philip's arm. "Easy, Wilton," he said. "Let the man breathe."

Reluctantly, Philip released his hold. Rawlings straightened his jacket, the look of confusion still stamped on his face.

"What is this?" he asked Porter. He looked back at Philip. "Is this about Maggie?"

"Don't say her name, you bastard!" Philip shouted, grabbing him once more.

"Wilton, please," Porter said, stepping between the gentlemen.

Philip took a deep breath to calm himself. His hands clenched, itching to squeeze the life out of his former friend.

"Maggie isn't at home, Rawlings," Philip said deliberately. "Tell me all you know of it."

Rawlings looked from him to Porter and back again. "I assure you, Wilton," he said, his hands held in front of him. "I don't know where your wife is."

Philip ran his eyes over the man. He read the sincerity in his demeanor and grudgingly believed his words. He sensed, however, that the man did indeed have something he was keeping secret. Rawlings fidgeted, his gaze flicking about the room. Philip narrowed his eyes at his former friend.

"What do you know of her?" he asked, bringing his face close to Rawlings's. "Tell me what happened between you and my wife."

A look of pain crossed Rawlings's face, confounding Philip. It took all of his patience to wait for him to collect his thoughts. After what felt like forever to Philip, Rawlings took a deep breath and began.

"I fell in love with her," he said.

Porter held tightly to Philip's arm, willing him to let the man tell his tale. Philip did not miss his friend's intent, reluctantly holding himself still.

"Go on," he ordered through clenched teeth.

"At first I was simply attracted to her," Rawlings said, sinking into his chair. "She's the most beautiful creature. But when I learned of her true nature, when she refused my advances time and again…," he trailed, shaking his head.

"She refused you?" Philip asked, desperate to believe him.

"Yes," Rawlings admitted. "Even yesterday, when she looked so utterly miserable, I couldn't persuade her to leave you."

Philip sat down in a chair facing the desk, his head in his hands. His mind raced with the events of the previous day: his hideous treatment of Maggie and his repeated accusations of her infidelity. He saw now the pain that had been so clear in her amber eyes.

He swore softly. "I'm a bloody fool."

"She's ever-faithful to you, Wilton," Rawlings stated.

Philip lifted his head to face the man. "What happened between the two of you last week?" he still needed to know. "When I found you together in my home?"

Rawlings shook his head, shame clear on his face. "I told her something that upset her," he said in a low voice. "Something that I thought would turn her away from you and toward myself."

Philip's heart pounded as he came to his feet. Had the man finally learned of Maggie's illegitimacy?

"What did you say to her?" he asked.

Rawlings's eyes flitted quickly to Porter, settling once more on Philip. Knowing that Porter could be trusted implicitly, Philip nodded his encouragement. At that, Rawlings continued.

"I know her secret," he said as before.

Philip knew in an instant that he did indeed speak of Maggie's illegitimacy and not of his past misconception of her character. Philip could well imagine Maggie's response to such a disclosure, her hurt and anguish to learn of her cloudy past.

"Ah, God," he groaned, raking his fingers through his hair. "What must she be thinking?"

Rawlings looked at him, his mouth agape. "You've known all this time?"

"Yes," he said wearily. "I wonder how the devil you learned of it," he added.

"Learned of what?" Porter cut in, wildly curious.

Philip looked at his friend.

"Maggie's mother was never married to her father," he explained quickly.

Porter let out a low whistle at that disclosure.

"Tell me, Rawlings," Philip urged again.

Rawlings reddened as he began to recount his story.

"I'm ashamed of myself, Wilton," he said. "I admit now that I became obsessed with your wife. I had to learn all about her, you see, so I traveled into Sussex."

"Sussex?" Philip asked. "What on earth could you have learned there?"

"The steward told me of it," Rawlings said in answer. "He didn't know the identity of Maggie's father, but he did assure me that they were never married."

Philip allowed himself to feel a bit of relief at the knowledge that Lord Bridgewater was not known to the steward.

It did little to ease his conscience regarding Maggie's certain distress, however. But as much of her anguish he owed to his own actions, he couldn't dismiss Rawlings's role in his telling her what must have shaken her.

He looked Rawlings directly in the eye. "You told Maggie what you learned?" he asked Rawlings, astounded. "Didn't you know what it would do to her?"

"I know now," Rawlings answered, his voice heavy with guilt. "She was devastated."

Philip's mind worked, reviewing every hateful deed he had done, every horrid word he had said to Maggie over the last week. He thought of last night, when he learned that Rawlings had once more called on her. She had been like a woman half alive, so cold that he could hardly bear to touch her. What had happened? He had to know all of it.

"What of yesterday, Rawlings?" he asked.

Rawlings's dark brows shot up in surprise. "You know of my visit?" he asked. At Philip's curt nod, he went on. "She looked so bloody miserable, Wilton. I begged her to come with me, but she refused."

"Why?" Philip asked, amazed that his wife would remain so steady in the face of his abuse.

"She loves you still," Rawlings answered. "And I couldn't force her to leave you, knowing that she carries your child."

Philip was shocked to the core.

"She carries my child?" he rasped, his heart pounding. "Are you certain?"

Rawlings gave a quick nod. "Forgive me, Wilton," he rushed out. "I thought you knew."

Philip allowed a smile to curve his lips as he thought of the growing child. His child, his mind happily amended. A son or daughter to raise with the woman he loved by his side. The reality of Maggie's situation soon broke into his thoughts.

"But if Maggie isn't here, where the devil is she?"

"Could she be with Bridgewater?" Porter offered.

Philip shook his head. "No," he said. "They returned to Somersetshire a few days ago."

The three gentlemen were quiet, thoughtful.

"Wilton," Rawlings said at last. "What do you know of the steward?"

"Nothing, I'm afraid," Philip answered. "Why do you ask?"

"I may have inadvertently informed the man of Maggie's location."

Philip immediately recalled Maggie's disturbing account of Lavery's words to her about her mother. He couldn't remember all of what she said to him and cursed himself for not trying to learn more at the time.

"Do you believe the man capable of such a foul deed?" he asked Rawlings.

Rawlings shrugged. "He was strange," he allowed. "Almost crazed. He spoke of a treasure, but I didn't know what he was talking about."

"That's it!" Philip exclaimed. "Maggie said the man was after her mother's treasure, whatever that may mean. He took her."

"Are you certain?" Porter asked the two of them.

"She isn't at Wilton's," Rawlings said.

Philip shot him a dark look. "She isn't here, either," he added with force. "Take us there, Rawlings. He must have taken her to Sussex."

Rawlings nodded vigorously as the three gentlemen rushed out, bound for the cottage of Maggie's childhood.

Chapter 27

Maggie knelt on the floor of the small parlor, a book held in her lap. The day having given over to night, a branch of candles lit the space, doing little to dispel the gloom. She brushed her tangled hair back from her face and stroked her hand lovingly over the leather-bound volume. It was a book of children's verses, one from which her mother had read often to her when she was growing up.

Maggie had come across the book during her long and as-yet-fruitless search for jewels or coins. Tears welled in her eyes as she imagined she could hear her mother's lilting voice washing over her.

When Lavery had brought her to the cottage what had to be three hours earlier, it had been painfully obvious to Maggie that he had been conducting his own faltering search since her departure many months ago. The furniture had been toppled, contents of drawers strewn about the rooms. Her mother's chamber was in remarkable disarray, as was Maggie's own small bedroom. Their clothes were ripped as well, due to Lavery's growing frustration. She sighed and hugged the book to her breast, one tear spilling over her lashes.

"Quit yer daydreaming, girl," Lavery growled from the doorway. "There's a treasure to be found, and you're going to find it for me."

Maggie wiped the tear from her cheek and set the book aside, turning her attention to the others set in piles around her.

"No," Lavery said, stepping further into the room. "There won't be any jewels in those books, I'd wager. Set those aside and come help me in the kitchen."

"The kitchen?" Maggie mused aloud. "Why on earth would anyone hide anything of value in the kitchen?"

"Exactly my thinking, girl," he said with a sly wink. "Yer mother was so good at hiding that man of hers—except from me, of course—I'm certain she'd be quite cunnin' regardin' her treasure."

"Oh, Mr. Lavery," Maggie sighed tiredly. "I tell you my mother had no treasure. Or a fancy man, for that matter."

He spat out a harsh laugh. "Think what ya' wish, girl," he sneered. "Now, get in here and help me search those cupboards."

With that, he turned and stalked out of the room. Maggie picked up a few of the books and stood, crossing to the shelves that lined one wall of the parlor. She slid them back into place, thumping them lightly against the paneled back of the shelves. She heard a hollow knock as one book hit against the back. Cocking her head to the side, she withdrew the book and again slid it forward, hearing the odd knock once more. Casting a quick glance toward the doorway, she shoved the books out of the way and rapped lightly on the panel with her knuckles.

Her eyes widened as she heard a different resonance over one particular section. Although the panel appeared flush with the others to her eyes, she could feel a slight indentation when she ran her fingers lightly over the wood. It was an area of nearly one foot square, and recessed ever so slightly into the surrounding wood. Could this be a secret compartment?

She pushed at one corner of the indentation, stunned as it gave a bit under her hand. It appeared to be hinged in the center, as the opposite side slid forward in reaction. Lavery yelled to her from the kitchen then, causing her to start. No, she thought with determination.

She wouldn't tell him of her discovery. If this compartment did indeed hold her mother's treasure, he wouldn't know of it. She refused to ponder what her discovery could truly mean: her mother had been kept by a wealthy man for his pleasure, a man who paid her for her services with jewels and coins. With a firm shake of her head, Maggie quickly placed more books over the section of paneling, effectively hiding it from the steward's eyes. Nervously brushing the dust from her skirts, she hurried to the kitchen at the back of the house.

After searching the large pantry and the many dark corners within, Maggie stood and stretched, her hands on the small of her back. Lavery took the opportunity to run his eyes hungrily over her figure, smiling slyly. She caught his gaze and straightened, shocked at the familiar way in which the man was staring at her.

"You've surely grown into a comely lass," he said, his eyes dark.

Maggie's eyes widened, quickly interpreting the lust in his gaze. "Don't look at me in that manner, Mr. Lavery," she said, her brow furrowed. "I'm a married woman."

Lavery curled his lip. "Aren't you the fancy one?" he jeered. "I know all about the other gentleman you've been bestowin' yer charms on."

Maggie brushed her hair from her eyes and glared at him.

"You know nothing," she said. "I have remained faithful to my husband. I love him."

Lavery laughed again. "No woman can remain faithful to any man," he stated, leering at her. "Not a woman what looks like you."

He suddenly lunged for her, grabbing her to him. She cried out in surprise.

"Unhand me!" she ordered, valiantly trying to dispel the fear that coiled in her belly.

"I aim to sample yer charms, missy," he said, grabbing her about her waist. "Yer mother was too good for me, with her fine gentleman to keep her in coins. But, you," he said, burying his face in her hair. "You're a bastard. I can do with ya' what I wish, and no one will speak of it."

"No!" Maggie cried, twisting away from him. "Leave me alone!"

She managed to free herself and turned to run from the room, tripping on an overturned chair. Lavery caught her easily and pulled her roughly against him.

"The search can wait," he rasped, squeezing her breast. "I believe I have a treasure right here."

"Let me go," she sobbed. "I can't bear for you to touch me."

"That's a shame, missy," he said, his breathing harsh in her ear. "I aim to touch ya'. All of ya'."

A loud crash was heard from the front of the house. Maggie and Lavery froze, their faces turned toward the doorway.

"What the devil…?" Lavery muttered.

"Maggie?" they heard Philip call. "Are you here?"

Maggie's heart soared with happiness. Philip had come for her! When she opened her mouth to respond to her husband's call, Lavery tightened his hold on her. Maggie's breath left her in a rush.

"Keep quiet," the steward hissed in her ear. "If he learns you're here, it won't go well fer ya'." He withdrew a wickedly sharp knife from his pocket. "Or fer him."

Maggie nodded quickly, praying that Philip wouldn't think to search the kitchen for her. Lavery backed into the darkness of the pantry, dragging Maggie with him. She happened a glance at the man's face, regretting her actions in an instant. His eyes were wild, his face contorted. She placed her hand protectively over her stomach, squeezing her eyes shut.

"Oh, Philip," she whispered in despair.

"I said to keep quiet, ya' trollop!" Lavery hissed, slapping her soundly.

She cried out, crumpling to the floor. She struggled to a sitting position, rubbing her cheek to rid it of the sting from his blow. Terrified, she watched as he advanced on her.

***

Philip and his friends quickly searched the poorly-lit front parlor with growing apprehension. They'd ridden from London at breakneck speed, with Rawlings leading them directly to the cottage. The place had a dark, deserted look about it, but Philip had known in his heart that Maggie was within. His confusion mingled with fear as he took in the disarray in the parlor.

"Where the devil is she?" he asked his friends.

Porter and Rawlings each shrugged their shoulders in answer.

"I'll check upstairs," Porter offered, turning to ascend the narrow staircase. "Perhaps she—"

A faint rustling noise drew the gentlemen's attentions to the back of the cottage. Philip urged his friends to keep silent as the three of them moved with caution toward the origin of the

375

sound. He'd known Maggie was in the cottage, and he now knew without question that she was at back of the house. As if to confirm his suspicions, he heard her cry out. Alarm beating in his breast, Philip stormed into the kitchen, the others following. They froze at the sight before them.

Lavery had Maggie by her arms, shaking her as she fought him. Her dress was dirty and torn, her hair a tangled mass as she shook her head in violent refusal.

"You won't hurt Philip!" she cried. "You won't!"

"Be quiet, girl!" Lavery ordered, raising his fist to deliver another blow. "Be quiet, or I'll—"

"Or you'll what, you miserable bastard?" Philip asked, a chill in his voice.

Maggie's amber eyes widened.

"Philip," she breathed.

Lavery looked over his shoulder at the three gentlemen, an ugly smile curving his thin lips.

"Well, well," he said, turning to face the men. "I recognize one of ya' fine gentlemen as Maggie's lover. Don't tell me the little missy gave herself to ya' others as well."

"Let my wife go, you scoundrel," Philip ground out, stepping toward them.

Lavery's smile widened. "Yer wife?" he goaded. "You're the cuckold?"

"Take your hands from her," Philip returned, reaching for her.

The steward lost his grin, his eyes glowing with madness.

"Don't come any closer!" Lavery ordered, brandishing his knife for all to see. He held Maggie in front of him like a shield "I won't hesitate to cut her."

Philip's gaze flew to Maggie's. He read her fear clearly in her eyes and felt his rage mix with worry. His eyes fell to the knife in Lavery's hand. It was pressed to her belly, bringing the growing child immediately to Philip's mind. He sought to maintain an air of calm, for he knew that one could never be certain of what a man as crazed as Lavery would do next.

"What is it you want?" Philip asked deliberately, his hands clenched in fists at his side.

Lavery's eyes shone as his mind worked.

"I want her mother's treasure," he said, his chin held high. "I want all of it."

Philip looked at Maggie in confusion. She gave an almost imperceptible shrug of her shoulders. He stared at Lavery, seeing the greed clear in the man's dark eyes. He held his hands in front of himself in a placating gesture.

"I know nothing of a treasure," Philip said cunningly. "Let her go. I'm quite wealthy. Surely I can offer you something for your trouble?"

Lavery contemplated Philip's tempting words, lifting one hand to scratch his chin. Maggie saw this as the opportunity to escape and pulled away from him. Lavery turned in reflex, his knife sinking into her thigh as she cried out. Her leg gave out beneath her and she fell to the floor.

"Maggie!" Philip cried.

He lunged at Lavery as the man turned from Maggie's crumpled form. Grabbing him around the throat, Philip brought him against the stone wall of the hearth again and again as he cursed his soul to Hell. Lavery struggled, his hands wrapped around Philip's wrists in a weak attempt to free himself.

"Wilton!" Rawlings shouted, attempting to pull Philip from the man. "Let go of him!"

Philip looked at Rawlings, barely seeing through his haze of rage. Porter pushed him roughly from the steward.

"Wilton!" Porter said, holding him back.

"I'll kill the bastard!" Philip growled, attempting to push Porter aside.

Porter held him off, pushing back hard. "See to your wife!"

Philip's eyes widened as Porter's words had their desired effect. He turned to gaze at Maggie's form, lying still on the floor. He could see the blood darkening her skirt as it seeped from her wound. Leaving the steward to his friends' capable hands, Philip rushed to her side.

"Maggie," he whispered. "My Maggie."

He cradled her in his arms as her eyes lifted to his. She gave him a weak smile.

"Philip," she breathed. "You came for me."

The astonishment in her voice pierced him to his soul. How cruel he had been to her to make her doubt him.

"Of course I came for you, love," he said, his voice hoarse. "You're my wife."

"But, I thought...," she began, tears in her eyes.

"Shh," he soothed. "Everything will be fine now. You'll see."

Rawlings turned his attention to the prone body of the steward. "He still lives." Porter patted Rawlings's shoulder and walked over to the couple, a smile on his face for Maggie.

"Hello, Lady Margaret," he intoned, bowing jauntily.

Maggie smiled up at the gentleman.

"Hello, Lord Porter."

"Are you hurt very badly?" he asked, looking pointedly at Philip.

Philip scowled at him and told him to turn away as he lifted Maggie's skirt, revealing her thigh. The gash was not a large one, and the bleeding had slowed to a trickle. Tearing a piece of her petticoat free, he attempted to fashion a bandage. His hands were shaking with such profound relief he could scarcely manage the task.

"Allow me?" Porter offered, kneeling beside them.

Philip cradled Maggie in both arms while Porter tied the soft fabric to her leg. Maggie thanked him and settled against Philip's chest with a sigh.

"There's so much I have to tell you, Philip," she said when Porter had rejoined Rawlings.

"And I you, darling," he returned. "I've been a bloody fool, Maggie. I never should have doubted you."

Her eyes widened in surprise. "You believe that I haven't betrayed you?" she asked, incredulous.

"You love me, Maggie," he said. "You will love me forever."

She smiled her agreement. Her brow suddenly furrowed. Philip puzzled over her change in demeanor.

"What is it?" he asked worriedly. "Is your leg paining you?"

She shook her head, tears coming to her eyes. "Last night, Philip," she said softly. "You left me and, and…"

He knew she spoke of her assumption that he'd taken another woman. He smiled softly.

"I didn't go to another woman, Maggie," he assured her.

"Truly?" she asked.

His smile widened as he recalled their long-ago discussion in the garden at Bridgewater Park. He brushed her hair from her face and cupped her cheek with his hand.

"How can I be tempted by another woman," he said, "when I have such perfection before me?"

He saw that she, too, remembered that long-ago afternoon. His words held such meaning for the two of them, and he saw that her eyes were soon filling with tears again.

"Oh, Philip," she sighed, hugging him tightly.

Philip closed his own eyes for a moment, savoring the incredible solace of holding her in his arms.

Porter returned to them a short while later.

"What do you want us to do with this reprobate?" he asked Philip.

"I'd like nothing better than to send his black soul to Hell," Philip answered. "Take him to the main house. They deserve to know what kind of man is running the estate."

Porter nodded as Rawlings pulled Lavery to his feet. The steward let out a groan of pain as Rawlings pulled his arms behind him.

"I'll see that the constable is sent for," he informed Philip.

Maggie took notice of Rawlings for the first time. She looked up at the viscount in obvious confusion, which Philip sought to dispel immediately.

"Rawlings led me to you, love."

Maggie nodded, giving Rawlings a look of profound relief and gratitude. He bowed stiffly to her, quickly turning his attention back to the villain in his charge. As he dragged Lavery from the room, the man began to shout.

"The treasure!" he cried. "Where's the treasure?"

Rawlings and Porter looked at Maggie, who simply shook her head. Philip saw something in her demeanor, something that indicated that she knew much more than she was telling. Her eyes stared into his, willing him to keep silent.

"Don't listen to that scoundrel's rantings, gentlemen," he said to put Maggie's mind at ease. "Please instruct the others to do likewise."

The two gentlemen nodded, bowing to both Philip's and Maggie's wishes.

Chapter 28

When Lords Rawlings and Porter had left—dragging the injured and subdued Lavery with them—Philip faced Maggie again.

"Maggie," he began, "I believe you know more of this treasure than you are saying."

"I simply discovered something of interest, Philip," she said. "I'm in no way certain that it's connected to the treasure."

He nodded, his curiosity piqued.

"Can you walk, love?" he asked, helping her to her feet.

Maggie nodded, leaning against him for support.

"It's in the front parlor, Philip," she said, excitement in her voice. "At the bookshelves."

The went into the parlor, Maggie walking gingerly on her injured leg. Philip kept his arm firmly around her shoulders.

"What have you found?" he wondered aloud.

She smiled as she pushed the books to the side, revealing her discovery to him. She ran her fingers over the recessed panel as he looked on in confusion. She pushed against the panel, causing it to depress again. Philip breathed in sharply.

"I can't open it any further, Philip," she said. "Perhaps you can."

He pushed against the panel, giving it a hard shove. The panel rotated open with a squeal. Philip's eyes widened in amazement.

"It's a hidden compartment of some sort," he marveled, peering into the inky blackness.

He reached in carefully, his fingers trailing over some very odd and some not-so-odd objects. He grabbed up the branch of candles from the floor and brought them to the bookshelf. Maggie took it from him, holding it close to the opening as he looked inside once more.

"My God," he said softly. "I can't believe it."

"What is it?" Maggie asked. "What did you find?"

Grinning broadly, he withdrew several large jeweler's boxes, along with a few leather pouches which he knew by their heft to contain coins. He opened one of the largest of the jeweler's boxes, astounded at the array of necklaces and rings and the like resting within.

"This is incredible," he said, quickly assessing the high quality of the pieces.

He picked up one of the leather pouches and opened it, amazed as gold sovereigns and silver crowns spilled into his hand. He turned to Maggie, losing his smile as he took in her demeanor. She'd lost all color, her eyes holding a sadness he'd rarely glimpse before. Slumped against the bookshelves, she appeared as limp as a rag doll.

"What is it, love?" he asked, alarmed.

Maggie shook her head as fat tears rolled down her cheeks.

"It's true," she said softly. "My mother was kept by a man, a man who paid for her favors with jewels and coins."

"No, Maggie," Philip said firmly. "Your father loved your mother. I'm sure of it."

Maggie shook her head again. "I'm a bastard, Philip," she said in despair. "My father paid for my mother's favors, not caring enough to marry her."

"Your father loved your mother," he stated again. "As he loves you."

His words affected her, causing her to straighten. She brushed her hands over her cheeks.

"How can you say such words?" she asked. "You don't know anything about this."

Philip returned his attention to the jeweler's box, searching for a particular item that had caught his eye upon first perusal. He plucked it from the box with a triumphant whoop, holding it out for Maggie to see. It was a gold signet ring, engraved with the Bridgewater crest. Maggie looked at the ring in disbelief, her eyes flying to Philip's as she sought to make some sense of it all. He laughed heartily, hugging her to him.

"The earl is your father, Maggie."

Maggie took the ring from his fingers, studying it in the candlelight.

"The Earl of Bridgewater," she murmured. "My uncle is my father?"

Philip nodded, smiling. She lifted round eyes to his.

"You knew of this?" she asked him.

"I've known for the longest time, sweetheart."

He took the candles from her and set them on the floor.

"How?" she asked. "When did you learn of it?"

"Before the country dance in Bridgewater."

Maggie blinked rapidly. "And you still wanted me?"

He enfolded her in his arms. "I'll always want you, Maggie," he assured her. "I'll always love you. You have my heart."

She smiled cheekily. "And the rest of you?"

Philip breathed in sharply as desire flared through him. He tamped it down, growling playfully at her.

"Minx," he gently admonished, hugging her tightly.

Maggie closed her eyes, rubbing her cheek against his chest as a beautiful smile curved her lips. Porter and Rawlings returned from the main house, coming to an abrupt halt at the sight of the jewels and coins spread out on the shelf.

"Good God," Rawlings said. "What is this?"

Philip turned to face them.

"It appears that my wife is an heiress," he said, draping his arm over Maggie's shoulders.

"Indeed," Porter said, gazing at the bounty.

"We must find something in which to carry this," Philip said, turning to Maggie. "Is there anything here at the cottage?"

Maggie told him of several hatboxes that remained in the chambers abovestairs. Porter offered to retrieve them, dragging Rawlings along with him. Philip took the signet ring from her hand and slipped it into his pocket. She gazed once more at the beautiful jewels.

"This is all so strange, Philip," she said, lightly fingering a particularly exquisite necklace. "Does my aunt know?"

"Yes," he said. "It doesn't matter, love. We've spoken of it."

"How did the earl become involved with my mother? Why did he stop calling on us at the cottage?" She lifted her chin in determination. "I must know all of it, Philip," she said firmly.

He agreed wholeheartedly, and told her so.

"We'll go to the earl directly upon our return to Bridgewater Park."

She nodded. Philip withdrew the necklace she had been admiring, holding it up to the light. It was delicately wrought, the lacy gold holding stones of topaz. The rich amber stones sparkled in the glow of the candles.

"These stones are nearly the color of your beautiful eyes, love," he marveled. "I believe I wish to see you in this," he added, a twinkle in his eye.

Maggie caught his meaning, blushing lightly.

"As with the pearls?" she asked, lowering her lashes.

He nodded slowly, bringing his mouth to hers to drop a lingering kiss there. Her hand flew to her belly.

"Philip," she began, "there's more I need to tell you."

Lords Porter and Rawlings rejoined them. They placed the treasure in the large box that the gentlemen had brought down to the parlor and climbed into the carriage. Philip and Maggie sat on the cushioned seat, Porter and Rawlings facing them on the seat opposite.

The carriage rolled over the country roads toward London. Jarred by the bumpy ride, Maggie winced and grabbed her leg. Philip saw her distress immediately, lifting her easily onto his lap and cradling her there. She shot a look of surprise at the two gentlemen sharing the carriage, quickly lowering her lashes.

"Philip," she whispered, embarrassed.

"Hush," he gently ordered, placing her head against his chest. "Do try and rest, Maggie. The trip is not overlong, but I believe you'll benefit from a bit of rest."

Maggie nodded, soothed as his hand gently stroked her injury. She closed her eyes and cuddled against him.

Philip dropped a kiss on her brow as she slipped rapidly toward sleep.

"I didn't know," Rawlings said softly. "I didn't realize how much you and she were to each other. Forgive me, Wilton."

"It's all right, Rawlings," Philip returned. "After all, you brought me to her."

Maggie sighed and let sleep claim her.

***

Philip gently shook Maggie awake some time later. She yawned and stretched languorously, a sleepy smile on her lips. Her eyes suddenly flew open in alarm, relief flooding through her when she realized that they were in front of their home and not still at the cottage. She saw that Lords Porter and Rawlings had taken their leave, furthering her ease. She turned to find Philip smiling down at her.

"Did you have a pleasant rest, love?"

"Yes," she answered. "I feel quite refreshed."

He assisted her from the carriage and carried her up the stairs to their chamber where he placed her gingerly on her feet.

"How's your leg?"

"It still pains me a bit, Philip."

He studied her, his brow furrowed.

"I'll send for the physician at once."

"Oh no, Philip," Maggie said. "It's nearly midnight. We shouldn't bother the man at this hour."

He dismissed her argument with a wave of his hand, striding toward the door.

"I'm sending for him," he stated. "That's the final word on the subject."

She placed her hands on her hips, her head cocked to the side.

"I suppose that you expect me to bend to your wishes, husband?" she teased.

He grinned, turning back to sweep her into his arms.

"You'll bend to my wishes in all matters, wife," he said, kissing her thoroughly.

He lifted his head and stared at her lips for a long moment. She gazed up at him, bemused.

"The physician," he said in answer to her unasked question. "I'll send Joan to you if you wish."

Maggie nodded as he left, her heart still racing from his kiss and the heat in his gaze following it. Joan assisted her mistress in readying for the physician's visit, bringing hot water with which she could wash. Maggie removed the makeshift bandage covering her thigh, wincing as the cloth pulled at her injury. It stung as she gently washed the dried blood away. She was relieved, however, to see that the gash was not as large as she had imagined. She donned her nightgown, covering it with the thickest wrapper she possessed. Joan brushed Maggie's hair and helped her climb into the big bed, fluffing the pillows behind her. Maggie thanked the maid and bade her good night.

A rapping soon came at the door.

"Maggie?" Philip called. "May we come in?"

"Yes," she answered, brushing her hands over the coverlet in mild nervousness.

Philip opened the door and entered, his worried frown making its reappearance. The doctor trailed in his wake, rubbing his eyes as if to rid them of sleep. The medical man stopped beside the bed and smiled at Maggie. She couldn't help but return the gesture, finding the man's appearance almost comical. He was an older man, and much shorter than Philip. The wispy white hairs on his head stood on end and his cravat was tied crookedly. Any remaining nervousness fled as she glimpse the kindness in his brown eyes.

"How are you feeling, Lady Wilton?" he asked, taking her hand.

"Very well," Maggie answered. "Although my leg is hurt."

"Her leg was cut with a sharp knife," Philip said. "It requires your attention, I'm certain."

The doctor nodded and averted his eyes as Maggie shifted the covers, exposing her thigh to his gentle ministrations. He carefully examined her, palpitating the skin around the injury. At Philip's insistence, he gave the rest of her a rudimentary examination as well, his hands gently prodding her limbs, her head, her stomach.

"The wound should heal quite nicely, I'd wager," the doctor said, straightening. "I won't need to sew you, if that was a worry."

"Thank goodness," Maggie breathed.

Philip echoed the sentiment, loudly expelling a breath.

"You're a lucky woman, Lady Wilton," the doctor continued. "The injury is minor and should have no impact on your condition whatsoever."

Maggie's eyes widened in shock. She looked quickly at Philip to gauge his reaction to the doctor's words. A smile teased the corner of his mouth, befuddling her. The smile quickly disappeared. The doctor bandaged her wound, leaving a salve for her to apply for the next few days. Maggie nodded absently, puzzling over the very odd expression she had glimpsed on Philip's face.

Philip thanked the man and led him from the chamber. He closed the door and crossed to the bed, now unable to keep the grin from his face. Maggie brushed her hair back from her face and gazed up at him.

"Philip," she began. "What are you thinking?"

He removed his jacket and settled himself beside her on the bed. "I believe there's something you need to tell me, love."

She smiled brightly as the truth hit her. "You know of the child."

He nodded.

"But, how?" she asked.

"Rawlings told me of it," he explained. "Although I daresay I allowed myself only the tiniest moment to feel happiness at the disclosure."

Maggie shook her head in confusion. He stretched out beside her and gently ran his fingers over her arm.

"I was far too worried about the child's mother to give more than a passing thought to anything else," he said.

Her heart beat faster. "You're happy, then?" she asked, still unsure.

"Ah, Maggie," he said, wrapping his arms around her. "I have never felt such happiness in my life."

Chapter 29

One week later, they departed London for Somersetshire.
Maggie was filled with apprehensions regarding her
confrontation with the earl. Would he welcome her as a
daughter? What would her aunt—for Maggie still thought of her
as such—have to say of all of this? Although Philip assured her
time and again that both Lord and Lady Bridgewater already
loved her dearly, her apprehensions remained.

Her morning sickness was a daily occurrence, causing only
mild discomfort now that she was certain of Philip's love for
both her and the growing child. He frequently patted her belly,
speaking in hushed tones to the babe nestled within. The wound
in her leg pained her little, as the salve the doctor had left
proving to be more than adequate treatment. Philip doubted this,
however, and still assisted her up and down the stairs as well as
into their bed. Maggie suspected him of merely wishing to have
the excuse to touch her, although when she accused him of this,
he laughingly told her he needed no such excuse.

This day, as the carriage rolled on toward Bridgewater
Park, Maggie once more gave voice to her worries.

"I assure you, love," Philip said, taking her hands in his. "The earl will accept you. He loves you."

Her brow furrowed.

"I don't doubt his affection for me, Philip," she stated. "I am apprehensive regarding what we may learn."

"No matter what we learn, sweetheart," he began, "I'll be beside you."

She felt inclined to push her worries aside, the love and support he had for her more than adequate comfort. Settling comfortably against his side, she willed the matter from her mind.

When they arrived at Bridgewater Park, it was nearly the dinner hour. Lord and Lady Bridgewater greeted them warmly, albeit with a touch of surprise.

"How wonderful it is to see you, children," the earl said with a wide smile.

"Yes," his wife concurred. "Although, I daresay we weren't expecting you until morning."

Maggie gave them a nervous smile. "We didn't wish to dally," Philip quickly explained. "Isn't that right, love?" he asked, taking Maggie's hand in his.

Maggie could only stare at the earl. He was her father! she marveled. Had he truly loved her mother? Philip gave her hand a gentle squeeze, effectively breaking her trance. She nodded to Lord and Lady Bridgewater.

"Go and ready yourselves for dinner," Lady Bridgewater said. "We'll await you in the parlor."

Maggie permitted Philip to lead her from the room. They went directly upstairs to their spacious chambers. Philip didn't take long to dress, and when he emerged from the dressing room, he found Maggie sitting before the vanity. She wore her chemise and petticoat, her hair upswept in a simple yet elegant style. He crossed to her and placed his hands on her bare shoulders.

"Are you quite all right, love?" he asked, caressing her skin.

"I will be, Philip," she said, turning. "Once I know all of it."

Dropping a kiss on her brow, he left her to finish her dress. With the help of Lady Bridgewater's maid, she donned a beautiful gown of topaz, nearly the color of the stones in her mother's necklace. They had brought the jewels with them, loath to leave them unattended at the townhouse. When she was alone once more, Maggie opened one of the jeweler's boxes, searching for one particular item. She found the necklace easily enough, running her fingers over the delicate stones once more. Leaving the necklace with the other items in the box, she withdrew the signet ring bearing Lord Bridgewater's crest. She slipped it into her reticule and closed it tight, looping the small purse over her wrist. She squared her shoulders and went downstairs to join her husband.

Maggie ate little at dinner, although Philip was the only who noticed anything amiss. Now and again, his hand found hers beneath the table, his fingers gently stroking hers. She caught his eye, pulling needed strength from him. Lord and Lady Bridgewater discussed the bashes they'd attended in town, expressing their great relief to be home in the country once more. Philip joined in the conversation, leaving Maggie to her own thoughts.

At the conclusion of dinner, the gentlemen stood. Philip requested an audience with the earl in his study, a request the older man was more than happy to honor. He bowed to the ladies and turned to leave the room. Maggie stood quickly and took

Philip's hand. Philip inclined his head toward her and called out to the earl.

"Maggie wishes to join us, sir," he said.

Lord Bridgewater came to a stop, turning to face the couple. An indecipherable look passed between the earl and his wife, the latter dropping a curtsy and taking herself off to the parlor. With a nod, Lord Bridgewater led Maggie and Philip to his study.

The earl closed the door as Philip led Maggie to one of the wing chairs facing the man's massive desk. She sat, watching closely as Lord Bridgewater came to sit behind the desk.

"What is this about, children?"

"She knows, sir," Philip stated, settling into the chair beside Maggie's.

"Ah," the earl groaned, rubbing his hands over his face. "Maggie, I don't know what to say. How could you tell her, Philip?"

"I didn't," Philip answered. "She learned of it from a different source entirely."

"Lord Rawlings learned of my illegitimacy and told me of it," Maggie said.

"Don't tell me it is known among the *ton*?" the earl asked worriedly. "I don't wish your mother's reputation to be sullied so."

Maggie shook her head. "He didn't know your identity, Uncle," she said. "I suppose," she added, reddening, "I can no longer address you as such."

"Dear Maggie," the earl said, coming to stand before her. "I hope that one day you may call me 'Father.'"

Maggie looked at Philip. "I don't know."

Lord Bridgewater gave her a bright smile. "Don't fret, dear," he said, patting her hand. "I know all of this must be a shock to you."

Maggie nodded, her eyes huge. The earl once more took his place behind the desk. Philip took the opportunity to inform the man of all that had transpired: from Lavery's kidnapping to their discovery of the treasure hidden behind the bookshelves. Lord Bridgewater listened intently, his face showing a strange mixture of relief and shame.

"I admit that I gave your mother those jewels, Maggie," he said in a low voice. "But the steward could have no inkling that that she and I were involved."

"Mr. Lavery didn't know your identity either," she said.

"But," the earl began, "however did you learn of it? If Philip didn't tell you."

Maggie reached into her reticule and withdrew the signet ring. The earl blinked as if it were some sort of vision. A wry smile soon spread across his face as he took it from her.

"I gave her this when she told me of your coming," he said, no doubt reliving that moment in his past. "I was so happy, although it was all so muddled. I wanted the child—you—to have something of its father."

Maggie looked to Philip, who gave her a nod of encouragement. She squared her shoulders and faced the earl once more.

"Pray, tell me all of it," she urged softly.

The earl handed her the ring and folded his hands on the desk. "I believe it may cause some pain in the telling," he warned them. He flicked his eyes toward Philip. "And not only to Maggie."

Philip shook his head in apparent confusion. "Sir, what are you saying?"

The earl sighed once more. "Your father, Philip," he said in explanation. "He was involved in the mess."

"My father?" Philip repeated. "But, how can he be connected to this?"

"He loved her, too," the earl answered.

"What!?" Philip asked, coming to his feet.

"Do calm down, son," the earl soothed. "You're upsetting your wife."

Philip took a deep breath and sat once more, leaning to take Maggie's hand in his. She once more requested the earl to tell his story. The man nodded and began.

"We were very close, your father and I," he told Philip. "More like brothers than cousins, truth be told. He was widowed so young, and he took to carousing and charming his way among the ladies of the *ton*. It pained me to see how little attention he paid you."

Philip swore under his breath at the memory of his father, a man who had little to nothing to do with his only child. It was Maggie's turn to soothe him. When she touched his leg, she felt the tension leave him.

"My own wife was quite ill," Lord Bridgewater said. "She'd been so nearly since our wedding. When her sister came to stay with us, I was most pleased to have the company." He smiled at Maggie then. "Cecilia was so like you, Maggie. So sweet, so beautiful. My heart was lost. We fought our attraction as best we could, for your mother was a lady of virtue. But, alas..." He shook his head at the bittersweet memory. "Loath to have my wife learn of our involvement, we agreed that she should settle in Sussex. It wasn't far from London and, as I had many occasions to go to town, we could be together that way. I'm not ashamed to admit that our time together was the most wonderful of my life. When you were born, Maggie, it only became sweeter. Those were precious years."

The earl gazed off in the distance, as if envisioning all he had just told them. Maggie gently urged him to continue, at which he cleared his throat and went on.

"Your father came to Bridgewater Park to visit, Philip. Cecilia was in attendance at the time, although she rarely made her presence known. Nevertheless, he saw her and wanted her for his own. He approached her—with more conviction each time—until Cecilia had no choice but to tell him of our involvement.

He was enraged and threatened her time and again that he would tell my wife of it, although I admit I didn't believe him capable of such a hurtful act. It became obvious to me that he was obsessed with your mother, Maggie."

Philip looked quickly at Maggie. They both knew full well the trouble that could arise from such an obsession. She returned his knowing glance, turning her attention again to the earl.

"Did he tell her?" Maggie asked, afraid to hear the truth.

"Yes," the earl said wearily. "He told my wife of our involvement. She took it very hard and, being most frail, her health worsened. She passed away soon after."

"I'm so sorry for my father's actions," Philip said thickly. "I can't believe anyone could be so cruel."

The earl wiped a tear from his eye and nodded. "That wasn't the end of it," he added. "Cecilia was heartbroken. She loved her sister dearly, a fact that only served to compound the guilt she felt over our involvement. Despite my entreaties to the opposite, she refused to see me anymore."

"I remember when you stopped coming to visit," Maggie mused aloud. "I was nearly Betsy's age, I believe."

"You were eight years old," the earl answered. "Your mother would only allow me to visit you a few times a year after that. She said that it hurt her to see us together when she knew that we could never be a family."

"But you could have married her," Philip pointed out.

"It wasn't possible," Lord Bridgewater said. "She was my deceased wife's sister. That fact notwithstanding, Cecilia felt such guilt over her sister's death, she couldn't bear to be reminded of what she referred to as her shame."

"But what of the jewels?" Maggie had to know.

The earl reddened. "I admit that I tried to buy your mother's forgiveness, Maggie. She evidently accepted the coins I sent for your support, but I suppose she felt too guilty to ever make use of the jewelry."

"What happened to my father?" Philip asked. "Did he continue to pursue her?"

"Yes," the earl answered. "But not for very much longer. He was in London, frequenting the seedy pubs where he chose to spend his time, when he apparently got into an argument with the wrong type of people. Someone from the watch found him, beaten to death down at the waterfront. I'm sorry to tell you of it, Philip."

Philip waved away the earl's words with his hand. "I shed no tears upon his passing more than ten years ago, sir," he said. "I won't shed any this day."

The earl nodded sagely. "When it became obvious to me that your mother would never change her position, I ceased to bother her. I was content to see you, Maggie, on occasion. I met Lady Bridgewater and, as a matter of course, we married."

Maggie nodded, relieved to finally know all of it.

"I've provided for you in my will, Maggie," the earl went on. "And as you have conveniently married my heir," he added with a grin, "I have no need to worry over your future."

"But what of the jewels?" she asked him again. "I don't believe they belong to me."

"You'll keep them, of course," he stated. "And wear them as your mother never did."

"Oh no," Maggie said, shaking her head. "They were to be my mother's."

"Maggie," the earl smiled. "You were your mother's treasure. It's only fitting that her treasure belong to you."

Maggie looked at Philip, who nodded his wholehearted agreement. Favoring her father with a smile, she accepted his offer.

They rejoined Lady Bridgewater in the parlor, finding the older woman wringing her hands in her nervousness.

"Is everything quite all right, husband?" she asked the earl pointedly.

"Yes, my dear," Lord Bridgewater answered.

He looked at Maggie with unrestrained warmth, causing her to flush hotly.

"Aunt, I…," she began awkwardly.

The earl held up his hand to still her. "Maggie knows all of it, wife," he told Lady Bridgewater.

Maggie held her breath and waited for the woman's response. She saw no animosity in Lady Bridgewater's countenance and breathed a sigh of relief. She hurried to the older woman's side.

"I'm so sorry for any pain this might have caused you, Aunt," she rushed out.

Lady Bridgewater smiled and patted Maggie's cheek. "Nonsense, Margaret," she responded. "You were but a child, and could take no responsibility for it. The earl and I have discussed all of this," she added, to which the earl nodded his agreement. "In fact, we had discussed our telling you of it before you arrived for this visit."

Maggie looked from the woman to her father and back again.

"We felt you were owed the truth, Maggie," Lord Bridgewater added. "No matter the discomfort to the two of us."

Maggie held tightly to Lady Bridgewater's hand, tears welling in her eyes at the warmth she sensed coming from the woman. Lady Bridgewater gave her hand a squeeze and led her to sit beside her on the settee.

"I believe we should tell Betsy of it," she told the others. "She's nearly of an age to learn of the connection between the two of you."

Maggie smiled again, nodding vigorously. "I love her as a sister already."

Philip and the earl shared a smile.

"Hmm," the other woman mused aloud, drawing their attention. "I believe you must have sensed something from the start, Margaret. Betsy as well, for she took to you immediately."

They decided to tell the child the next day, anticipating Betsy's response to be quite positive as well as vocal. When Philip suddenly grew quiet, Maggie looked at him searchingly. His brow was furrowed and his mouth turned down in a frown.

"What is it, Philip?" she asked.

Philip shook his head. "I still can't put aside the tremendous guilt I feel over my father's actions," he said with regret. He turned to the earl. "I fell in love with Maggie almost immediately, sir, so I can at least fathom why he did the horrid deeds he did."

"Never mind that, son," the earl said. "What your father felt for Maggie's mother was in no way the same as the love you obviously have for our Maggie."

Philip gazed a Maggie. She gave a quick nod of her head, still smiling. At Maggie's unspoken encouragement, Philip announced their blessed news. Lady Bridgewater cried out happily. She wrapped Maggie tightly in an embrace while the earl slapped Philip heartily on the back. The earl took Maggie's hand in his.

"A child," Lord Bridgewater said with a sniffle.

"Another treasure," Philip put in with a grin.

Epilogue
Spring 1819

Philip returned to the townhouse in London, a bit tired from a late evening out with his friends. He had met with Lords Rawlings and Porter to celebrate the recent betrothal of the latter. It was nearly four years to the day since Philip had encountered Maggie at the Inn at Salisbury, and much had happened in that time.

The Earl of Bridgewater—while he couldn't claim Maggie legally as his daughter—made little secret of their relationship. Betsy and Mary loved their half-sister as dearly as ever, with their mother filling a maternal role in Maggie's life as well. Her mother's treasure was spoken of often, and Philip insisted that she wear the beautiful jewels whenever they went out for the evening. He assured her time again that she was his treasure, and that he had discovered her at the inn and claimed her for his own. A smile teased his lips at the memory. Shrugging off his jacket, he entered the parlor, finding his wife within as he had fully expected.

Maggie smiled sweetly as she crossed to him, a thick dressing gown of brocade wrapping her slender figure. She looked pointedly at the clock and placed her hands on her hips in a show of annoyance.

"You're quite late, husband," she teased.

He arched a brow at her. "Is that so, wife?" he countered, crossing to her.

"Yes," she responded, coming into his arms. "Your little love was quite put out."

Philip laughed out loud. Their daughter, Cecilia—nearly three years old now—had her father wrapped around her little finger, a fact of which all who knew them were well-aware.

"Did she give you much trouble?" he asked, leading her from the room.

Maggie's eyes twinkled. "I believe I know how to handle the little miss."

"That's no small wonder," he said wryly.

They climbed the stairs to the nursery, set on the floor above the sleeping chambers. Walking quietly into the room, Maggie pulled him to the small bed in the corner. Curled within the covers was their daughter, Cecilia. Golden curls encircled her cherubic face, her tiny mouth pursed like a rosebud. A light sleeper by nature—a fact that confounded her parents—the child raised thick lashes to regard the two of them closely.

"Papa?" the tot asked sleepily.

Philip smiled down into the green eyes so like his own.

"Yes, little love?" he asked softly.

Her tiny brow furrowed. "You dint read me a story, Papa," she pouted.

"Tomorrow, sweet," he said, reaching down to brush her curls away from her cheek. "I'll read you as many stories as you wish tomorrow."

"Three stories," she demanded with a yawn. "Read three stories."

Philip bit back his laughter. "Yes, Cecilia," he answered. "I'll read you three stories tomorrow."

Cecilia nodded and closed her eyes, asleep in moments. Philip cast a sidelong glance at Maggie.

"She has a stubborn streak as wide as the Thames," he chuckled softly, escorting Maggie into their chamber.

"I do wonder from where she inherited it?" Maggie asked in feigned innocence.

"Minx," Philip growled, pulling her into his arms. "And how was your evening, love?"

"Utterly miserable," she said, working his cravat loose. "I've sorely missed you, husband," she added, her voice husky.

He lowered his head to hers, kissing her hungrily. He nibbled her ear as he removed her wrapper, sharply drawing in a breath as he realized that she wore nothing beneath. He quickly removed his own clothes and grabbed her once more, falling upon the bed. Taking a long moment, he stared into her eyes.

"My Maggie," he murmured, running his hands over her. "My treasure."

When he had loved her as thoroughly as he wished, he held her close.

"That was wonderful, Philip," Maggie sighed contentedly.

He smiled at the satisfaction in her voice. "I wonder, Maggie, if it's time for us to begin thinking about giving Cecilia a brother or sister?" he mused aloud.

Her answering silence caused him to lift his head to stare at her.

"It's strange that you should mention that," she hinted, her eyes sparkling.

"Do you mean…?"

She nodded, a bright smile lighting up her face.

He grinned and hugged her once more. At last he had the family he'd longed for the whole of his life. And Maggie claimed one of the finest families on England as her own. Together they would raise their children as their own parents had been either unable or unwilling—with the love of two parents who recognized their worth.

The love they shared was their treasure: worth more than all the jewels and coins on earth, more than the fool's gold that sparkled so brilliantly on the surface. What they had was real and they would hold it close forever.

About the Author

JoMarie DeGioia is a bestselling author of Historical and Contemporary Romance. She's known Mickey Mouse from the "inside," has been a copyeditor for her tiny town's newspaper, and a bookseller. A hybrid author, she also writes Young Adult Fantasy/Adventure stories, New Adult Romance and Paranormal Romance. She gets lost in DIY projects around the house and works out plot ideas during long runs. She divides her time between Central Florida and New England.

Discover other books by JoMarie DeGioia

The Bridgewater Brides series, including

The Heir's Treasure

The Gentlemen Undercover series, including

A Hero and a Gentleman

The Shopgirls of Bond Street series, including

That Determined Mister Latham

The Dashing Nobles series, including

More Than Passion

Pride and Fire

Just Perfect

More Than Charming

The Gentlemen Undercover series, including

A Hero and a Gentleman

The Cypress Corners series, including

Finding Harmony

Taming Jake

Loving Cassie

Winning Ben

Showing Jessie

Seeing Shannon (Barefoot Bay Kindle Worlds Novella)

Dreaming Eli

Giving Chase (Barefoot Bay Kindle Worlds Novella)

Kissing Bree

The Gifted YA Fantasy/Adventure Trilogy, including

Gifted

Braunachs of the Dell series, including

Luke's Gold

Patrick's Promise

Connect with me online

Twitter: https://twitter.com/JoMarieDeGioia

Facebook: https://www.facebook.com/JoMarie.DeGioia.Author

Website: www.jomariedegioia.com